Love by the Book

MAGNOLIA COVE MAGIC BOOK TWO

NOEL BAILEY

Edited by Milly Bellegris

Proofread by Megan Cox

Cover design by Bring Design

www.authornoelbailey.com

For my dad—cool enough not to mind having a romcom dedicated to him. The one who taught me that life needs a good soundtrack—and whose music now plays through these pages.

I love you.

Author's Note

Hey there lovely reader,

Welcome back to Magnolia Cove—where the cinnamon rolls are sweet, the magic is subtle, and the love stories will sneak up on you when you least expect them.

While this book is full of cozy, small-town charm (including a truly iconic karaoke scene and all the bookish vibes your heart can handle), *Love by the Book* dips a little deeper than *Whisked Away*. It touches on themes of grief, the ache of relationships that don't go the way we hoped, and what it means to open your heart again after loss.

There's plenty of laughter, a fair amount of glitter, and cameos from a few fan favorites (yes, Ethan is still baking, and Alex still has opinions). You can also expect a bit of mild language, some swoon-worthy moments, and references to intimacy, though nothing happens on the page.

At its heart, this story is about healing. About learning to believe—maybe for the first time—that love doesn't have to be perfect to be worth the risk. I hope these pages wrap you in warmth and leave you with a little more hope than when you started.

Thanks for being here.

With love (and a playlist full of Stevie Nicks and second chances),

-Noel

Music Playlist

A playlist that feels like moonlight on old book pages, sounds like laughter echoing after midnight karaoke, and aches with the kind of longing that comes when life gives you a second chance at new love. These songs are the perfect soundtrack to Rhianna and Eli's story.

Click here to listen now!

Rhianna

"The secret to perfect matchmaking is... glitter. Lots of it. Like, unreasonable amounts," I whisper dramatically, leaning toward the circle of wide-eyed children gathered around my booth at the Magnolia Cove Farmers Market. The morning sun streams through colorful banners overhead, casting rainbow patterns across our table.

I laugh, stirring a mason jar filled with shimmering pink slime. "Also maybe a sprinkle of moonlight and a really good playlist."

The kids lean in closer, completely enchanted—which is exactly how I want them. The *Magnolia Cove Library Presents: Magical Potion Workshop* sign flutters in the breeze above us. On the table, a dozen jars sparkle with various concoctions, each one more glittery than the last.

Magnolia Cove is what we call a magical pocket community—one of a handful of hidden places in the world where people with magic can live freely. Wards cast by the town's magical council keep the energy veiled from non-magical eyes, letting us enchant the world just enough to make it sweeter. Around here, the flowers always bloom on time, the library smells like whatever mood the head librarian decides to bottle —this summer, it's lemon sunshine—and the brick streets never seem to crack. Even the cinnamon rolls taste like comfort itself, thanks to a bit of mood-lifting magic infused in the sugar. It's subtle, mostly. Gentle. Like someone brushing a charm over the ordinary and making it glow.

"Now, who's ready to make a magical jar that can totally— not officially—spark romantic destiny?" I wink, holding up my creation.

"ME!" shouts a chorus of excited voices, hands shooting into the air.

"Miss Wilder, can mine help my mom find a boyfriend?" asks Lily, a gap-toothed seven-year-old with pigtails and the most serious expression I've ever seen on a child.

"Mine is for my turtle!" declares Jamie, already reaching for the gold glitter.

I grin, pushing my sleeves up as I distribute empty jars. The table is a Jackson Pollock painting of art supplies, and a fine dusting of sequins already clings to my cardigan. It's perfect chaos.

As the kids dive enthusiastically into their potions, my gaze drifts across the market. That's when my magic lifts my attention to someone—Karl, early thirties, dark hair curling slightly at the ends as he leans over a display of sun-ripened tomatoes at Robert Hart's farm stand. He's arranging them with the same quiet focus he brings to everything—thoughtful, gentle, the kind of man who hands out strawberries to local kids and remembers your cat's name.

And then I notice her—a woman with brunette hair tucked behind one ear, cute tortoiseshell glasses perched on her nose as she samples a spoonful of Grammie Rae's spun honey. Her yellow sundress glows in the morning light, and a canvas tote bag with a faded literary quote swings at her hip. The visitor that Grammie Rae—the town's unofficial gossip columnist and walking database of everyone's business—was telling me about earlier. Brooke.

Something flickers between Karl and Brooke—like a golden thread connecting their energies across the market. It's subtle, but unmistakable to someone like me who can read those vibrations.

Oh. *Oh.*

My magic senses are tingling.

"Oh no," comes a familiar voice. "I've seen that look before."

I glance up to see Alex approaching, two iced coffees in hand. Her expression shifts—tight lips, flared nostrils, that familiar mix of amusement and judgment that makes her look every inch the New York City food critic who waltzed into Magnolia Cove to try the cinnamon rolls and ended up stirring up more than cookie batter.

She hands me one of the iced coffees. It's from The Whimsical Whisk, of course—Ethan's working the booth today, which explains why Alex is out here instead of holed up inside her café, *Sinclair's Sips and Savories*. They have a system, the two of them. And if there's one thing better than Ethan's cinnamon rolls, it's the iced caramel cold brew he makes with some kind of espresso-magic blend that should be illegal.

"Rhianna Wilder, what are you plotting now?"

"See Karl over at Robert's stand?" I nod toward the stall where he's carefully helping a woman pick out the ripest tomatoes. "Single. Sweet. The type of guy who carries extra bags for customers and brings fresh herbs to the diner just because he thought they might need some."

Alex arches a brow. "And?"

I tip my chin toward the honey booth. "Now look at her. Cute glasses, sundress, tote bag full of main-character energy."

"The tourist with the fancy reusable bags? What about her?"

I lower my voice, glancing around. Not that any of the kids are paying attention—they're too busy turning the booth into a glitter-coated war zone. One is furiously shaking a jar of what looks like purple slime, another is sprinkling sequins with the intensity of someone warding off evil spirits. A stray puff of glitter explodes into the air like fairy dust from a faulty wand.

"Her name's Brooke. She's staying at the bed-and-breakfast for the week. Grammie Rae says she's a children's book illustrator visiting for inspiration. And their energies are perfectly compatible. Like peanut butter and chocolate. Like Stevie Nicks and that microphone with all the scarves. Like—"

"Like two random strangers who have never met each other and probably have no reason to?" Alex interjects, though the corners of her mouth are twitching.

"That's the beauty of it! They've never had the opportunity." I tap my temple knowingly. "But I can feel it. Their energies sing together like they're both parts of the same song."

Glitter crunches under Alex's sandal as she shifts her weight. One of the potion jars has tipped over on the edge of the table, forming a slow-moving pink ooze that's dangerously close to dripping onto someone's backpack. I swoop in with a napkin and nudge it back before disaster strikes.

Alex lifts an unimpressed brow. "And you're going to be that catalyst, I suppose?"

"Watch and learn." I stand up, smoothing down my sea-green dress covered in tiny embroidered books. "Jamie, you're in charge of the glitter for exactly two minutes. Make sure no one eats it."

Jamie, a freckle-faced 9th grader who used to play trumpet in Rachel's band, gives me a solemn salute that scatters glitter onto three nearby patrons.

I weave through the market, the scent of fresh bread and spun honey filling the air as I plot my approach. It needs to seem casual, natural—a chance encounter orchestrated by fate, not a wild-haired librarian with questionable decision-making skills.

Grabbing an empty basket, I position myself near the honey booth, pretending to examine jars while keeping an eye on Karl across the way. He's helping a young boy choose a pint of strawberries, crouching down to offer one with a smile and a gentle nod. A moment later, he ties the boy's shoelace, then hands the berries to the kid's mom with a quiet word and that easy warmth he always carries. The woman—Brooke—is moving toward the display that sits between the honey booth and Robert's stand.

Perfect. The universe is already helping.

I time my approach, stepping out just as she's passing by, ready to create a casual collision that will send her gently toward Karl's berry arrangement. What I don't expect is the small child darting across my path, chasing a butterfly.

My evasive maneuver to avoid the child sends me careening into a display of Grammie Rae's specialty honey jars. My elbow connects with the carefully stacked pyramid, creating a domino effect that's both horrifying and, if I'm being honest, aesthetically impressive.

"Oh my gosh—" I lunge to catch them, but my reflexes are about three jars too slow.

Glass doesn't shatter, thankfully—magic wards against breakage are standard at the Magnolia Cove market—but the jars roll wildly, one spinning directly into the strawberry display, toppling baskets that tumble toward Robert's stand.

"Watch out!" I call, my voice far too late to be useful.

Karl lunges forward to catch the falling strawberries, colliding with Brooke who's stepped forward to help. Her tote bag swings around and snags on the edge of a table stacked with baskets of green beans, sending it wobbling dangerously.

In an impressive display of reflexes, Karl steadies both

Brooke and the berry baskets with one graceful movement, his hands at her waist.

"I'm so sorry," Brooke says, looking mortified.

"Not your fault," Karl replies. "Though I think these berries might need a safety net."

There's a moment—a perfect, crystalline moment—where their eyes meet, and even through my mortification, I can see it: that spark, that recognition, that possibility.

"I'm the one who should apologize," I say, extracting myself from the scene and trying to look dignified while grabbing a few stray honey jars and sliding them back onto their shelf. "Completely my fault. Total accident."

Karl helps Brooke right her bag, then offers her a basket of berries. "For the trouble," he says with a smile I've never seen on him before. "I'm Karl, by the way."

"Brooke," she replies, her cheeks flushing a shade that matches the strawberries. "You know, I was actually hoping to find someone who knows the island well. I'm looking for inspiration for my next book..."

I back away slowly, trying to contain my triumphant grin as they continue talking, Karl already pointing out features of the island on a market map he's pulled from beneath the counter.

When I return to the library booth, Alex is waiting with her arms crossed, but her lips are twitching with barely suppressed laughter. Meanwhile, the kids have taken full advantage of my absence—glitter coats the table like fairy dust after a storm, and one of the potion jars is bubbling suspiciously.

"That," she says dryly, "was the most chaotic display of attempted matchmaking I have ever witnessed. You're like a bull in a romance novel shop."

"But did it work?" I ask, grabbing a napkin to dab at honey residue staining my dress.

We both turn to look. Karl is pointing to something on the map, and Brooke is nodding eagerly, jotting notes in a small sketchbook she's pulled from her tote. They're standing closer than strictly necessary, and his eyes have a twinkle in them I can see even from here, like the moment has a little extra sparkle around the edges.

"I can't believe that actually worked," Alex murmurs, sounding impressed despite herself.

"It's a gift," I say, fanning myself dramatically. "I can read energy. I can match books with readers, I've never given anyone a book recommendation they didn't love. And now, I can match *people*."

"One accidental success doesn't make you Cupid, Rhi."

But I'm already reaching for my notebook, mind racing with possibilities. I flip to a fresh page and write in large letters: *Magnolia Cove's Premier Matchmaking Service*.

"I could actually do this," I say, more to myself than to Alex. "I could help people find their perfect matches. I already sense which books will resonate with people—this is just the next logical step!"

"Well, if you're taking on clients, I know someone who could use your help." Alex takes a long drink of her iced coffee. "Dean Markham."

I spin around. "Where?"

If there's anyone to avoid on the island, it's Head Warlock Dean Markham. That man's a dark specter who manages to stand at the corner of every road at all times. It's unsettling, even for someone who grew up in a magical pocket community like I did.

"No, he's not here." Alex chuckles. "He could be one of your first clients."

"Oh my gosh, no. Of all the bad ideas that have ever existed in the history of bad ideas, that one is the worst."

She rolls her eyes then swoops in to catch a teetering jar

before it hits the ground and hands it back to its wide-eyed owner with a reassuring nod. She turns back to me. "Dean's single. And I don't think he's as bad as he seems."

"A glowing recommendation from a food critic."

"He's not food."

"Nor datable. So he's out of the discussion."

She huffs and gives her coffee cup a shake. "Tom, then."

"Tom is like me, allergic to romance."

"What does that even mean?"

"It means we grew up in a small town where everyone knows your grandmother's name and you can only miss in relationships so many times before you strike out and decide to take up bird watching and afghan knitting instead."

"You hated both of those."

"Right. But think of the tragedy if I'd dated someone and never even tried them. It could have been the love of my life."

"The person you dated?"

"The hobbies, Alex, stay with me."

She snorts and I grin, letting the moment pass with a joke, as always. It's easier than explaining how the idea of loving someone that deeply—and watching them walk away when things get too hard—makes my chest feel too tight. It's easier to play matchmaker than risk being the one who falls, who reveals too much, who ends up alone.

In the distance, Karl appears to be saying something to Robert, gesturing toward the far end of the market. A moment later, he falls into step beside Brooke, the two of them walking away together, laughing in the summer sunshine like they've known each other for years. I slap my notebook shut, already mentally designing flyers—pink ones, with glitter. I could even do this as an extra extension of library services. My boss loves anything that sounds community-driven and vaguely morale-boosting. I'll need a system for tracking potential matches. And maybe a logo, too, something with hearts and books...

"Miss Wilder!" Jamie's panicked voice breaks through my plotting. "The potions are EXPLODING!"

I turn to see a geyser of pink slime erupting from what was supposed to be a sensible craft project. Three children are covered head-to-toe in sparkles, and the rest are gleefully adding more ingredients to the bubbling concoctions.

Alex steps back with the reflexes of someone who's witnessed one too many glitter-related incidents in my presence. "And on that note, I'm going to check on Ethan. Good luck with... everything." She gestures vaguely at the growing chaos.

I roll up my sleeves, grinning despite the impending mess. If I can handle this, I can definitely handle a little matchmaking.

After all, what could possibly go wrong?

Well... aside from the glitter, the slime, and the magical energy fizzing around the edges of the craft table. If I don't get this under control, Dean is definitely going to show up to 'handle' it—and I really don't need a visit from Mr. Rules and Regulations right now. Especially not with that judgy eyebrow thing he does.

"Coming, Lily! Just don't add any more—" A jar makes a concerning gurgling sound. "Oh sweet honey candy, did someone add baking soda to the moonlight essence?"

As I wade into the craft disaster, I can't help but feel a thrill of excitement. I'm practically made for this new plan: reading energies, creating connections, bringing a little magic to the people of the island.

Watch out, Magnolia Cove. Cupid's got nothing on this witch with a mission. Let the matchmaking begin!

And if my heart stays safely on the sidelines? Well, you

can't get hurt if you're just the one holding the bows and arrows, right? No one leaves the matchmaker.

Eli

"You *moved* to—" My sister's voice cuts in and out, the static crackling through my phone speaker. "—Magnolia Cove?" The connection stabilizes just enough for me to hear her pitch up several notches. "Tell me it's a lie."

I'm actually surprised my phone is working at all. The locals had warned me that Magnolia Cove is notorious for having terrible cell service—something about the island's unique geography or, as one cryptic shopkeeper suggested, "the veil being too thick here." Whatever that means. Magical pocket communities use wards to keep their secrets hidden from non-magical eyes—but even for someone like me, who knows how that works, the way the locals discuss magic feels... different. Magnolia Cove plays by its own rules.

"It's true." I step carefully around a flower planter on the cobblestone walkway, lifting my phone higher as if those extra few inches might improve the connection. My gaze fixes on the small café ahead as I walk. *Sinclair's Sips & Savories* gleams in the mid-morning sun, its sleek steel and glass behind its windows looking almost comically metropolitan against the quaint charm of the island's main street. An interesting location for a meeting.

"And I had to hear about you moving from *Mom*?" I chuckle which apparently acts as tinder to Piper's irritation. Her voice grows sharp. "I called her a liar, Eli. To her face."

"Well, that was rude." The call breaks up again, and I pause, waiting for the connection to return.

"—never—" Piper's voice fades in and out before suddenly coming through with surprising clarity. A scoff blares over the line. "—not once in the history of our entire life done something impulsive. Even as a kid you returned library books early and waited for walk signals at crosswalks even if there wasn't a car in sight."

"Notice we never paid late fees or got hit by a car. You're welcome." I pause at the corner, letting a family with small children pass. The town's morning bustle has a different rhythm than what I'm used to—less frantic, more meandering. Like everyone knows exactly where they're going but sees no reason to rush.

She sighs dramatically. I'm pretty sure she's pressing her mouth close to the phone so the sound comes through loud and clear. "You're impossible. Why did you move? Did something happen?"

I pause, the memory of Mark slumped over his desk flashing through my mind, unbidden. He was a dozen years older than me, but he'd become the first colleague I truly considered a friend.

And then he was gone. Two days before anyone noticed. Except me.

"Let's just say I needed a change. It's only for summer, anyway. I'm taking a break."

"You? A change?" There's a sloshing—creamer hitting coffee if I know my sister.

"I just felt like trying something new and the spring

semester ended early this year. Plus, Magnolia Cove was once home to Cyrus Whitlock."

Even as the words leave my mouth, I can feel their hollowness. How could I explain that watching Mark slumped over his desk, gone for two days before anyone noticed, had shattered everything I thought I knew? That finding my colleague —my mirror image in so many ways—had forced me to confront the terrifying possibility that I too could disappear without leaving a ripple. That a life spent meticulously organizing books and thoughts and schedules might add up to nothing more than an empty office and a brief mention in the department newsletter.

The truth felt too raw, too vulnerable to share. That I'd spent that night staring at my own perfectly ordered bookshelves, my color-coded planner, my carefully curated life, and for the first time saw not achievement but a prison of my own making. That I'd set myself a challenge—because of course I needed structure even in spontaneity—to make three bold choices. Not planned in advance, but recognized when the moment arose. Moving to Magnolia Cove had been the first, a decision made almost overnight. Two more undefined acts of courage waited, opportunities to feel something real before I returned to the life that was waiting for me.

No, that wasn't casual conversation material. Better to let them think this was just a whim, a Cyrus-Whitlock-signature-chasing adventure, than admit I was running from the ghost of what I might become.

The call drops completely for a moment before reconnecting with a burst of static. I switch the phone to my other ear and make a mental note to only take calls from my apartment when I'm on Wi-Fi—lesson learned.

"Oh my god, you're STILL obsessed with finding that signed Whitlock book? Brubba, I should've known!" Piper laughs through the phone. "And here I thought you'd actually done something wild for once. There's always a perfectly logical explanation with you, isn't there?"

"That's me. Mr. Logical."

The words taste flat, almost bitter on my tongue. For the first time in my life, I'm hoping to escape myself—to outrun the carefully constructed framework that's defined every decision I've ever made. To find something that doesn't fit neatly into the boxes I've drawn around my existence.

I reach for the door of *Sinclair's Sips & Savories*, the scent of freshly ground coffee beans greeting me as I step inside. The interior is even more surprising than the outside—exposed brick contrasting with polished steel fixtures, Edison bulbs hanging from industrial ceiling pipes, and a sprawling espresso machine that looks like it belongs in a science laboratory sits on the counter. It's sleek, modern, and utterly foreign to the island's aesthetic, yet buzzing with people. And somehow, the clatter of mugs and low hum of conversation wraps around the sleek space like a quilt, softening every sharp edge with small-town charm.

I'm suddenly grateful I stuck to my usual habit of arriving early. I enjoy having a moment to take everything in before things start—scoping out the space, settling my nerves, and not walking in mid-chaos.

It's a trick I've relied on since childhood—arriving fifteen minutes before any appointment, class, or social gathering. Giving myself time to breathe. Organize. Prepare. My therapist in graduate school called it an adaptive coping mechanism for anxiety. I've always preferred to think of it as simple efficiency.

But lately, I've started wondering if my careful organization—my color-coded tabs and alphabetized bookcase and precisely timed morning routine—is less about managing anxiety and more about avoiding life altogether. If I've been so busy constructing the perfect framework that I've forgotten to fill it with anything meaningful.

"I've always loved the logical, predictable you," Piper says in that singsong voice she uses whenever she's half-teasing, half-sentimental.

I scan the menu board written in impeccably stylized chalk lettering. "Yeah, sure you do."

I step up to the counter where a barista with bright red lips and a name tag reading 'Kasey' smiles at me. "What can I get for you today, handsome?"

"I, uh—" I fumble, unprepared for the casual flirtation. Of course this would happen the one time I didn't rehearse my coffee order in advance. My ears burn and I stutter, "J-just a medium coffee, I guess. Um, black. Please."

This is exactly why I detest unexpected social interactions. No matter how many degrees I accumulate, how many academic papers I publish, or how precisely I organize my life, I still freeze like a first-year undergraduate when caught off guard. It's embarrassing. If I had a dollar for every time my tongue has tied itself into knots during an unscripted conversation, I could fund an entire library wing.

My dissertation advisor once told me I had "the most brilliant mind and the most awkward social presence" he'd ever encountered. He meant it as a compliment. I think.

So much for my grand self-reinvention. One hint of unexpected social interaction and I'm reduced to fragmented sentences. The barista's friendly smile doesn't waver as she waits for me to elaborate on my order, which only increases my discomfort. I can feel sweat forming at my hairline. Why didn't I anticipate this? I should have practiced ordering at an unfamiliar coffee shop. Should have considered the variables. Should have—

"Brubba," Piper's voice is smug in my ear. "Please tell me

you didn't just black-coffee your way through a flirtation opportunity."

I turn slightly away from the counter, lowering my voice. "I'm fine, Pipes."

"Any chance you want to try our signature drink?" Kasey offers, leaning forward slightly. "It's an espresso blend with hints of cardamom and vanilla. Won an award this year."

"Yes, I mean no, I mean—"

"He'd love to try it," Piper yells loudly enough for Kasey to hear. "My brother is all about new experiences these days."

I reluctantly nod, mostly because backtracking now would be even more awkward. Kasey's smile widens, and I mentally add 'unsolicited personal growth' to today's agenda. "Great! Room for cream?"

"He likes it hot and sweet," Piper shouts once more, and I nearly drop my phone.

"Pipes!" I hiss, then force a smile at Kasey. "Just as you make it is fine, thank you."

As I step to the side, Piper is cackling in my ear. "That was painful to listen to. If that's how you're handling meeting new people, I'm genuinely worried about this break of yours."

"Shouldn't you be off saving reluctant readers somewhere?" I mutter, finding a small table by the window. I set my leather messenger bag down carefully, arranging it so the strap doesn't crease.

"I don't have any students for another hour. So tell me, what exactly are you doing in Magnolia Cove? Besides butchering conversations with cute-sounding baristas?"

I pinch the bridge of my nose, shifting my glasses up. "I'm working on my research. Being somewhere that isn't..." I trail off, unwilling to finish the thought. Somewhere that isn't the office where I found Mark. Somewhere that doesn't remind me of how easily a life can slip away, unnoticed and unfulfilled.

"Ah," Piper says, and I can hear the understanding in that single syllable. She knows me well enough to fill in the blanks. "And how's the apartment?"

"It's... fine. Minimalism suits me."

"Meaning you've already arranged it exactly like your place here," she guesses, correctly.

I don't respond, which is answer enough. The truth is, I spent my first night meticulously recreating the layout of my Misty Pines apartment—books categorized by subject and then alphabetically by author, record player positioned at the precise angle for optimal sound, even my coffee mugs arranged by size and frequency of use. The familiarity was comforting, but also vaguely disappointing. So much for turning over a new leaf.

"Promise you'll keep me updated?" Piper asks, her voice gentling.

"I promise," I say. "Now, I've got to go. I have a meeting in ten minutes." Twenty-five, actually. I'd rather be settled than caught mid-phone-call, looking unfocused.

"Bye, Brubba."

"Bye, Pipes."

I slip my phone into my pocket just as Kasey approaches with my drink. "Here's your signature blend. And my number." She slides a napkin toward me with a wink.

"Oh, I—thank you, but I'm not—I mean, I just moved here and—" I stammer, heat creeping up my neck.

Kasey laughs good-naturedly. "No pressure. Just thought I'd shoot my shot. Enjoy your coffee!"

As she walks away, I take a careful sip of the coffee and am surprised by how much I enjoy the sweetness contrasting the complex coffee tones. Perhaps there's something to this 'trying new things' concept after all.

Twenty minutes and one nearly finished coffee later, the café door swings open, bringing with it a rush of warm air and a woman with silver-streaked hair pinned in an elegant chignon. She spots me immediately and makes her way over with purposeful strides.

"Professor Lancaster!" Her voice carries with it the confident authority of someone used to speaking in rooms designed for silence. "I hope I haven't kept you waiting long."

I stand, extending my hand. "Not at all, Ms.—"

"Maria Delgado, Library Director." Her handshake is firm, professional. "I can't tell you how thrilled we are to have someone of your expertise joining us, even temporarily. Your department head spoke so highly of your cataloging skills and your protection magic."

"Thank you, that's very—"

"And of course, we're eternally grateful you've agreed to help with our backlog of ancient texts," she continues, pulling out the chair across from me. "Some of these volumes haven't been properly examined in decades. Who knows what treasures might lurk in our collection?"

I nod automatically, even as confusion settles in my stomach. Cataloging backlog?

That hadn't been part of the plan.

I'd only arranged to use an office space during my break to continue my research. This was supposed to be a break. A slower pace. Not filling my hours doing the tedious work better suited to graduate assistants armed with coffee and a fear of disappointing their advisors.

My brain, which can recite entire passages from obscure Welsh mythological texts at academic conferences, has apparently gone offline. It's always like this—an impromptu conversation short-circuits my ability to form basic sentences. I can deliver a flawless three-hour lecture on comparative folklore traditions, but ask me to make small talk about the weather without preparation and suddenly I'm linguistically challenged.

The words I need are scattered somewhere in the fog between my academic vocabulary and basic human communication. I should decline politely. Set boundaries. Explain that my plan is for focused research, not inventory management.

Instead, I find myself nodding. Agreeing. Smiling even.

"Your expertise in determining which volumes might be valuable will be indispensable," Maria adds, her eyes bright with enthusiasm. "And your protection wards! Your department chair mentioned they're some of the strongest she's seen in academic circles."

"I, I look forward to examining them," I manage to say, my voice steadier than I feel. A professional mask sliding into place despite the internal panic.

"Excellent!" A warm smile spreads across her face. "I've prepared a preliminary list of the texts we're most concerned about. Some are showing signs of deterioration despite our best efforts, and we suspect a few might have significant historical value. Michael in acquisitions can show you to your office once you're ready. He's working today if you want to pop by."

A familiar tightness grips my chest. This wasn't the plan. Today was meticulously scheduled: unpack boxes 15 through 18—containing my reference materials on Welsh mythology and more obscure book collections—organize my desk according to the diagram I'd sketched last week, and begin preliminary research on local Whitlock connections. I'd even allotted a precise forty-five minutes for lunch.

Now my carefully constructed day has collapsed like a house of cards. The thought of improvising a new schedule sends tendrils of anxiety curling through my stomach. My fingers itch to pull out my planner and frantically rework things.

But isn't this exactly why I came here? To break free from the rigid framework I've built around myself? To step into the unknown without a safety net of schedules and contingency plans?

I take a deep breath, forcing my shoulders to relax. The boxes will still be there tomorrow. The desk can wait. Perhaps this unexpected detour will lead somewhere interesting—or at the very least, prove I can survive an unplanned afternoon without dissolving into a puddle of anxiety.

"I'll do that, then."

Maria beams, clearly delighted. "Wonderful! I won't keep you any longer—I know how scholars value their time. But please let me know if you need anything at all to make your work more comfortable."

As she sweeps out of the café with the same efficiency with which she arrived, I sink back into my chair, disappointment settling over me like a heavy cloak. So much for my grand transformation. Not even a full day in Magnolia Cove, and I'm already falling back into my old patterns—taking on responsibilities I didn't seek, organizing my space exactly as it was before, and barely managing social interactions without sounding like a malfunctioning audiobook.

At this rate, I might as well have stayed in Misty Pines. What was the point of moving if I was just going to recreate my old life in a new location?

I think of Mark again—his meticulous office, his carefully ordered life, the way he worked through dinner most nights. He was reliable, steady Mark. And look where that got him. No one even noticed he was missing until I came looking for a book he'd borrowed.

I came here for a reason and swore to myself three bold choices. I've already made the first by moving. The second will be whatever opportunity I see next that scares the hell out of me. No backing down, no pros and cons list, no careful deliberation. The next terrifying chance that presents itself, I'm taking it. No matter what. Because if I don't push myself now,

I'll slip right back into the comfortable patterns that led me nowhere.

Gathering my bag, I finish the last of my now-lukewarm coffee—which really was excellent—and head toward the library. Outside, the morning sun warms the cobblestones, a light breeze carrying the scent of something sweet from a nearby bakery. A wind chime tinkles from a porch as I pass, and a few locals exchange cheerful greetings on their way down the street.

The library appears ahead, its weathered brick facade softened by climbing ivy. Stained glass windows catch the sunlight and send glimmers of light dancing over a massive oak tree. I pause just inside the entrance, taking in the comforting smell of books and the warm, well-lit atmosphere. Even the library's foyer feels like home.

A large cork board has a dozen flyers on it advertising a children's 'read to the dogs' library program, the town's upcoming Blue Moon Festival, and a variety of book clubs that meet around the town.

I'm about to turn and walk into the main entrance when another flyer catches my eye.

It's fluorescent pink and sparkly. Some glitter has fallen off it to dust the surrounding pages. The words *Magnolia Cove Matchmaking Service* are splashed across the top in a whimsical font beneath an even more flourished title, *Love by the Book*. Below, it reads: *Let our town's very own Cupid find your perfect match! Ask for Rhianna at the circulation desk.*

My stomach drops and I feel like I might throw up despite the lack of food. I can't imagine anything more horrifying than working with a matchmaker. No, actually I can. Working with a matchmaker in a new town when I'm trying to establish myself as a professional and reasonable person.

It's horrifying, but it's also... bold.

No, no, I won't. It's too terrible. I'll sign up for a submarine dive or that thing where people crawl through caves with those awful headlamps. I'll do anything else. My challenge is private anyway. No one will know if I skip this one. I won't be letting anyone down. I can just... walk away. Pretend I never saw it.

Except I *did* see it. And now it's glittering at me like it knows something I don't.

A sigh pushes past my lips. The door opens, and someone walks past me but I don't even look at them. I'm standing like a statue staring at a multi-colored poster with my hands in my slacks' pockets like if I focus enough, it'll disappear. Or maybe I will.

But it doesn't. And neither do I.

A particularly large piece of gold glitter on the flyer catches the light when the door opens again and twinkles at me like it's privy to some cosmic joke. I can almost hear Piper's voice in my head: "Where's your courage at, Brubba?"

Fine. This is all an experiment, anyway. Three bold moves, a wild search for the mythical signed Whitlock books, then I can revert to my previous, boring life and let all these horrifying decisions fade into distant memory. Just another chapter in the tale of my life, one I can quietly close and never revisit.

With a shaky hand,—and a silent prayer that none of my students ever get word of this—I reach out and tear off one of the contact strips. The sound of ripping paper is impossibly loud in the quiet foyer. I quickly stuff the strip into my pocket, as if hiding evidence of a crime.

There. I've done it. Sort of.

Now all I have to do is actually talk to this Rhianna person. At the circulation desk. Where I'll be working. Every day.

My heart races. What if word gets around that the new guy is so desperate he immediately signed up for a matchmaking service? What if it makes its way back to my actual job and life?

I take a deep breath and smooth the cuffs of my favorite tweed blazer. No backing out now. This is bold move number two. It's terrifying, yes, but that's the point, isn't it? To do things that scare me, to live life instead of observing it from behind the safety of my books.

With one last glance at the glittery monstrosity of a flyer, I turn and walk toward the circulation desk. Time to start this new chapter.

The library smells of lemons. That's not something I would have guessed. My loafers tap softly, echoing in the quiet space as I force myself to move toward the circulation desk.

That's when I hear it—a soft humming and the occasional lyric sung under someone's breath. The sound draws me toward the circulation desk, where a whirlwind of movement catches my eye.

She's a blur of color and energy, her dark hair swaying as she bobs her head to whatever tune is playing through her earbuds. Her fingers dance over book spines as she sorts through a cart of returns. She's wearing a turquoise skirt that whirls as she bops around. It's paired with a white graphic tee and a mustard-yellow cardigan adorned with pins that say things like 'Prose before Bros' and 'Talk Wordy to Me.'

I clear my throat, suddenly feeling like an intruder in this moment of joyful solitude. "Excuse me, are you Rhianna?"

She spins around, thick lashes framing warm brown eyes that brighten when she smiles. My heart stops pounding for a moment as she pulls out an earbud and answers me. "The very one. The only one, in fact!"

Something unexpected flutters in my chest—a sensation entirely foreign to my carefully regulated emotional landscape. Her smile hits me with an almost physical impact, and I find myself momentarily transfixed by the curve of her lips, the sparkle in her eyes that seems to illuminate her entire face. I've never been distracted by someone's mere presence before, yet here I am, suddenly aware of the subtle floral scent of her perfume, the graceful way she tucks a strand of hair behind her ear.

Somehow I find my voice. "Well, there's also the one cemented forever in song form."

Her full lips part in an even larger grin. "I spell my name differently than that one, but I concur. It's only the very best song that's ever existed, after all."

"I'm afraid you're incorrect on that," my voice is a tease. And who the hell is this version of Eli Lancaster? I don't know, but YOLO or whatever it is that Piper says all the time.

The words flow out of me with an ease that's startling. I'm bantering. I'm teasing. With a complete stranger. Without rehearsing or weighing each potential response for its risk of awkwardness. The realization is almost dizzying—this isn't me, or at least, it hasn't been me for as long as I can remember.

"Please." Rhianna rolls her eyes playfully. "Fine, name one that's better."

"Dreams, also by Fleetwood Mac."

She pauses, her smile dropping and her eyes going wide. "Oh my gosh, you're right."

Heat creeps up my neck but I shrug. "Fleetwood Mac is the best soft rock band of all time, though. Full stop."

"As much as it pains me, I do have questions." She leans on her arms, close to me, like she's about to whisper a secret. "Like, first of all, how dare you relegate Fleetwood Mac to 'soft rock' as if they weren't producing revolutionary music that spanned a dozen genres." Her smile is infectious and I find myself mirroring it. "Second of all, what about The Eagles? Or Bread?"

I can't contain my laughter. "Bread? I mean, they're good... but they have nothing on Stevie Nicks."

"Just because they don't have Stevie's notoriety,"—she pauses and crosses herself, then presses her hands together for a moment of silence—"doesn't mean they weren't excellent. I suppose we can at least agree that the 70s were the best era for rock."

"What about the 80s?" I can't resist asking. "I mean, some of the best Queen and AC/DC music came out in that decade." It amazes me how easily the words are flowing. Music and books are my two safest topics—familiar ground I can usually count on, even if I still stumble through them in group settings or with new people. But with Rhianna, it feels easy. Natural. Like we've been having this conversation for years.

She gasps in mock horror. "Sir, I'm sorry, but I'm going to need to ask you to leave the library."

We both dissolve into laughter, and I'm struck again by how simple this feels. It's been a long time since I've connected with anyone like this. Too long, if I'm being honest.

Most of my conversations are structured, predictable—intellectual sparring in academic settings, polite small talk over catered university dinners, surface-level exchanges with acquaintances who don't really know me beyond my credentials. Even my last relationship, steady and reasonable as it was, had a rhythm to it. Safe. Comfortable.

But this?

This is something else entirely. It's effortless, like stepping into a conversation that's already been happening, like finding a melody I somehow know the words to before the chorus even begins.

And I don't know what to do with that.

"I'm Eli Lancaster." I extend my hand. "Starting tomorrow I'll be working at the library."

And, apparently, spending most of my time there too, now that I've somehow agreed to what sounds suspiciously like a full-time job. But then she smiles again—wide and bright and entirely unbothered by my internal grumbling—and I find myself thinking that maybe being here every day won't be so bad after all.

She gives my hand a shake. Her hand is small in mine, soft and cool. I want to keep holding onto it but I'm also relieved when she drops the contact. "Oh, welcome to Magnolia Cove! I'm Rhianna Wilder, librarian extraordinaire and a woman of excellent music taste."

Before I can talk myself out of it, I pull the glittery strip of pink paper from my pocket. "Are you also the Rhianna from this flyer?"

Her entire face lights up. I've heard that expression before, but never understood it. Now I do. It's like plugging a Christmas tree in and watching the transformation. I want to see her face do that a hundred more times.

"Yes! Oh my gosh, are you interested in the matchmaking service? I'm so excited! This is perfect timing—I was just thinking about how to get started, and here you are!"

I nod, trying to match her excitement even as my stomach twists. "Yes. I'm... trying new things."

"Well, you've come to the right place." Rhianna beams. Her smile could power the entire library, and probably half the town. "I'm 100% going to help you find the love of your life in no time!"

I release a breathy chuckle, suddenly struck by the horrifying reality of what I've just agreed to do. Rhianna's presence is soothing—no, more than soothing. But this matchmaking service? This means sitting across from strangers. Stammering. Sweating. Trying to articulate my deepest hopes and fears to people who will stare at me, waiting for coherent sentences that will never come. My heart begins to race, the familiar panic of unpredictable social interactions crawling up my spine. What was I thinking? This isn't a bold move. This is a disaster in the making.

My heart thunders to the point that it pounds in my temples, caught between panic and something else entirely—a spark of attraction I haven't felt in years. Rhianna's energy pulls at me like a gravitational force, and for a moment, I'm captivated by the way her hands move when she speaks, the subtle curve of her smile, the golden flecks dancing in her brown eyes. But reality crashes back with brutal efficiency.

The woman before me is practically bouncing on her toes with excitement, vibrant and full of life—the kind of woman who turns heads when she walks into a room. Her turquoise skirt swirls around her legs as she moves, her cardigan adorned with playful pins that speak to a personality so different from my own. Someone like her would never be interested in a quiet, bookish professor like me. I can already imagine the conversation dying, her growing restless with my careful words, my studied silences. I'd probably bore her to tears within a week.

Still, there's something about her enthusiasm that's infectious. Maybe that's exactly why she's perfect for this role. Her energy, so different from mine, might be just what I need to shake up my routine during my stay. Maybe bold move number two isn't about finding love at all, thank god, but an opportunity to experience some of the spontaneity I came for.

"So, when do we start?" My playful tone is gone, and a rasp has entered my voice as I force the words out.

Rhianna's grin widens, if that's even possible. "How about we set up an initial consultation for tomorrow afternoon? We can go over your preferences, deal breakers, and all that good stuff."

I nod, hoping the look I give is *interested* and not *absolutely terrified.* "Sounds perfect."

As I walk away from the circulation desk, the citrusy library scents mingle with Rhianna's fruity-floral perfume and I can't help but wonder what I've gotten myself into. But then

I remember Mark, and my promise to myself. Three bold moves. This is number two.

I take a deep breath, straighten my cuffs again, and step out into the warm Magnolia Cove afternoon. The sun is bright, almost blinding after the peaceful, dim library interior and I blink rapidly to adjust. It's only when I'm halfway down the street that I realize something.

I stop dead in my tracks. "Damn it," I mutter under my breath, earning a curious glance from a woman holding a Pomeranian.

I forgot to look at my office. The entire reason I went to the library today, and I completely forgot about it. How did that happen? One conversation with Rhianna, and my carefully laid plans flew right out the window.

A rueful chuckle escapes me as I shake my head. Is this what Rhianna does to people? Is this what I'm in for with this matchmaking business? My ordered, predictable, comfortable life suddenly seems very far away.

Part of me wants to turn around, go back inside, and ask to see Michael as I'd planned. It would be the sensible thing to do. The Eli thing to do.

Instead, I continue down the sidewalk, away from the library. Whatever happens next, at least it won't be boring. And maybe that's exactly what I need.

Welcome to bold move number two, Eli. Let's see where this leads.

Rhianna

I practically skip through the side door of our family's house, then toss my keys into the bowl on the counter with a satisfying clink. Look, I know few adults live with their parents, but few people have historical family homes on Main Street, either. Besides, it's just me, and I have saving goals, okay? Helping cover the utilities with my parents is much cheaper than renting one of the resident's cottages. Because of that, in a couple more years I'll be boarding a plane to somewhere warm and wonderful.

Anyway, there's just something about home. Copper pots hang above the center island—pots Dad used to teach me and my older brother how to make pralines, stirring the sugar and pecans until they were just right. A wire basket of fruit perches on the counter's edge, alongside a glass cookie jar—both mainstays of my childhood. Mom still keeps them stocked even though Gavin moved out almost a decade ago and it's only the three of us left here. Art prints from friends of Dad at the university hang in frames near the fridge.

It's eclectic, a bit cluttered—and home.

I let out a long, contented sigh. Maybe it's just me but the sun seems to glisten through the windows with an extra sparkle today. I glimpse myself in a mirror and—oh my gosh, I'm smiling. Like a real, genuine, I-just-won-the-magical-lottery smile. What in the name of The Whisk's blessed cinnamon rolls is happening?

"Well, don't you look chipper." Mom's voice floats in a moment before her. She's wearing her paint-speckled smock and her art-therapist assessing gaze. "Good day at work?"

I bounce over to the cookie jar and pull out one of Mom's polvorones, the delicate, crumbly dough melting on my tongue as powdered sugar dusts my fingertips. The touch of magic she imbued them with sends warmth unfurling in my chest, like a hug in dessert form. "Every day has been a good day at work since I got the activity director role."

Mom grabs a stack of envelopes from the mail basket and shuffles through them. "Mhmm, Grammie Rae told me about your newest venture. Do you think this reflects an inner desire, Rhi?"

I groan. "Mom, we've talked about this. You can't do the therapist thing on me."

We've been having this conversation since I moved back home, all broken pieces and stubborn pride. I wasn't ready to be fixed then—especially after Jacob left. I'm not sure I am now.

Jacob and I met in college—he played guitar, I did theater. We showed up to each other's performances, stayed out too late, danced in dorm hallways, laughed like the world was always going to be golden. When we were still together a year after graduation, it felt like maybe we'd outrun the odds. Like maybe we had the kind of love that could last.

He said he loved me. And maybe he did.

But maybe there are different kinds of love. There's sunshine love—the kind that only blooms when everything is bright and easy. There's snowflake love too—like what I had with my grandmother, who lived with us when I was a kid. Delicate and rare and beautiful in a way that stays with you long after it melts.

But what I needed most was storm-season love. The kind that sits with you through the downpour and doesn't flinch. Jacob didn't have that kind. He wanted the girl who laughed through the sunny days, not the one crying on the floor in a tangle of grief and Grandma Ida's old scarves.

So he left. Not just me—he left Magnolia Cove.

And maybe he was right. Maybe my storms were too long. Too loud. Too much.

Maybe I am.

I haven't let anyone get that close since.

And my mother hasn't let me forget it. She's gentle about it—mostly. But with every passing year, her nudges have gotten less subtle and more determined. She wants to see me happy, dang it. And she'll cheer, scheme, or strong-arm the universe into making it happen.

What she doesn't see—what no one sees—is that deep down, I'm not built for the kind of love that stays. I burn too hot in the highs, sink too deep in the lows. Even the good ones get tired of weathering that kind of intensity. Some people are meant to go it alone. I think I'm one of them.

Mom drops the mail and puts both hands on her hips, a mock look of offense raising her brows. "Is it 'doing the therapy thing' if I ask about your life?"

"Yes, if you say 'reflection of inner desires' it is. I'm happy single. I have my big trip in the works."

But of course, she gives me that look—the one that says she's a coon hound who's just treed a squirrel and she's not backing down until I admit I've got feelings.

The worst part? She's usually right. Annoyingly, frustratingly, magically right.

I inherited my energy-reading magic from her, after all.

She just uses hers for art therapy and emotional break-throughs, while I use mine to match people with their perfect book and to occasionally avoid my own emotional growth. Balance.

She calls it mother's intuition. I call it magical meddling. But deep down, I know she sees right through me—especially when it comes to my commitment issues, which she brings up approximately once a week, always with a gentle smile and a not-so-subtle raised eyebrow.

She walks up and presses a kiss on my cheek and surprisingly lets the subject fade. "I heard there's a new employee at the library as well."

"Oh, Eli Lancaster. He's not actually an employee, he's just helping the library with managing and warding our backlog of ancient texts. He's a professor and a rare book curator, though—don't you think that's a fascinating job?"

"Your father certainly would." We exchange chuckles. "Did you get to meet him?"

"I did! He's actually hilarious and knows 70s rock bands which is an immediate point in anyone's favor." I pause and shove another bite of cookie into my mouth. I'm sounding a bit too enthusiastic. And I don't do enthusiastic about potential romantic interests.

Even if Eli has kind eyes, a voice made for poetry readings, and the kind of slow-burn banter that could melt the spine off a first edition. Still. I've read this story before, and I know how it ends. "You know, I mean it's nice to have someone new around who appreciates good music."

Mom's eyebrow arches in a way that means she's shifted into therapist-mode again. "Oh? Tell me more about this Eli?"

I try to keep my voice casual, but it's like trying to keep Grammie Rae away from gossip—nearly impossible. "I don't know. He's got this whole understated-but-sophisticated vibe going on. Like, he's the type that could pull off a sweater vest and not make you cringe. He also wears these black-rimmed glasses but somehow they set off his eyes and make him look intellectual, you know?"

Mom stares at me, and a flush warms my cheeks. I'm gushing like a romance novel heroine. But, come on, can you blame me? Eli's got this unassuming yet quietly charismatic presence that practically screams 'intelligent hottie who probably knows the Dewey Decimal System by heart.' All of that to say, he's going to make an excellent matchmaking client.

Because that's all I'm interested in with him. Truly. Strictly professional. Even if he makes my heart do that ridiculous flutter-patter thing when he looked at me like I was more interesting than his favorite footnote. And even though my magic hummed toward his like a needle finding true north. It doesn't mean anything. I learned the hard way what happens when you let someone in too deep—when you let yourself *love* someone like that. It breaks you. And I promised myself I wouldn't open myself up to that again.

"Anyway, he seems nice. Professional. A good addition to the community."

"A good addition to the community," mom repeats in the same tone of voice that I mimicked her therapy-talk. "Are you going to be working closely with him?"

"We'll both work at the library, so I'm sure we'll see each other around," I say, perhaps a bit too quickly. "But you know I'm focused on my career. The only interest I have in dating is helping facilitate relationships for other people. Not for me. Because I'm not looking. At all."

Mom's lips twitch into a smile. "Of course, love."

"I'm serious. I'm building my dream life—solo adventures, passport stamps, and all that jazz. Plus, he works at the library! Can you imagine how awkward it would be if we dated and broke up?" It would be the worst. I repress a shudder. "I'd have to find a new job, and then where would I be?

Jobless, dateless, and probably living in a cardboard box by the beach."

I can only hope this argument is convincing enough to throw Mom off the scent. Her hound-dog instincts are already zeroing in on the fact that the new, undeniably attractive employee will be working with me *every day*.

I want to be the matchmaker—not the match-made.

"You seem to have given this a lot of thought for someone who's not interested." Mom's eyebrows are now raised in full mom-mode and I don't even fight my eye roll. So much for my hopes that she'd nod politely and move on like a normal person.

"Look, if you're hoping for grandkids or whatever this is, you're going to need to put more pressure on Gavin. He's the oldest, anyway. Don't they talk about birth order in therapy school? The oldest is the responsible kid. I'm the young, free spirited one."

She offers me an eye roll that reminds me where I get the tendency from. "You're just like your father. And that has nothing to do with birth order."

"So she's devilishly handsome and a lot of fun?" Dad walks in, tossing his house keys into the basket next to mine and I jump toward him and give him a giant hug. He teaches at a university on the mainland during the week and only comes home over weekends and school breaks.

"Dad!" I exclaim, breathing in the familiar scent of his cologne mixed with the faint smell of chalk that always seems to cling to him. "You're home early."

He squeezes me tight before releasing me and grinning at Mom. "Now, what's this about Rhianna being like me?"

Mom laughs and gives him a kiss which causes him to sweep her into a dip. I finish my cookie and turn away. That's the thing about my parents—they're still in love. They married before social media existed and they still slow dance in the kitchen. Come to think of it, this is probably why Gavin and I have yet to find someone. When you grow up with the perfect relationship on display, it makes everything else feel subpar.

When Mom is back on her feet, her eyes dart to me again. "Rhianna was just deflecting from talking about the new man in town."

I groan. "Mom, there's no 'new man.' He's just a new coworker. At the library. Where I work. Professionally."

Dad leans toward me conspiratorially. "Fresh blood? What's his thoughts on William Carlos Williams?"

"Not sure yet." I give side-eye to Mom. "I've barely spoken with him."

"A book man, though? Not from the island?"

"Dad," I whine. "Not you too! He's a professor like you, but that's not the point. The point is—"

"The point is," Mom interjects with a sly smile, "that our daughter is getting all flustered over a man who apparently knows his 70s rock bands and looks good in a pair of black glasses."

I splutter, looking between my parents in disbelief. They're acting like I'm sixteen again and crushing on the boy who worked with me at the ice-cream shop. "I am not flustered! I'm just... glad to have a fresh conversational option, okay? It's been the same three faces at the water cooler for years."

"Mhm." Mom pats my arm. "I have one more client before I can call it quits today. Rich, honey, dinner is on you tonight."

"You've got it, love." As soon as Mom walks out, he turns to me. "So, which pizza shop should we patronize?"

I laugh. Mom definitely meant for him to cook. Maybe she's right that I'm just like my father. "Love you, Dad."

"You too, chicken." His hand is already inside the cookie jar.

I dart up the stairs two at a time until I reach the safety of my room. The family cat, Mr. Whiskers, sprawls across my bed, sunning himself in a patch of late afternoon light. I yank a book off an overstuffed shelf, intent on escaping into someone else's story for an hour.

But when I lay down on my bed, my eyes dart to the Fleetwood Mac poster that I'd taped over the floral wallpaper as a teen. Then I'm thinking of *him* again. Of his hazel eyes that changed colors as different light hit them. Of the richness of his laughter and our easy banter. Of his sharp jawline and the curl of his lips.

The way my magic seemed to reach for his without permission. Like it recognized something in him. Something that fit. A little too perfectly and—

I jump to my feet, toss the book onto my side table, and march myself to my mirror. I give myself the sternest look I can muster. "Listen here, Rhianna Wilder. You are not, I repeat, NOT interested in Eli Lancaster. Mom is just putting that into your head. He's a client and a coworker. A very handsome, intelligent, book-loving coworker who probably smells like old parchment and— No! Stop that! Focus on your work. On your savings goals. On your grand adventure around the world. You're not falling for someone again. Not seriously." I pause and give myself a firm look. "You know how that ends. Got it?"

I point two fingers at my eyes then back at my reflection. She gives me a nod that looks more convinced than I feel.

Beside the mirror, I'd taped a savings chart when I moved back in—after a few years working as a librarian post-grad, stacking up experience while quietly plotting my grand escape. Two more years and I'll have enough. The hard part is almost done and now it's just the fun planning—and a few more years of living with my parents who quietly hate the entire idea.

At the bottom of the chart, I'd taped a birthday card from Grandma Ida so I could always see her loopy signature and remember her last words to me. If I close my eyes, I can hear them as clearly as the day she said them from her hospital bed.

"Promise me, Rhianna." Her once-powerful voice had turned into a whisper. "Promise me you'll take that trip we always talked about. Even if I can't make it."

Her frail hand gripped mine with surprising strength, and I hiccuped a breath, fighting the sting of tears.

"Paris, Buenos Aires, Cairo," she murmured. "We planned it for so long. I used to fill journals with the places we'd go, the stories we'd collect." A weary smile ghosted her lips. "But now... it's your turn. Don't wait for the perfect time. Go. See it all—for both of us."

The lump in my throat thickened. "It won't be the same without you."

"Promise me you'll go," she whispered. "Really go. And when you do... you'll find me there. In the sea spray, in the café music, in the pages of your travel journal. I'll be with you. Always."

I nodded and attempted to fight tears that streamed down my cheeks. The savings chart is nearly half colored now. Grandma Ida would be so proud. I run my fingers over it and remember the pain in her eyes.

Jacob thought the way I grieved my grandmother was... too much. Like it was strange to hurt that deeply over someone who wasn't a parent or a partner. But Grandma Ida wasn't just my grandmother—she was my best friend. When you're an awkward kid who struggles to fit in—even on an island full of magical people—having someone who walks to the beat of the same odd drum you thought only you could hear... that kind of connection changes everything.

We snuck candy into matinee movies. We swam in the

ocean under the moonlight. We made a vow to see the world together, one grand adventure at a time.

But then she got sick.

And she left before we could.

With a determined huff, I plop down at my desk and pull out a new notebook I'd purchased for the matchmaking service. Enough of the moping. Enough of the what-ifs and whispered memories.

Time to brainstorm potential matches for Eli. Someone who's not me and doesn't have relationship non-compatible plans. Someone perfect for him. Someone who likes charmingly nerdy men with a passion for books, surprisingly good music taste, and the ability to banter like he stepped out of a Jane Austen novel and... and...

Someone who isn't terrified of loving someone again.

Because Mom's right. I do avoid love. She knows it. I know it. It's the unspoken elephant in every conversation we have.

And no matter how much the energy sparked between Eli and me—because yes, of course I felt how our magic practically hummed in the air together—Eli seems like a good guy. The kind who's steady and genuine and open-hearted. And he doesn't deserve someone like me.

Someone who builds walls and calls them boundaries.

Someone who learned the hard way that vulnerability doesn't guarantee closeness—it can be the very thing that pushes people away. I've kept things light, surface-level, safe.

It's easier to help other people fall in love than to risk showing someone the mess underneath and being abandoned all over again.

Because once was enough.

Once was *too much*.

So I pick up my pen, pretend the flutter in my chest means

nothing, and start planning the perfect match—anyone but me.

* * *

The scent of fresh coffee wafts into my room, followed by a gentle knock. Dad pokes his head in, two steaming mugs in hand, his reading glasses perched on his nose and a well-worn poetry journal tucked under his arm.

"Early bird gets the coffee," he says, padding into my room in his worn leather slippers. I'm already at my desk, notebook open, pen in hand—because apparently my brain decided to wake up at dawn, buzzing with matchmaking ideas and, fine, maybe a few lingering thoughts about Eli. Strictly professional ones, of course. Totally reasonable. Completely manageable.

Just don't ask me to say that out loud.

"You're my favorite father," I say, making grabby hands at the coffee. He gives me a mug—the one with little books printed all over it that Mom got me for Christmas—and settles into my reading chair, the one by the window that used to be Grandma Ida's.

"I brought you something else too." He pulls a glossy brochure from his back pocket. "A colleague mentioned this at yesterday's faculty meeting. It took a bit of digging but I managed to find some information."

The brochure's title makes me set my cup down with a clink against my desk. The *World Library Tour Fellowship*. My heart thunders as I scan the details. Six months. Twenty-four destinations. Libraries around the world.

It's like someone reached into mine and Grandma Ida's dreams and turned them into a real opportunity.

"Dad..." My voice comes out all wobbly.

"I know you've been saving," he whispers. "But this seemed like a perfect opportunity—libraries and worldwide travel. And it would keep you from dipping into your savings. Maybe you can spend that on your next adventure."

"Next adventure?"

Even for me, that feels like a lot. I won't lie, I love to take massive, oversized, regret-everything bites... but one gigantically ambitious idea at a time, please.

Dad's eyes twinkle, and he takes a sip of his coffee before answering. "You know, your grandmother was right to encourage you to see the world. But she was also right about another thing she used to say—that magic finds its way home." He gestures around my childhood bedroom, at the marks on the doorframe showing my height through the years, at the window seat where I spent countless hours reading. "Magnolia Cove has a way of holding space for what you need. Sometimes that's distance for a time. Sometimes it's stillness. A chance to let yourself be known. That's the hardest part of life, I think."

He must see something in my face because he quickly adds, "Hey, I didn't mean to push, chicken. I know it's not simple. Just—whatever happens, whatever you choose... just know that Magnolia Cove will still be here. *We* will still be here. What matters is that you choose. That it's your life. Your story."

I let out a breath. Leave it to Dad to know exactly what to say, to make both holding on and letting go feel like choices, not failures.

Staying in Magnolia Cove is hard. Not just because Grandma Ida's memory lingers in every creaky boardwalk and lopsided sandcastle. But because this town also watched me fall apart.

Jacob didn't just break up with me—he left. Packed up, moved away, and made it pretty clear to everyone that my grief was the reason.

And Magnolia Cove is small. People talk. People remember. I became the girl who was *too much*. The one who lost her grandmother and then her boyfriend, and who hasn't dated seriously since.

Sometimes it feels like I'm living inside a snow globe that everyone else keeps shaking.

What I want—what I've wanted ever since—is to run. To find somewhere new, where no one looks at me like I'm fragile or broken or still trying to hold herself together. Somewhere I can breathe without the weight of old stories pressing down on my chest.

Dad blows on his coffee. "Besides, life catches you by surprise sometimes. I had my own plans, then I met your mother." His smile goes a little dreamy. "Then we had Gavin and you. That's been the very best adventure."

He thumbs under my chin, and I return his goofy grin. Sometimes Dad makes it feel free again. Like I could be the version of me that existed before everything fell apart.

I look back at the fellowship papers. "But the application requirements—"

"Three innovative community projects," Dad finishes, because of course he's already read every detail. "How's that matchmaking service coming along?"

"It's one," I say, my brain firing on all cylinders now. "And Library Alive Night is happening in three months—that's two." I've been planning that event forever: a night where literary characters come to life through living book characters, complete with themed food and interactive storytelling. "I just need one more."

Dad kicks a knee over an ankle. "You know your mother worries about you leaving."

"I know." I glance at the photo on my desk—me and Grandma Ida at my high school graduation, both of us beaming. "That's not really living, is it? Focusing on the worries?"

"Well, Mary Oliver would take your side," he answers. I

clutch my mug, warmth seeping into my bones. Neither Gavin nor me had followed Dad's passion for poetry, but I'd always had a soft spot for Oliver. She just said things so dang perfectly. Dad stands and presses a kiss to the top of my head. "Just promise me one thing?"

"What's that?"

"Don't let the fear of losing something good make you run from it," he says gently.

The words hit harder than I expect. It's like he's not just giving advice but naming something I haven't said out loud.

His eyes twinkle in a way that makes me suspect he's not just talking about travel. He says nothing about the new, albeit handsome and surprisingly good-at-banter man working at the library—but that look says he and Mom have discussed it. Extensively.

After Dad leaves, I spread the brochure out on my desk, tracing the photos of libraries in Paris, Marrakesh, Cape Town. My heart races at the possibilities. But there's also this weird ache in my chest when I think about leaving Magnolia Cove, about leaving the library, about leaving my friends, and maybe even about... leaving certain people I've not gotten to know yet who I absolutely am not thinking about.

I pull out a fresh notebook—because every new project deserves its own notebook—and start listing potential ideas for my third innovative project. The pages are crisp and clean, full of possibility. Just like this fellowship. Just like my future. The application deadline is in two months. If I'm going to do this, I need to go all in.

Project Ideas for Fellowship Application:

1. Virtual Reality Library Tours
2. Senior Tech Literacy Program
3. Storybook Kitchen Story Hour

I tap my pen against the page, frowning. They're all... fine. But none of them feel special enough. None of them feel like something that would make the fellowship committee sit up and take notice.

Mom would have good ideas—she's the best at making lists and listening with her whole person. But, Mom would also have *opinions*. Opinions about why I want to leave, about what I'm running from, about how sometimes we create elaborate escape plans to avoid dealing with our feelings. If I try to explain this Fellowship opportunity to her, she'll start throwing around words like *emotional bypassing* and *fear of commitment*.

Maybe I'll keep it to myself for now. Just until I know if I can craft a third community project and if they accept me into the program. No need to upset Mom or get the town gossip mill churning. Once it's an actual plan, I'll share it with her.

Grandma Ida's photo sits in a puddle of golden morning light. "I'm doing it," I whisper to her smiling face. "I'm really doing it."

Now I just have to figure out how to balance planning a global adventure with working my job and finding perfect matches for others in town—including one frustratingly attractive book curator who makes my heart flutter in ways I can't afford to feel.

Right. Simple.

I take another sip of coffee and start writing, trying to ignore the way my stomach flutters every time I think about leaving. Or staying. Or Eli.

Maybe I need something stronger than coffee.

Eli

My first reaction upon entering the room is disbelief.

"This is..." I trail off, unable to find the right words as I take in the staggering collection before me. Floor-to-ceiling bookshelves stretch in every direction, seemingly defying the physical dimensions of the library itself. Ancient texts line each shelf, their leather bindings in various states of preservation, from crumbling to surprisingly pristine.

The air carries the unmistakable scent of old paper—that distinct combination of dust, leather, and something else. Something almost sweet, like vanilla but earthier. The perfume of centuries.

"Impressive, right?" Michael says, clearly pleased by my stunned reaction. He's been chattering happily since collecting me from the entrance, and I'm grateful for his ability to carry the conversation. It allows me to absorb everything without the pressure of maintaining small talk.

I run my fingers along a shelf, the raised spines humming beneath my touch. "How did you even collect this many books on an island? The salt air alone would—"

"Destroy them?" Michael finishes with a knowing smile. "That's where the magic comes in."

As he says it, I notice the shimmer in the air—almost imperceptible unless you know what to look for. Protective wards. The ones around the room are strong, steady, humming with quiet power. But the ones surrounding the books themselves... they're different. Still present, but dulled, like a once-vibrant painting left too long in the sun.

"The entire room is warded," I murmur, feeling the gentle buzz of magic against my skin.

Michael nods enthusiastically. "One of the strongest magical containments on the island. Has to be. Some of these texts date back to the 1500s." He gestures to a glass case in the corner. "We've got a first edition Malleus Maleficarum over there, though I don't recommend reading it—terrible propaganda, obviously."

My initial frustration about agreeing to this full-time position during my break dissolves as I scan the shelves with growing excitement. This is a treasure trove of knowledge that could contain almost anything.

Including, perhaps...

My heart rate quickens at the thought.

Cyrus Whitlock spent twelve years on Magnolia Cove. Twelve incredibly productive years, during which he wrote some of his most groundbreaking work on Welsh mythology. If there were any signed copies of his books—any at all—they would likely be here, perhaps gathering dust in this very room.

I can almost hear Dr. Chen's voice in my head, her knowing smirk when I'd mentioned my summer plans. *Still chasing one of the mythical signed copies?* I'd shrugged it off like it didn't matter, but of course it did. Finding a signed Whitlock would be more than just a rare book acquisition; it would be the culmination of my entire academic career.

"You must have a powerful witch or warlock to maintain

this room," I comment, noting how the space seems to expand beyond what should be physically possible. Magic like this requires constant attention, regular renewal.

Michael laughs and rolls his eyes good-naturedly. "Oh yeah. Head Warlock, Dean Markham. Have you met him?"

"I have." The memory of my meeting with Dean Markham is still vivid. I'd needed his approval to stay on the island for the season, magical pocket communities being cautious about long-term residences to protect their secrets. Being in his presence had been like sitting before a roiling fire of magic—intense, almost uncomfortable. Though in all fairness, I find most social situations uncomfortable, so perhaps that was nothing unusual.

"He's... a lot," Michael continues, "but he takes the protection of these texts seriously. We couldn't maintain this collection without him."

I nod, absorbing this information as we continue our tour. Michael points out sections organized by era, by subject matter, by magical properties. My fingers itch to begin examining them immediately, to lose myself in their pages.

"—and if you want to join us for lunch some days," Michael is saying, "the break room is behind the circulation desk. Maria brings homemade cookies on Fridays."

"What are the other librarians like?" The question comes out smoothly, surprising me with its ease. But I know immediately why it flows so naturally—I'm asking about Rhianna. I'm thinking about Rhianna.

I haven't stopped thinking about her since our encounter yesterday. Her laughter still rings in my ears, the cadence of her voice like a song I can't get out of my head. The way she'd argued with me about music with such passion, such conviction—it was magnetizing.

This morning, walking into the library to meet Michael, I'd passed her. She crouched down to speak with a child, her flowing skirt draped like a flower petal across the polished floor. Dark curls tumbled down her back, catching the light from the stained glass windows above.

"Of course I can find the perfect book for you," she'd said to a wide-eyed little girl. "It's my specialty."

Then she'd accepted the child's outstretched hand and skipped—actually skipped—to the children's section, her bracelets jingling with each movement.

It was like watching joy embodied. I came to Magnolia Cove seeking something to make me feel alive again, to break me out of the monotony I'd fallen into—especially after Mark's death. And stumbled directly into Rhianna Wilder, the most vibrantly alive person I've ever encountered.

I've tried to think of a plausible excuse to talk to her again, rolling possibilities around in my mind until they're worn smooth like river stones. But everything I come up with sounds contrived, forced.

"—mostly keep to themselves," Michael is saying, and I realize I've missed part of his response. "Claire handles non-fiction, she's super organized. Rhianna runs the circulation desk and children's programming, she's basically the heart of the place. Everyone loves her."

I try not to look too interested at the mention of her name. "I met Rhianna. She seems... passionate about her work."

Michael chuckles. "That's one way to put it. Rhianna's passionate about pretty much everything. Last month she convinced the entire staff to dress as characters from Greek mythology for a special storytime. Dean Markham even attended. He didn't participate, of course, but she somehow got the rest of us to go along with it." He shakes his head, fondness evident in his expression. "I was Apollo. Had to wear a laurel wreath for six hours."

The image makes me smile despite myself. I can easily

picture Rhianna orchestrating such an event, her enthusiasm sweeping everyone along in its wake.

"You'll get to know everyone soon enough," Michael assures me. "It's a small staff. We're like family."

Family. The word sits oddly in my chest. I've never really belonged anywhere outside of my own family and academic circles, where connections are formed through shared intellectual interests rather than emotional bonds. The idea of this close-knit library community both appeals to me and makes me nervous. What if I don't fit in? What if my social awkwardness keeps them at a distance?

But then I think of Rhianna again, of how easily she drew me into conversation despite my usual reticence. Perhaps this place is different. Perhaps I could be different here.

"So," Michael says, gesturing expansively around the room, "this will be your domain for the next few months. We desperately need someone with your expertise to catalog everything properly, assess what needs restoration, and strengthen the protective wards where needed. Maria mentioned you have a particularly strong talent for book preservation spells?"

I nod, grateful to be back on comfortable ground. "Yes, it's been my focus alongside my academic work. Books are... well, they're more than just objects to me."

"I can tell," Michael says with a knowing smile. "Well, I'll leave you to get acquainted with your new charges. You've seen your office already. If you need anything, I'll be at the reference desk until closing."

As Michael's footsteps fade, I'm left alone in the hushed sanctuary of ancient texts. The silence wraps around me like a comfortable blanket, broken only by the occasional creak of old wood and the whisper of magic sustaining the room.

I graze the book spines nearest me again, feeling the subtle variations in leather and binding techniques. Some of these books have survived centuries, outliving their creators, their readers, entire civilizations. There's something profoundly humbling about that.

Rhianna dances back into my mind as she's done repeatedly for the last 24 hours. We're meeting tomorrow at The Whimsical Whisk. It's not a date, I remind myself firmly. It's a consultation so she can try to match me with someone else—someone who might be compatible with my quiet, ordered life. Someone who isn't her.

The thought makes my chest tighten inexplicably. Which is ridiculous. I barely know her.

And yet... There was something about our interaction yesterday. The way conversation flowed between us without the usual awkward pauses and stilted responses that plague my interactions with new people. The way her eyes lit up when she talked about music, even when disagreeing with me. The natural ease of it all.

I pull a book from the shelf—a treatise on Welsh dragons from the 1700s—and carefully open it. The pages are brittle but intact, protected by fading preservation spells that need reinforcement. As I begin examining it, letting my magic assess the condition of the binding, I find myself smiling.

Tomorrow, I'll see Rhianna again. I'll have a reason to talk to her, to hear her laugh, to watch her hands gesture animatedly as she speaks. I'd face any level of social anxiety for that.

For now, though, I have these books. This quiet, this peace, this purpose. I settle deeper into the work, letting the familiar process of examination and preservation ground me. But even as I lose myself in centuries-old texts, a part of my mind remains fixed on tomorrow.

On her.

On the possibility of something I hadn't come to Magnolia Cove expecting to find.

Rhianna

The bell over The Whimsical Whisk's door jingles as Eli and I step inside. The smell of cinnamon and butter hits me like a sugar-coated freight train, and I have to physically restrain myself from doing the happy dance I usually perform when walking into my favorite bakery. *Play it cool, Rhianna. Act professional. Don't be too much.*

"And this," I say with a flourish that would make a game show host proud, "is the crown jewel of Magnolia Cove's culinary scene. Home of the 'I'd sell my soul for another bite' cinnamon rolls. And, as of today, the official headquarters for our matchmaking consultation."

Eli's grin tugs up the corners of his mouth, emphasizing the dark stubble on his jaw. My stomach twists but it's only because I'm hungry and for absolutely no other reason.

"That good, huh?" he asks.

"Trust me, one bite and you'll plot your way to marrying into the family just for the recipe. Unfortunately, Ethan is an only child."

"A shame," Eli whispers, like it's a secret joke just between the two of us. My heart flutters and I find myself in the strange position of being at a loss for words.

Our energetic vibrations brush together, soft and electric, like the crackle of static before a storm. His aura mingles with mine in that quiet, unmistakable way that happens when two energies align just a little too well.

But it doesn't matter.

It doesn't.

I'm the matchmaker. And I'll find someone who sparks with him even better. Someone open. Someone brave. Someone who doesn't flinch at the thought of love.

I'm about to pray desperately for any intervention when, as if on cue, Ethan emerges from the back, his apron flour-dusted. His eyes light up when they land on me. "Rhianna! And you must be the newest resident. Eli, right?"

Eli shakes his hand and there's a little spark of magic recognition—the tiniest flicker that passes between magical beings. It's like a secret handshake, but with more sparkle and less awkward finger movements. I notice the moment Eli realizes he's shaking hands with a shifter—when the magic becomes apparent. His eyes widen slightly but to his credit, his smile doesn't falter, and he only bobs his head.

We settle into a cozy booth, and I pull out my new notebook. I've already covered it with stickers of books and cats, because apparently, I never outgrew my middle school aesthetic. I flip it open to reveal a list of names that would make Santa's naughty-or-nice roster look brief. My head hurts from the brainstorming—and from the mental gymnastics I've been doing to avoid considering the one name that keeps popping up anyway: mine.

"All right, let's get down to business." I tap my pen against the page. "I have several suggestions that would make Cupid himself jealous."

Before Eli can respond, a familiar voice cuts through the air like a sugar-coated knife.

"Well, well, well, if it isn't our love guru and the town's newest resident." Zoe saunters over, carrying two glasses of milk and a plate piled with gooey, icing-dripping cinnamon rolls. "Or is this a date? Please tell me before Mia. She'd be so jealous if I brought the tea home first!"

She's twisted her purple highlights into what can only be described as a pastry-chef-chic messy bun, and her apron looks like it's been through a sprinkle-war and back. Typical Zoe. I grin.

"Zoe! Do you have no filter? This is my new coworker, Eli. I had to introduce him to The Whisk's cinnamon rolls."

"Zero filter." She winks at Eli as she slides the pastries between us. "coworker, sure. You're in for a treat, newbie. These rolls are so good they've been known to cause people to fall instantly in love."

Heat spools across my cheeks. It would really not hurt my feelings if this town could get a little less interested in my romantic life. I'm about to interject when Eli, charming smile in place, replies, "Love-inducing pastries? I knew I should have read the fine print better before moving to Magnolia Cove. Is there a return policy on small-town magic, or am I stuck here forever?"

Zoe laughs. "Oh, let's hang onto this one, Rhianna. He can keep up."

I shrug. "It looks like you're stuck here now. Sorry, Eli, I don't make the rules."

"Damn." His eyes are a different color in every single light and that's the only reason I'm staring at them so intensely.

Zoe smirks at me, and I clear my throat and grab for the glass of milk. I don't even like milk, really, I just need something to do with my hands.

"Well, I think the pastry case needs to be cleaned." Zoe

continues grinning like a cat that found a dish full of cream. "Let me know if you need anything else, Sugar."

"Thanks," Eli says, either missing the silent conversation Zoe was burning into me with her eyes or choosing to politely ignore it. He leans forward. "Before we dive in"—and I don't know if he means the food or the conversation—"can you tell me about the Blue Moon Festival I keep hearing about? Something about an Elvis impersonation contest?"

Oh for the love of moon pies. Of all the things for him to experience as his first major Magnolia Cove event it would be the corniest one of the year. Well, maybe they're all corny. "Ah, yes, the festival. There may or may not be an Elvis theme."

"May or may not be? That's cryptic. Are you preserving the mystery or denying your involvement in said festival?"

I snort. "Oh, there's no denying it. If you were born here, or even visited at the right times of year, you've attended the Blue Moon Festival. Elvis has as much of a starring role as the moon itself, if not more."

"Well, The King is classic for a reason. His music is timeless."

"His voice was timeless. His hips were timeless. His songwriting? Nonexistent."

Eli's eyebrows shoot up. "Ouch. Tell me how you really feel about Elvis."

I lean in and lower my voice conspiratorially. "Let's just say if I had to choose between listening to *Love Me Tender* on repeat or dealing with an overtired toddler and a melted popsicle, hand me the diaper bag."

Eli grins. He hasn't looked away from me for so long it wouldn't surprise me if a dozen other people had walked in and I'd missed them. "I guess he had great charisma and charm and loved sparkly clothing. I can see why people would be into that."

My cheeks flood with so much heat I look down, hoping

to hide it. Eli can't be talking about me. He's a coworker. Plus, we're very specifically meeting so I can introduce him to eligible singles on the island. He literally brought the flyer tab to me. He's interested in dating—real dating. Not... whatever this is. Whatever we're doing.

Because it's definitely not flirting. Right?

I swipe at a bit of lint on my shirt only to realize I'm wearing a bedazzled t-shirt that gleams in the light, reflecting sparkles onto the table. Sparkly clothing. Like he just complimented. I have to redirect this conversation.

Because even if he *is* flirting with me, I'm decidedly not available for falling in love. Love always feels good at this stage —when you're eating cinnamon rolls and staring into warm eyes and suddenly convinced you could run a marathon or take up interpretive dance or finally finish your taxes.

But later?

Love has a cost. It sinks into you—the way you care for someone, the way you start building your life with them in the center of it. And when they see the messiest, truest part of you? They leave. And I'm never letting anyone close enough to hurt me like that again.

It's casual or nothing—and with the fellowship hanging in the balance, with the possibility of traveling the world finally within reach, it's probably nothing.

I need to keep my head down. Focused. No distractions.

Especially not ones with hazel eyes that somehow manage to look like every comforting coffee shop I've ever wanted to live in.

"Okay, fine. Elvis had a great voice and yes there's definitely an Elvis impersonation contest at the Blue Moon Festival. It's a whole thing. 'Blue Moon of Kentucky' and all that. The town council fifty years ago thought it would be hilarious. Now we're stuck with glittering jumpsuits and questionable hip thrusts every year."

Eli's laugh is as warm and rich as hot chocolate. It does funny things to my insides that I promptly ignore. "That sounds amazing. I can't wait to see it."

And then, because apparently I've lost all control of my mouth, I blurt out, "I'll find you the perfect date for the festival! By the blue moon. Scout's honor."

Eli's lips pinch slightly, and I tell myself it has nothing to do with me. Still, a part of me hopes—stupidly, dangerously— that he doesn't want to date someone else.

I shake the thought off. No. That way lies trouble. Attachment. Risk.

I'm not doing that again.

He claps his hand around his milk, but doesn't take a drink. "Were you even a scout?"

"Umm, no."

"All right, that sounds like a very reliable oath for my fate to rest on. I'm game."

I chuckle. "We should dive into these cinnamon rolls. They're best warm."

We reach out at the same moment. Our hands brush, and I swear a jolt of electricity races down my arm. I snatch my hand back like the touch burned me. Eli does the same and mumbles something about "after you" that doesn't help the heat that has to be burning my face into an apple-red color.

We both grab separate rolls the second time. Eli takes a bite and groans.

"Good, huh?" I can't help but grin. Several big food magazines have featured Ethan's baking. His secret cinnamon rolls are objectively the best thing since coffee shops discovered the power of pumpkin flavor.

"You weren't kidding."

The way he's looking at me makes me wonder if he's referencing my comment about how good the rolls are or how they'll make you spontaneously burst into a marriage proposal. I rush the conversation forward, eager to move away from that kind of thinking.

"So, what's your type? Tall, dark, and handsome? Petite blonde with a wicked sense of humor? Someone with a penchant for obscure trivia?"

With each description, I catch myself mentally comparing these potential matches to... me. Which is pointless. And not the plan. And definitely not safe. And one-hundred-percent not happening.

Eli chews another bite of cinnamon roll and seems to consider for a moment. "Women for sure. Otherwise, I guess I don't really have a type. I'm more interested in someone who's passionate about what they do, someone who can make me laugh. Someone who sees the magic in everyday things, maybe."

I nod, jot down notes, and definitely don't think about how I might match that description. "What about past relationships? Any deal breakers?"

For the first time in the night, Eli looks away and seems hesitant to respond. He wipes his fingers on a napkin and shrugs. "I was in a serious relationship for a couple of years. She was actually everything I thought I wanted—consistent, steady."

Ugh. Consistent and steady. Those are definitely not words anyone would use to describe me. I'm more like a glitter tornado with a solid Spotify playlist. I can see it, though—someone like Eli, who probably thrives on routine, on knowing where everything stands. He seems like the kind of guy who has a morning routine that extends over an hour where he must go through each step in a specific order or it ruins his day. I'm more of a never-put-my-hairbrush-in-the-same-place-twice type.

"The relationship ended, though?" I prompt gently.

He grips the back of his neck. "Yeah, well, when I started

thinking about forever, I just couldn't see it. Maybe it felt too routine. When we discussed it, she felt the same. Neither of us were heartbroken, and it felt more like we were closing a chapter than losing each other. Like we both knew we'd outgrown what we had."

My stomach does a weird little flip—and not the kind it's been doing around him lately. This one feels more like a freefall, the kind where you can't quite see what's waiting at the bottom.

He just made leaving sound so logical. So clean. Like it was just another chapter to close.

And sure, maybe his breakup was mutual and mature and full of deep conversations over tea or whatever grown-ups do... but still. It adds him to the mental list of *People Who Leave When Things Get Hard*.

I shake the thought off before it can settle. "That's, um, very insightful. Recognizing when something doesn't feel right is important." Great. Now I sound like a fortune cookie. Maybe if I stuff this entire cinnamon roll into my mouth, it will keep me from saying any other ridiculous things.

I don't know why I'm struggling so much—talking to people is usually easy for me. Effortless, even. But something about Eli's quiet intensity, the way his energy hums just beneath the surface, it throws me off. Like my own magic doesn't know how to behave around his.

"Maybe I'm trying to figure out what does feel right." Eli leans in closer to me as he says this. He's ignoring the cinnamon roll—which is basically a crime. I can't breathe.

Everything in me leans toward him. Like my magic knows before my mind does—*this could be something*. But right behind that flutter is fear. The kind that sinks into your chest and whispers, *he just admitted he's good at walking away*.

I want to believe that his situation was different. I also

want to believe I'm the kind of person people don't leave. But here we are.

Right as I'm attempting to find something to say, Claire walks up. Apparently it's coworker hang out day. "Rhianna! Funny to run into you at The Whisk. The librarians must all have the same cravings today."

She's talking to me, but her eyes have fixed on Eli. Of course they have. Who wouldn't focus on him? He's like Mr. Darcy if Mr. Darcy had modern music tastes and a Clark Kent glasses thing going on.

I paste on my best librarian smile, the one I used when someone tries to return a book that they've dropped in the bathtub. "Claire! What a surprise. Have you met Eli? He's new in town and working at the library—he's handling all those dusty old magical texts in the back room no one's dared to organize in, like, a century."

Claire's green eyes light up like she's just discovered a first edition in the bargain bin. "No, I haven't had the pleasure. I'm Claire, head of the non-fiction section."

Eli isn't looking at Claire, though. He's still leaning toward me. He clears his throat and turns toward her. "Nice to meet you. I'm Eli Lancaster, the, um, book guy that will be getting in everyone's way at the library."

Claire's smile grows even wider. "Oh, I can't imagine you'll be in anyone's way."

Great. Just great. I can practically see the wheels turning in her head, probably already planning their bookish wedding. And why shouldn't she? They both have similar tastes and are both single. Their energies are a good fit. Not perfect, maybe, but good. Clean energy, no static.

So why does the thought of connecting them make me want to 'accidentally' spill my milk all over Claire's sensible shoes?

I clear my throat, trying to remember I'm supposed to be

setting Eli up, not sabotaging his potential relationships. "Claire's also an expert on local history. Maybe she could give you a tour of our local museum sometime, Eli?"

The words taste like burnt Brussels sprouts in my mouth, but I force them out, anyway. Because I'm a professional, damn it. And professionals don't get flustered over someone they're supposed to help.

Eli glances over, like he's waiting for something—maybe even hoping I'll say no. Maybe even hoping I'll offer to show him around instead.

It's suddenly warm in here. Probably just me.

I nod. He winces, then turns to Claire with a smile that doesn't reach his eyes. Not like the real one. The one that crinkles the corners and makes him duck his chin like he's shy. "That would be, um, great, Claire," Eli says, his voice not quite matching his words. "I-I'd love that."

Claire beams, looking like the time she won our annual book sorting competition at the library. "Wonderful! Are you available tomorrow, by chance?"

As they exchange details, I feel like I'm watching a train wreck in slow motion. A train wreck I orchestrated. Suddenly I feel bad for Cupid. The man has a tougher job than people think.

When Claire finally leaves, practically floating on air, Eli turns back to me. He fiddles with the cinnamon roll on his plate, not eating any more. The faceplate of the leather watch on his wrist catches the sunset's light and bounces it around.

I force myself to sound chipper. "Well, that's a great start! How about we debrief after the date? We can discuss the pros and cons, see if Claire might be a good match for you?"

Eli lifts his face, and his smile is back. The one that makes my stomach do the good-weird little flips I'm trying not to think about. Trying but failing.

"That sounds perfect," he says. "Maybe we could grab dinner afterwards? To, uh, discuss the date."

The bell chimes as someone steps into The Whisk and that's what causes my heart to leap forward, not Eli's words. "Sure, we can analyze everything over some food."

"Great. I'm looking forward to... analyzing things with you." He digs back into his cinnamon roll.

As we part ways, I can't help but wonder what I've gotten myself into. I'm the world's most unprofessional matchmaker —not that I'd ever admit it to my friends or family. My first client and I have a big, sappy, sixteen-year-old-me-laying-on-my-bedroom-floor-singing-Everywhere crush on him. Ugh.

And the worst part? I swore I wouldn't do this again. That I wouldn't fall. That if someone *ever* made me feel that vulnerable again, I'd bolt.

But as I watch Eli walk away, something in me starts to hope. And hope is the most dangerous feeling of all. It's the one that tries to convince you that maybe this time... someone might stay.

Eli

The bell above *Vinyl & Verses* tinkles as I push open the door, and the scent of old books and vinyl hits me like a welcome embrace. It's exactly the kind of shop that makes small towns magical—shelves crammed with books reaching toward the ceiling, vintage album covers decorating the walls, and that indefinable atmosphere of possibility that comes with places where treasures wait to be discovered.

I've spent a good portion of my adult life seeking stores like this along the East Coast. It's how I've found a few of the gems in my book collection. Most small shops don't differentiate between dusty over-printed classics and the rare, forgotten treasures tucked into back shelves. A bit of digging and knowing what to look for, though, and you're suddenly holding a first edition, or a copy with penciled notes from a professor who is now as famous as the original author. Those are the finds that make it worth the hunt—books with their own stories woven in, waiting to be discovered.

I run my fingers along spines, scanning titles methodically. My colleagues back at the university would call this a fool's errand. *No one's ever found one.* I hear Dr. Chen's voice again.

But I know better. Cyrus Whitlock spent a decade in Magnolia Cove. There has to be something here, some trace he left behind.

The shop owner, a woman with silver-streaked hair and kind eyes, points me toward the folklore section when I ask about Whitlock's works. "Good luck," she says. "That's a popular shelf."

I lose track of time as I search, carefully examining each book. My fingers are dusty, but I don't care. This methodical work, this treasure hunt—it's what drives me. Or at least, it was until recently. Lately, though, everything's shifted. Mark's death has a way of echoing even in quiet rooms. This three bold moves idea was supposed to shake something loose.

But it's not the books pulling me anymore.

It's Rhianna.

Rhianna Wilder, with her sticker-covered journals, her impossible laugh, and her maddening ability to make me start questioning everything I thought I wanted.

My attention drifts to the vinyl section visible through the gap in the shelves. Just a quick browse, I tell myself. Five minutes, tops. But the moment I step into the music area, time slips away again. There's something meditative about flipping through albums, the soft whisper of cardboard against cardboard, each cover a piece of art in itself.

My fingers pause on a pristine copy of Queen's *A Night at the Opera*. The corners are barely worn, the sleeve still crisp. I carefully slide it from between its neighbors, examining the cover with the reverence it deserves. Getting lost in record stores was my salvation during grad school—the one place where precision and passion met perfectly.

The bell chimes again, and familiar laughter floods the shop. I peek around the corner of a bookshelf, and my heart does that strange stutter-step it's started doing whenever I see Rhianna. She's with Zoe from the bakery and another woman

I don't recognize, her hands animated as she talks, familiar quirky pins on her cloth bag catching the light. Today's say, "Reading is Lit" and "Bookworm & Proud."

I should focus on my search. I have a date tomorrow with Claire, after all. A date I agreed to because... well, because Rhianna suggested it, which in hindsight was the worst reason to say yes. But watching Rhianna wander into the shop, pulling out an earbud—she's probably listening to some carefully curated Spotify playlist even while hanging out with friends—it's impossible to look away.

The group breezes in together and it's exactly the friends I'd imagine Rhianna having—Zoe with striking purple-streaked hair and tattooed arms, the other laughing uninhibitedly at something Rhianna whispered, completely unbothered by the fact that she's wearing an oversized cardigan during summer. I wish I could have heard whatever Rhianna said, could catch that easy warmth that seems to follow her. They're all talking at once, gesturing animatedly, practically vibrating with energy.

They're the kind of people who make playlists called things like *Summer Vibes* or *Main Character Energy*. The kind of people who probably go to music festivals and could understand the slang my students speak.

The kind of people who would find my methodically organized record collection—and me—absolutely horrifying.

Rhianna's gaze flits around the shop and she drifts away from her friends before she disappears behind a row of shelves. I glimpse her through the gaps—pausing here, tilting her head at something there, her lips parting slightly as she studies something that's caught her attention.

When she finally reemerges, it's as if she's in her own world, her fingers trailing along the record spines in a slow, deliberate way that makes my pulse kick up. There's a gentle intensity in her movements, and I can't help but follow the line of her hand, the delicate curl of her fingers. It's impossible not to notice her, or to ignore the way my gaze keeps returning to her, like she's a mystery I suddenly, desperately want to solve.

"Found anything good?" Her voice snaps me back, and I startle. I hadn't even realized she'd spotted me.

"Just browsing." I hold up the Queen album, trying to look casual despite the way my pulse picks up when she moves closer.

"Queen?" She peers at the cover. "And in a vintage format. Very hipster of you."

I can't help but laugh. "There's nothing hipster about appreciating classic rock in its original format."

"If you say so." She's grinning now, reaching for the album. She flips it over and scans the song list. "Now this is the real Queen. Not like that 80s stuff you went on about."

"You're joking." The words come out more horrified than I intend. "Have you ever heard 'Another One Bites the Dust'? 'Under Pressure'?"

She hums the chorus of their iconic duet with David Bowie then does a little shoulder shimmy like it's the most natural thing in the world. "Those make excellent commercial jingles."

"First, how dare you." We both laugh, and it hits me again just how easy this is—how easy *she* is to talk to.

I pull another album free from its case and flip it so she can see the track list. "And second, may I present 'Bohemian Rhapsody'? The greatest rock opera ever written?"

"'Bohemian Rhapsody' is a masterpiece." Her slim fingers accept that album from me as well. She studies it with an intensity that makes my chest feel tight. "But I bet you only like it because it's popular." She smirks, glancing up at me with a mischievous glint in her eyes.

I pretend to be scandalized and place a hand over my heart.

"You wound me. I'll have you know that's the first time I've ever been accused of following the crowd. Besides, I've ruined this album forever. I once made my students do a comparative analysis of it with Hamlet."

"You did not."

"I did. They never forgave me. The dean called it an interesting departure from traditional literary analysis."

"Of course he did, you pretentious academic." She bumps my shoulder with hers, and the casual contact sparks all my nerve endings. "I'm guessing you're one of those people who can't hear a love song without turning it into a metaphor for mortality."

"I have opinions about everything."

Rhianna's laugh makes something warm unfurl in my chest. "Color me shocked." She slides the Queen albums back into their places with careful precision. "So what other opinions are you hiding behind your terrible music taste?"

I laugh, and when she walks, I follow. I should walk away. There's work I need to do—research to complete and articles I need to write before I return for the fall semester. Instead, I follow her down the aisle as she trails her finger along album spines, trying not to think about how she'd nodded encouragingly at me yesterday, her expression brightening when Claire suggested we get together.

Opinions, though, I have plenty of those. It's practically a job requirement for a liberal arts professor. "Well, I think vinyl is superior to digital in every way." She rolls her eyes and I can't help my smile as I continue. "The Beatles are overrated—"

"How dare you!"

"—and anyone who says they don't like ABBA is lying to themselves."

She stops so abruptly I almost run into her. "'Dancing Queen'?"

"Undeniable classic."

"'Mamma Mia'?"

"Changed musical theater forever."

She spins to face me, and we're standing much closer than I expected. Close enough that I can see the tiny silver compass charm on one of her necklaces, and the flowing curve of her lips.

"Professor Lancaster," she says solemnly, "I think we might actually be friends."

The word 'friends' hits like a bucket of ice water, reminding me of how I ended up agreeing to the date. Because Rhianna's expression had brightened when she'd suggested it, and I'd nodded along like an idiot just to keep that smile going. Because Rhianna Wilder is everything I'm not—effortlessly outgoing, beautiful in a natural way, and magnetic to everyone around her. The kind of person who shines in any crowd, while I... Well, I'd rather be buried in a stack of books than face any attention.

In short, she's exactly the kind of woman who'd never fall for someone like me.

I take a step back, putting distance between us. "My research calls. I should return."

Something flickers across her face—disappointment? Relief? But her smile doesn't waver. "Yeah, of course." She turns away, then pauses. "You know, if you're interested in local work, talk to Marcus at *A Novel Idea*. He's got an incredible collection of local history stuff tucked away in the back room."

I hesitate. I've passed *A Novel Idea* a dozen times since moving in, but I wrote it off as another small-town shop catering to tourists—the kind that stocks overpriced paperbacks and novelty mugs. I never thought to look beyond the curated front displays.

But a hidden section of local history? That's different. That's interesting.

A nagging curiosity tugs at me. If Marcus really has rare or forgotten records tucked away, there's a chance something valuable—something connected to Whitlock—might be buried there.

I nod slowly, filing the name away. "Didn't realize he carried local archives," I admit. "I'll check it out." I try to ignore how my pulse picks up when she beams at me.

"Good luck!" She gives me a little wave and practically bounces away, rejoining her friends who've clustered near the front counter.

I watch her go. The tightness in my chest is just anxiety about tomorrow's date, about this entire moving and taking bold actions thing. It's probably just the lingering tension that never really left after Mark. It has nothing to do with the warmth that bloomed between Rhianna and me, or the way she makes me feel like I'm something more than I am, or how much I want to know what other charms she's wearing on those delicate necklaces.

I turn back to the folklore section with determination. I'm here to find Whitlock's work, write a few papers I can get published to maintain my academic credibility, and maybe shake up my life a little. Not to develop inconvenient feelings for the woman who's enthusiastically trying to set me up with someone else.

But as I pull another book from the shelf, her laughter floats to me from the store's front, bright and musical as a favorite song.

Rhianna

I spin in slow circles on my desk chair, watching the ceiling fan make its hypnotic rotation above me. My usual stack of half-read novels sits abandoned on my nightstand. I've tried three different books in the past hour, but none of them hold my attention.

With a sigh, I plant my foot and stop the spinning. My gaze drifts to the clock on my bedside table. Eli and Claire should be well into their museum tour by now. Not that I'm counting minutes or anything. Absolutely not. I'm definitely not wondering if they're having a marvelous time exploring Magnolia Cove's tame little museum, with Claire pointing out historical details in that earnest way of hers, Eli nodding thoughtfully, his glasses catching the light just so—

Nope. Not thinking about that.

Though I am looking forward to dinner with him later. Just to hear how it went. For matchmaking evaluation purposes. Purely professional curiosity.

I spring up from the chair and flop onto my bed, arms splayed like a starfish washed ashore. Mr. Whiskers, who had been napping in a patch of sunlight on my quilt, shoots me an offended glare before leaping away. "Sorry," I mutter, as if the cat understands or cares about my apology. As if explaining that I'm losing my mind over a man—a man I've known for a handful of days, no less—would somehow justify disturbing his precious slumber.

The house creaks around me, empty and too quiet. Dad's at the university, Mom and Gavin joined the Blackwoods on their boat for the day, and all my friends are either working or helping at the farmer's market. Which I'm specifically avoiding because a certain professor with ridiculously perfect hair might see me there after his date with Claire, and I refuse to seem like I'm hovering.

I roll onto my stomach and kick my feet in the air, feeling like a teenager waiting for her crush to call. Something hot and uncomfortable prickles under my skin. Is this what jealousy feels like? I barely recognize the sensation. I'm not supposed to feel this way.

I don't get attached. Not anymore. Not after learning how much it hurts to let someone in and have them walk away anyway. So I keep things safe. Contained. Manageable.

Because if Eli really saw all of me—the highs, the lows, the mess—he'd leave. They always do.

This restless energy isn't jealousy. It can't be. It's just... anticipation. About dinner. About helping my client find his perfect match. Even if a traitorous part of me hopes Claire isn't it. And maybe there's also a smug little voice in my head, the one that already knows their magic aligns, but doesn't spark. Not like it does when it's meant-to-be.

Not like our magic does when we're together.

The thought slips in before I can stop it and I shove it down so fast, it nearly takes my breath with it.

I sit up and drum my fingers against my thigh, too fidgety to settle on any one task. My gaze falls on my desk, where the application for the *World Library Tour Fellowship* sits half-completed.

"Focus on that," I tell myself. "That's your actual dream. Not some... summer fling with the new professor in town."

But the words feel hollow, even to my own ears. My fingers drumming picks up pace, my whole body twitching with the need to move, to distract myself from this inexplicable discomfort. The living room seems too empty, and yet my bedroom feels suddenly claustrophobic.

Before I fully realize it, my feet are already moving—down the stairs, through the back hallway, toward the door I deliberately avoid at all costs. My hand hovers over the crystal doorknob—the one Grandma Ida special-ordered because, "doorknobs should sparkle just like the people who turn them, Rhianna-bean."

The childhood nickname echoes in my head, and something cracks inside my chest.

I haven't been in this room for at least a year. After she died, I spent weeks curled up in her bed, breathing in her fading scent, sobbing until my throat was raw. Then came the months of avoidance—hurrying past the door, looking away when it entered my peripheral vision, pretending the room didn't exist. Now I can enter without dissolving into tears, but I still don't. Not often. Not without purpose.

What's my purpose now?

My fingers close around the doorknob, cool crystal pressing into my palm. The latch clicks, and I step inside.

The blinds are drawn shut, casting the space in gloomy shadows. It feels wrong. Grandma Ida hated closed blinds. "What's the point of windows if you block out the light?" she'd say, tugging the cords to flood the room with sunshine that would turn the hardwood floors golden and make her colorful quilts shimmer like jewels.

I cross to the window and pull the blinds up. Dust motes

dance in the sudden beam of light, and I sneeze. The room smells stale, nothing like Grandma Ida's potpourri of cinnamon gum, the floral perfume she ordered from a catalogue, and the endless varieties of tea she brewed in eclectic porcelain cups she picked up at antique stores.

"Sorry," I whisper to the empty room. "I should visit more."

My thoughts have been revolving around Eli all morning, and suddenly I'm here, in Grandma Ida's room, running my fingers over her quilts instead of obsessing over whether he's enjoying Claire's detailed explanation of our town's dubious historical artifacts.

I pause, the realization hitting me with uncomfortable clarity. Did I wander in here because I needed comfort, or because I needed a distraction? Is this what I'm doing? Using my grandmother's memory to distract myself from thinking about Eli? How messed up is that? No wonder Jacob ran. I really am too much.

Or maybe I'm here to remember. To remind myself why getting too close to anyone—especially someone like Eli Lancaster with his earnest eyes and his ridiculous music opinions and his way of making me feel both seen and heard in a way that terrifies me—is a terrible idea.

Because Jacob seemed like the best thing since cinnamon sugar toast at one point too. Our magic glistened together—maybe not like my magic does with Eli, but still. There was sparkle. There was hope. And Eli already admitted he ended a relationship when it got too routine. I read a book my mom recommended once that said we repeat patterns until we deal with our stuff. (The book used much fancier therapy words, but the point stands.)

That's all this is. Me repeating a pattern. One that already burned me badly enough to leave a scar. And I'm not going to let myself go through that again. I can't. I'm not strong enough to survive that again.

I sink onto the edge of the bed, running my fingers over the quilt. I still remember sitting here as Grandma Ida brushed my hair before bed, telling me stories about the goddess I was named for. Rhiannon, forever riding her magical white horse, too swift for any suitor to catch.

"You're just like her," Grandma Ida would say, pride warming her voice. "Wild and free and true to your own rhythm."

Grandma Ida always knew how to spin things. Honestly, she should've worked in PR. Despite her encouragement, before I found my people in middle school band—the oddballs who liked me exactly as I was—there were years I felt like a walking, talking personification of *too much*.

I didn't have words for it then, but I think I've always feared being too much. And Jacob proved me right.

A memory surfaces, sharp and vivid. I'm ten years old, sobbing into Grandma Ida's shoulder after another day of eating lunch alone. "No one wants to be my friend," I hiccup. "I'm too weird. I talk too much. I'm too... too..."

"Too much like Rhiannon," Grandma finished, stroking my hair. The Welsh goddess—always following her own path. "And that," she says, "is exactly what makes you wonderful."

And maybe she was right. After all, the only man Rhiannon ever slowed down for ended up betraying her. My life is patterns within patterns. Maybe I've echoed my namesake's path all along.

I blink back tears and stand, needing to move. My fingers trail over Grandma Ida's belongings—the collection of driftwood pieces lined along the windowsill, the framed photographs, the bookshelf stuffed with volumes organized by color rather than any logical system. Dad used to drive himself crazy trying to find specific books in her "rainbow chaos," as he called it.

I'm about to turn away when something happens—a sensation I've felt many times before but can never quite explain. An energy pulses from the bookshelf, drawing my attention like a magnet. My ability to sense when a book matches someone is what makes me great as a librarian, why Tom trusts me to find the weirdest monster romances I can get my hands on, the ones he'll absolutely devour, and why Claire comes to me when she's in a reading slump.

But this is different. This feels like... a match. A perfect match, but not for me.

For Eli.

I step closer, my fingertips skating over spines until they settle on a moss-green leather binding tucked between a scarlet romance novel and a cobalt book of poetry. The energy vibrates stronger, and I slide the book free.

My breath catches. *Welsh Gods and Goddesses* by Cyrus Whitlock. I've seen this book a hundred times, but today it feels like I'm holding something sacred. I open the cover, and the pages naturally fall to the most-read section: *Rhiannon: The Enigmatic Goddess of the Moon.*

The pages are soft with age and handling, the margins filled with Grandma Ida's elegant script. Little notes, observations, connections to other myths. She'd drawn a tiny horse beside one paragraph, and a small heart next to a line about Rhiannon's independence.

This book is precious. A piece of my grandmother, a connection to my namesake, a treasure I've taken comfort in since I was old enough to read. I couldn't possibly give it to Eli Lancaster. Even if its energy is utterly aligned with his in a way I can't explain. Even if the connection feels deeper than the usual book-to-reader match I sense.

I barely know him, I remind myself sternly. And besides,

he's out on a date with someone else right now. With Claire, who's sensible and grounded and probably doesn't have a wanderlust itch under her skin or the instinct to keep love at arm's length just in case it disappears.

I hate the twist in my stomach at the thought of them together. Hate that I'm standing in my late grandmother's bedroom, clutching a book to my chest, fretting over a man like some lovesick teenager. This isn't me. I don't do this.

But the book pulses with that undeniable energy, like it's already decided it belongs to Eli. Like it's just waiting for me to admit it.

I press my forehead against the bookshelf, breathing in the faint, lingering scent of Grandma Ida. My gaze falls on a framed photograph—me at seven, gap-toothed and grinning, her arm around my shoulders as we proudly display mud pies we'd made after a summer rainstorm. We're both laughing so hard our eyes are nearly closed.

"What would you tell me to do?" I whisper to her image.

The silence that follows isn't really an answer, but I imagine her saying what she always did when I faced a choice: "Follow your joy, Rhianna-bean. The rest will sort itself out."

I straighten up, adjust the frame to its proper position, and tuck the book under my arm as I leave the room. I'm not going to give it to him, I tell myself firmly. But I'll keep it close, just in case.

The book's energy signature is unmistakable. Every reader leaves a trace of themselves behind—emotions, thoughts, dreams embedded in the pages like invisible fingerprints. Over the years, this book has collected a unique energetic aura, one that resonates in perfect harmony with the essence I sense in Eli. It's not that the book has chosen him specifically, but that its accumulated energy aligns with him in a way I've rarely felt before—like two pieces of a puzzle meant to fit together.

That's what books are meant for, aren't they? To be read,

to be shared, to find the readers who need them most. Grandma Ida never hoarded her books. She lent them freely, gave them as gifts, passed them to strangers she met who mentioned an interest. "Books have their own journeys," she'd say. "We're just temporary caretakers."

I close Grandma Ida's door behind me, the crystal knob cool against my palm. The book feels warm under my arm, almost expectant, like it knows something I don't.

"Don't get smug," I mutter to it. "I haven't decided anything yet."

But even as I say it, I know I'm lying to myself. The book has already chosen its new owner. The question is whether I can honor that choice—whether I can let go of this piece of my past to follow what my magic is telling me is right.

I check my clock one more time as I head back to my room, the book tucked safely against my side. Dinner with Eli is still over an hour away. He'll tell me all about the date with Claire, and I'll be the perfect, professional matchmaker. And maybe—maybe—I'll know then whether this book is meant to find its way to him after all. It would be so convenient if magic could just hand me a big, sparkly "yes, this is the right thing to do" sign. Maybe with glitter. Or at the very least, less emotional confusion.

With a sigh, I settle on my windowsill seat, open my worn copy of *Pride and Prejudice*, and try to lose myself in Elizabeth Bennet's world instead of obsessing over mine. But the Whitlock book rests beside me, a quiet but intense presence, like it's insisting that it's already made up its mind.

Eli

I adjust my collar for the hundredth time, wondering if I've made a terrible mistake. The sun gleams over Magnolia Cove, casting a golden glow over the quaint storefronts as I make my way to meet Claire for our 'history tour' date. It seemed like a reasonable idea when Rhianna suggested it—a perfect blend of my love for knowledge and Claire's apparent passion for local lore. Claire seems like the type I'd be interested in as well —steady, routine-driven, and probably appreciative of a well-organized coffee cabinet. It all seemed so logical, but now I'm not so sure.

Claire meets me with a nervous smile outside the Magnolia Cove Museum, a small building that looks like someone's grandmother's house more than a repository of historical artifacts. It's a stormy ocean blue and has a long porch that runs the house's length.

"Ready to dive into some fascinating Magnolia Cove history?" She shrugs but her voice pitches high. "Keeping in mind, of course, that this is the *tourist-approved* version of history. But you have the perfect guide to give you the back-stage stories."

I nod, trying to muster some enthusiasm. I should be thrilled about this. It's a perfect opportunity to see what the locals know about Whitlock. Instead, dread gnaws at my stomach but I try to force casualness into my voice. "Lead the way."

Claire grins and walks us through the entrance.

What follows is two of the most excruciating hours of me attempting and failing to make small talk I've ever endured. The only moments of success are when I imagine Rhianna there and what I might say to her. Claire's efforts to make every mundane object sound thrilling fall flat, and I long for Rhianna's zany comments.

"And this," Claire says, gesturing to a faded photograph, "is Magnolia Cove's famous cat, Buttercup." She leans in to whisper. "She belonged to the Head Warlock during the 50s."

I make a noncommittal noise, wondering how many more exhibits we have left. I'd hoped there might be something about Cyrus Whitlock, but like everywhere else, there's no trace of him beyond a single mention in the *Local Authors* display that lists his birth and death dates wrong. Probably just a mistake, the kind of minor oversight that happens when no one's paying much attention. Whitlock might be who I wrote my thesis on, but around Magnolia Cove, he's just another half-forgotten name in the archives. When I ask Claire, she waves it off with a dismissive "Oh, he's overrated, honestly" that makes me cringe.

Claire seems perfectly nice, exactly my type on paper, the lack of Whitlock appreciation aside. Normally quirky historical details would fascinate me, but my eyes keep darting toward the door, my mind rushing ahead to dinner with Rhianna.

Rhianna who is anything but my type. If she was giving the tour of this museum, she'd make unexpected jokes that would have me laughing and batting back comments. This date, on the other hand, is an accurate reflection of how most of my attempts at relationships go—and why whatever I have with Rhianna feels so different.

By the time we reach a final exhibit showing off the various shells found on the beach—spiraling Knobbed Whelks, glossy Olive Shells, and sleek, dark ones that are charmingly nicknamed Shark Eyes—I'm silently praying for the minutes to pass.

Piper will analyze and tear this date apart later. She actually popped popcorn for our conversation the other night when I'd mentioned dating at all. *Oh, I hope your schedule is clear; I have questions*, she'd quipped. The matchmaker aspect I'd left out. I do have some sense of dignity I'm attempting to preserve.

Claire continues to discuss the shells and I continue struggling to find anything to say. I hope Piper is busy and I can get away with a simple text conversation later. I attempt not to look at my watch too obviously.

"Thank you for the tour," I say as we finally exit the museum.

Claire looks up at me. "Are you hungry? Do you want to get dinner?"

"Ah, I'm afraid I already have plans this evening," I reply, guilt creeping in.

Her face falls, and she looks away so her hair drifts between us like a curtain. "Maybe another time, then."

"Sure." I say, knowing full well it's a lie.

"Well, I'll see you on Monday." She forces a smile on, waves, then practically runs down the steps. I want to follow her and try to explain myself. But nothing I'd offer would console. A pang of guilt swirls through me. It's not Claire's fault we lack chemistry. Or that I didn't come to Magnolia Cove looking for love. Or that natural conversation for me only happens with those who already know me inside and out.

Well, unless you're someone who wears quirky pins, debates classic rock like its life or death, and has brown eyes deep enough I could drown in.

That heaviness hangs over me as I make my way toward Seabreeze Avenue, the street that overlooks the ocean. I'm going to have to tell Rhianna that I can't do anymore matches. My gut twists knowing she'll be disappointed. The last two hours were excruciating, though, and I hurt Claire's feelings as well. Not just the anxiety—though that's always there, humming like an air conditioner I can't shut off. It's that I've never met anyone who quieted the noise in my head long enough to feel possible. Connection has always felt like something to brace for, not something to want.

Even my one long-term relationship just... happened. Sarah and I liked the same coffee shop, worked at the same university, hit the same gym. Eventually, it felt easier to date than not.

But with Rhianna nothing about her blends in. She's not routine. She's wildfire. We've shared one breakfast, a handful of conversations, and already she's in my head like a spark I can't put out.

It doesn't feel like folding into someone else's life. It feels like something cracked open the moment we met and now I can't look away.

The Siren's Song, a seafood bistro with a wooden pier-like exterior and twinkling lights, is bustling when I arrive. The restaurant overlooks the harbor where the orange of sunset reflects in the water and splashes color over dozens of sailboats. I walk in and offer my name. The server smiles and tells me to follow her. Inside, the restaurant is cozier, defined by weathered wood, soft blues, and strategically placed mermaid sculptures that manage to be whimsical without crossing into kitschy.

Rhianna sits at a corner table, illuminated by a softly

glowing lantern. She's wearing a flowing emerald dress that sets off her skin and makes her dark hair seem even glossier. When she turns in my direction, a smile spreads across her face and she waves. She's chosen dangling earrings made of glass beads and they clatter together as I return the wave and walk over.

Even in this dim restaurant she sparkles like starlight reflected on a still lake. I've longed to see her all afternoon, but wasn't prepared for it. For how beautiful she looks or how my heart feels like it's going to explode at the sight of her.

As I take my seat, I steel myself for the conversation ahead. How do I tell her that her matchmaking efforts are in vain? Even though I want to quit, I dread disappointing her.

"So," she says. "How was your date with destiny?"

She emphasizes the last part by spreading her hands out in front of her, maroon and gold bracelets sliding down her arm. I groan and drop my head into my hands. "More like a date with disaster."

Is it just me hoping or do her shoulders drop and she smiles a bit at my response? She chuckles and the sound is as light and musical as wind chimes. "That bad, huh? Spill the tea, Lancaster."

And so I do. I recount how a three-room museum felt like it lasted for a hundred miserable years, about Claire's desperate attempts to engage me in conversation, and the awkward silence (thanks to me) that felt longer than the tour itself. I finish with the uncomfortable parting.

Rhianna listens, her eyes dancing with amusement at first, but softening as I describe Claire's disappointment. "Oh no," she gasps, but she's laughing a bit too. "Poor Claire. And poor you! It must have been *really* rough if it got you that tongue-tied. You? Struggling with conversation? Hard to believe. You're pretty smooth."

Heat rushes up my neck. "Not most of the time, I'm afraid."

"Only when you're saying sub-par bands are on the same level with Stevie Nicks."

"Bread is not sub-par!" We're both grinning at each other like idiots right as the server arrives with nothing other than a basket of cornbread and butter.

Rhianna thanks the woman then pulls a slice. "Funny and able to summon things with your mind. Is there anything you can't do?"

I chuckle, the earlier heaviness in my chest lifting. "I think I'm only those things when I'm with you."

I say the words before I think it through, then immediately regret them. Rhianna's eyebrows raise and color sweeps over her face. It emphasizes freckles I hadn't noticed before and I have the desperate urge to brush my fingers across her cheekbone. Or to excuse myself from the table, go back to my apartment, then pack and leave town before I can make more of a fool of myself than I already have.

Rhianna laughs and takes another bite of her cornbread, chews slowly and swallows. "I'm adding 'brings out the best in others' to my resume."

"You should." My smile fades as I force myself to continue. "But... I think I need to take a break from this dating experiment. It's not fair to the women you'd set me up with if I'm not ready."

After all, I tried it. I walked up to the counter, signed up for the humiliating and terrifying matchmaking service, and went on an entire date. I'm pretty sure that qualifies as my second bold move. One more to go. Mark would've laughed and probably said it didn't count unless there was skydiving involved.

But I'm trying. Even if these bold moves feel more like

cautious nudges than the leaps I'd expected. Even if I'm not sure they're changing anything yet.

"That's okay. Dating is tough, especially when you're not aligned with the person." Rhianna's smile falters a bit. "I definitely had that issue in my last relationship." Her gaze drops to her plate, and something shadows her expression—just for a moment—before she blinks it away. Then her eyes brighten like she's flipped a switch. "Oh! And the guy before him? Everything had to be a giant romantic production all the time with him."

The server arrives with our plates—scallops and orzo for Rhianna, buttery shrimp and grits with lemon garlic sauce for me.

Rhianna dives into her food but I hesitate. Something in her shift felt... off. Like she'd skipped a chapter. The kind you leave out when it still hurts too much to say aloud.

I don't ask. It's not the time, and I don't have the right. But I wish I could protect her from whatever left that shadow on her face. Wish I could go back and undo it—whoever he was, whatever he did to make her tuck that hurt so neatly behind a smile.

"Is romantic bad?" I ask about the previous boyfriend instead, keeping my tone light.

She chews through her bite before answering. "Not bad, necessarily, just not for me. Everything had to be such a big deal." She rolls her eyes and I can't help but smile at the gesture as she continues. "I swear, if I had to sit through one more candlelit dinner where a violinist played so close to our table that I got bow hair in my soup, I was going to snap that Stradivarius over my knee and use it as kindling for a bonfire instead." She hovers her fork in the air for a moment before adding, "I actually think that would be a more fun date."

A laugh spills from me. "I could see why that might be annoying."

"Oh, it gets worse. Once he decided a picnic at the beach would be the most romantic gesture."

"And it wasn't?" I ask, food forgotten. I can't care about dinner no matter how beautifully plated or magic-infused it is when Rhianna sits directly across from me, telling a story with her glistening eyes and dancing hands as much as her words.

"It was terrible. A whole flock of seagulls attacked us. Dive-bombed us like something out of an Alfred Hitchcock movie. Let's just say, I've become an expert at speed-eating outdoors. No lingering with food in the open for this girl!"

We're both laughing now. "So," I say once we catch our breath, "I take it you're not big on the dating scene these days?"

Her smile turns wry. "Not so much, no. I figure I'll stick to matchmaking for others. It's safer that way—less chance of seagull attacks."

I pop a bite of food in my mouth and ignore the little pang in my chest at her words. Because this—whatever feeling this is —can't happen. Rhianna is my coworker and I should avoid dating her on that point alone. I've already created an awkward situation with one coworker. Rhianna just said she's not interested in romance. And besides, we're too different. I'd bore her within a few months.

"I guess you probably think me wanting to drop out over a little dull conversation and awkwardness seems pretty ridiculous compared to vicious seagulls."

She's laughing again, and it's all I want—to make her laugh, to listen to the rich sound of it and watch her face brighten.

"Deranged birds are too high of a standard for comparison. Awkward conversation is worse anyway. Oh my gosh, though it makes for one of my favorite romance tropes."

"Which one?" I couldn't name a single romance trope, actually. I've spent my entire career researching and teaching

Comparative Literature or reading old mythology tomes. Romance makes rare appearances and is usually tragic.

"Stuck in an elevator together."

Being stuck in an elevator sounds like a nightmare and somehow I'd love to get trapped in one with Rhianna. Hours of conversation with her with no excuse for it to end. I imagine she'd have me chuckling within minutes and forgetting the situation not long after that. Disappointment would fill me when the electricity finally returned, and we began moving again.

"And this happens enough in romance novels to be a trope?"

She gives a dramatic gasp and places a hand over her chest. "Don't tell me you've never read romance?"

I shuffle my spoon through the grits. "I can't say it's my primary genre."

"Those are basically relationship manuals. Read a man-written-by-a-woman and you'll understand so much."

"Well, I'm open to the idea if you have a suggestion. I'm usually reading folklore."

"Ha." She grins so her eyes squeeze together. "I can find the perfect romance for you. Trust me, I'm able to match people with just the right book. Give me a few weeks to really think about it and I'll bring you one."

"I can't wait."

We've both leaned in across the table. Her skin is luminous in the lamplight. The sun has disappeared and everything outside is blue, making her face the brightest thing. It might have been true before the lights dimmed.

"Maybe I shouldn't give up on dating so quickly," I say. If I quit the matchmaking service, I give up having an excuse to spend time with Rhianna.

She licks her lips which is excruciatingly distracting.

"What you need is a more laid-back approach. I have an idea." Even before she explains, I already know I'll say yes. "I'm going with some friends to *The Tipsy Mermaid* tonight. Why don't you come with us?"

My heart leaps at the invitation even as my mind spirals through a dozen potential excuses. I'm not typically a 'last-minute plans' kind of man. In fact, the idea usually sends me into a mild panic. No time to mentally prepare, no idea what to expect, no exit strategy if it all goes awkwardly sideways.

And *The Tipsy Mermaid*? That name alone sounds like a sensory overload waiting to happen.

But the thought of spending more time with Rhianna overrides the noise in my head. It's irrational. Entirely out of character. And yet... I don't want to say no.

"*The Tipsy Mermaid*?" I ask. "Let me guess, it's a nautical-themed bar where the bartenders wear seashell bras?"

"So close, Lancaster." Rhianna's earrings dance as she shakes her head. "No seashell bras, but it is a bar." She pauses, her grin slowly spreading wider. "A karaoke bar. It would be a great opportunity for you to meet some people without the pressures of one-on-one dating?"

I take a deep breath, steeling myself. I actually grew up taking vocal lessons. Not for my sake, but because Piper wanted them and was too scared to go by herself. Singing I can do. Karaoke, though?

The thought of getting up on a stage, with all eyes on me and a microphone in my hand, makes my chest tighten. My palms are already damp. My heart pounds against my ribs like it's trying to escape. I can practically feel the heat of the lights, the silence of the crowd just before the music starts, the pressure to be *good*, or at least *not embarrassing*.

What if I miss a note? What if my voice cracks? What if I forget the lyrics entirely and just stand there while everyone stares and wonders how someone so clearly uncomfortable ended up in front of a karaoke machine in the first place?

The logical part of my brain tells me I can do this—I've sung before, in lessons, in recitals, even in front of strangers. But that was different. That was structured. Controlled. This is public vulnerability disguised as entertainment.

But then I look at Rhianna's expectant face, her warm brown eyes twinkling with excitement, I nod.

"You know what? Why not?"

Rhianna fist pumps the air in a way that's entirely inappropriate for the setting which makes it only that much more charming. "Perfect! Trust me, Eli, you're going to love it. We are going to have the best time tonight!"

My heart stutters over that *we*. It's just a word, two letters, and yet it sends a rush of warmth through me. Like it might be just enough to keep me from having a panic attack.

As we finish our meal and prepare to head out, I'm filled with a lightness that doesn't match the situation. Eli Lancaster does not go to karaoke bars. He doesn't sing in front of people. He doesn't make last-minute plans.

Well, Eli Lancaster didn't. Eli Lancaster with Rhianna Wilder, though?

That man, it seems, is capable of anything.

"So," I ask as we step out into the cooling evening air, "what's your go-to karaoke song? Let me guess, something by Fleetwood Mac?"

Rhianna links her arm through mine. The casual contact sends another jolt through me. I hope she doesn't notice how my breath catches. "You know me so well already," she says. "But I like to keep people guessing. You'll just have to wait and see. Now, go home and change. I'll meet you at the bar at nine?"

"Nine o'clock."

She gives my arm a squeeze before parting ways. I struggle

to tear my gaze from her retreating form, to force myself to keep walking.

As I reach my apartment, I realize I'm still smiling. Whatever happens tonight, one thing's for certain—this experiment is already changing me. And I think I like it.

That is, until I open my closet and the reality of the situation hits me like a ton of leather-bound books.

What does one wear to a karaoke bar?

I stare at my wardrobe, a sea of muted colors and sensible fabrics, and feel a wave of panic. The tweed jackets and button-down shirts that usually bring me comfort now seem to mock me.

"Come on, Lancaster," I mutter to myself, rifling through hangers. "You can identify a 15th-century manuscript at twenty paces, surely you can find something to wear to a bar."

I pull out a sweater, then immediately stuff it back in. Too librarian. A suit jacket? Too formal. A t-shirt with 'I'd rather be reading' printed on it—a gag gift from Piper—is quickly discarded.

In desperation, I call my sister.

"Pipes, help. What does one wear to a karaoke bar?"

There's a pause on the other end of the line, then an eruption of laughter. "Oh, Brubba," she wheezes, "please tell me you're not planning to show up in a bow tie and loafers."

"Of course not," I lie, kicking said loafers under the bed.

Fifteen minutes and much sisterly teasing later, I'm dressed in dark jeans, a navy button-down with the sleeves rolled up, and the least professor-like shoes I own.

As I give myself a final once-over in the mirror, I shake my head. All this fuss over clothes, and for what? It's not like this is a date. It's just a night out with Rhianna and her friends. Rhianna, who probably isn't giving a second thought to what I'll be wearing.

I take a deep breath. It's just karaoke, just a night with

friends. *You can do this, Lancaster.* It's then that I realize I've started calling myself by my last name the way Rhianna does.

As I head out the door, I grin. Rhianna Wilder has already changed how I dress, how I spend my evenings, and even how I talk to myself. I wonder as a cool ocean breeze reaches me what else she might change before this adventure is over with.

Rhianna

The Tipsy Mermaid buzzes tonight, all neon lights and laughter. I'm nestled in our usual booth, sandwiched between Alex and Rachel, when I spot him: Eli Lancaster looking like he's walked straight out of a J. Crew catalog.

I wiggle my way out of the booth and wave him over. "Well, well, well, Lancaster, look at you all dressed up."

Eli's smile falters but then his eyes skim over me. "You as well."

I scoff at my shimmering sea-foam colored top and jeans. His gaze lingers on my bare shoulders a moment before jumping back up to my eyes. I smile and grab his arm to weave him through the crowded room. "Let me introduce you to everyone."

As the rest of our crew files in, I rattle off names, but I can't help but notice how Violet's eyes linger on Eli a beat too long. Something twists in my stomach. And I use the rest of my brainpower to convince myself it's just the questionable package of cookies I munched on as I got dressed earlier. Still, I focus with my magic—just enough to check. It's with a quiet flood of relief that I can tell their energies don't match at all.

Violet is fire and precision. Eli's energy is more reserved than I'd realized—quiet in a way I wouldn't have noticed if not for the contrast.

Definitely not a match.

Not like... well.

I shove that thought down before it can finish forming.

Eli slides into the booth next to me and shakes Tom and Grant's hands. His smile is smooth, his countenance relaxed, but I understand what he meant about his date now. He's so quiet, scarcely giving single word answers to questions the group peppers him with.

"Ethan didn't want to come out tonight?" I ask Alex, trying to divert attention from Eli and also distract myself from the way his knee rests against mine.

Alex shakes her head. "You know baker's hours. He says he can't manage on three hours of sleep anymore."

"But Zoe is here!" I whine playfully, gesturing to our resident firecracker who has braided her hair into a French crown and donned shimmering emerald lipstick.

Zoe grins and wraps an arm around Mia's shoulders. "That's because fun is always the priority over sleep. Tomorrow-Zoe will hate me, but tonight-Zoe plans to sing her heart out. Besides, Mia can sleep in for the both of us."

Mia rolls her eyes affectionately. "She acts like the bookstore doesn't also open early."

"But you're so beautiful when you're sleepy," Zoe coos then plants a kiss on Mia's cheek. "I look like a hag. You don't need beauty sleep the way I do."

The DJ's voice booms over the speakers. "And now we have Zoe singing 'Girls Just Want to Have Fun'!"

Zoe squeals and grabs Mia's hand, pulling her out of the booth. "Eek, that's me! Come on, babe!"

As they dash off and the electric, glittery sound of the song blares over the speakers, I turn to Eli who's watching the chaos with a soft smile. "So, Mr. Year of Spontaneity, are you going to grace us with a song?"

He brushes his dark bangs back from his forehead and chuckles. "I don't think so. I mean, how am I supposed to top that?"

He gestures to the stage where Zoe has donned a feather boa and is leaning toward her mic, one arm raising the roof. The crowd is already in her clutches, clapping and waving in rhythm.

I bump into his shoulder. The rich scent of his cologne makes my head spin a little. "Oh, come on, Lancaster. Live a little. Aren't you all about trying new things?"

His eyes flash. He's so close to me I can see the flecks of gold in his irises, count each of his unfairly long eyelashes. For a moment, the cacophony of the bar fades away, and all I can hear is the quickening of my heartbeat. His gaze drops to my lips for a fraction of a second before snapping back up to meet mine.

The air between us crackles with an electricity that has nothing to do with magic and everything to do with the way he's looking at me right now.

"You're right," he says, his voice low and husky. "I am currently all about trying new things."

For a wild moment, I think he might kiss me. Part of me hopes he will. I'm considering drowning the part of me—the Rhianna who is screaming a million excuses why that's a bad idea—in enough Mermaid's Kiss Cocktails she'll forget every one of them. She gets the best of me, though, reminding me I'm supposed to be finding Eli's perfect match, not auditioning for the role myself. Especially not in front of the whole town.

That Rhianna also remembers what it felt like to be left behind by someone who once claimed to love her—someone who couldn't stay when things got hard. And it's not her era for pain anymore. It's her era for plane tickets and possibility. For traveling the world unencumbered. For being young and alive and selfish in the best kind of way. Not for risking everything on a pair of soft eyes and a quiet voice that makes her wonder what it might feel like to risk her heart again.

I clear my throat and shift away from Eli the smallest amount, ignoring the way my skin tingles where we touched. I wiggle my eyebrows, hoping we can move past whatever almost happened between us. "So, a song?"

Eli looks at me for a long moment as the last beats of the music blare through the speakers. There's something unreadable in his eyes. Then he grins in an adorable half-smile. "All right, Wilder. You're on. But only if you sing one too."

"Done." After all, I don't care what people think about my singing and I've always been comfortable on stage. Eli shifts like he's going to leave the booth and request his song but I grab his arm gently to stall him. "Wait, your outfit needs a slight adjustment. Do you mind if I—?"

He hesitates, and we're back in the previous moment again. And the ideas of cocktails and poor decisions sound perfect. Then he nods. My fingers tremble slightly as I reach out to undo the top few buttons of his shirt. The brush of my knuckles against his skin causes him to shiver and my breath catches. Suddenly it's very warm in here.

"There," I say, my voice breathier than I'd like. "Now you look the part. Go knock 'em dead with your rendition of 'Blue Moon of Kentucky', champ."

He laughs and stands, walking over to the DJ. I regret sending him away the moment the air cools around me. I slump back into the booth, my heart racing.

Alex glides over next to me. "So, want to tell me what that was all about?"

Tom has taken the stage along with Violet, Mia, and Zoe as swoony boy band music plays. Tom even gives a little hip wiggle as he belts out the chorus of 'I Want it That Way'. Rachel and Grant stand in front of the stage fist-pumping in rhythm. For a book club, we're pretty cool, I have to say.

Alex isn't paying attention to the performance, though. She's smirking at me, one eyebrow raised. I shrug. "What are you talking about?"

"Oh, I don't know," she says, stretching the words out. "Maybe the fact that what your fingers didn't do in unbuttoning Eli's shirt, your eyes were finishing?"

My cheeks catch fire. "They weren't! I was just… helping him get into the karaoke spirit."

"Mhmm." Alex takes a sip of her drink in the mermaid-tail shaped goblet. "Just friendly encouragement?"

"Exactly. I'm his matchmaker, remember? I'm just trying to help him come out of his shell."

Alex's expression softens. "Rhianna, I think you might be—"

But whatever she thinks I might be is cut off by the DJ's booming voice. "All right, folks! Next up we have Eli with 'Go Your Own Way' by Fleetwood Mac!"

My jaw drops. "Fleetwood Mac? But why would he—"

"Looks like he knows your favorite band already." Alex pats my hand.

I can't pay attention to her, though, as Eli takes the stage. His hands shake as he accepts the mic, but he juts his jaw up as the first guitar chords come on, and then…

Holy. Crap.

Eli Lancaster can sing. Like, really sing. His voice is rich and soulful, filling every corner of the room. Gone is the buttoned-up professor. For a moment, the entire bar is transfixed, then as Eli hits a long note perfectly, the place explodes.

Zoe still stands at the front with the rest of the group and they're singing the backup lyrics loudly enough that they carry even without a mic.

But I'm completely fixed on Eli who loosens up as the song carries on. His eyes, which had been closed in concentration, suddenly open and lock onto mine. The intensity in his gaze nearly knocks me out of my seat.

As he belts out the chorus, the meaning of the lyrics hits me like a tidal wave. This is a song about a man who's in love with a woman but knows she wants to go her own way. He's saying he would give her his world if he could. Is Eli... is he trying to tell me something?

My heart races, and it's not just with the energy in this room. It's the realization that I *feel* something for him. Something real. Not crush-level, not fling-level, but gut-deep, maybe-don't-leave-level feeling. And that's the most terrifying feeling of all.

Eli's voice soars on the high notes, raw emotions pouring out of him. Our club members have become his own personal hype squad, hooting and dancing when they aren't singing. Despite the atmosphere, the words seem to hang in the air between us, heavy with meaning.

I feel like I'm seeing him for the first time. He'd explained how he has difficulty carrying conversations. Not with me, though. Now watching him pour his soul into a song at a cheesy karaoke bar has me staring slack-jawed.

As the final chords fade away, the bar erupts in cheers and applause. Eli blinks, as if coming out of a trance. A slow, shy smile spreads across his face as he takes in the crowd's reaction. But his eyes find mine again, and in that moment, it feels like we're the only two people in the room.

Alex nudges me and gives me a knowing look that I pointedly ignore. She hops up, offering to bring me a drink. I'm not even sure if I say yes or not. As Eli makes his way back to our table, he accepts high-fives and pats on the back from other patrons. I'm still frozen in place, my mind reeling.

"So," Eli says as he drops beside me, his knee bracketing

mine. He's slightly out of breath and flushed, his cologne stronger than ever. "A worthy enough attempt for my first performance at *The Tipsy Mermaid*?"

I open my mouth, but for once in my life, I'm at a loss for words. How do I tell him he just turned my world upside down with a single song? That I just saw a side of him I didn't know existed and I want to see it again?

"I... wow," I finally manage with the absolute elegance you'd expect from someone who works with words for a career. *Come on, Rhianna, get it together.* "Eli, that was... you're an amazing singer."

He ducks his head which only slightly obscures the smile blooming on his face. "Thanks. I guess I felt inspired."

Our eyes meet again, and the air between us crackles with unspoken words and possibilities. I know I should look away, should remember that I'm supposed to be his matchmaker. But right now, with Eli looking at me like that, a flush still coloring his cheeks, I can't bring myself to care about anything else.

I'm in trouble. Big, Fleetwood Mac-Rumors-tour sized trouble. Because somewhere between the cinnamon rolls and the karaoke and the quiet, steady way he looks at me like he *sees* me...

I stopped pretending this was a casual crush.

I think I'm falling.

And the scariest part is that a small, reckless part of me *wants* to. Even knowing how it ended last time. Even knowing what it cost.

Rhianna

The library at midnight is my personal brand of magic—quiet, cozy, and just eerie enough to keep things interesting. There's something enchanting about being alone here after hours, surrounded by all these stories just waiting to be discovered. The building creaks and groans around me like it's trying to tell its own tales while I dig through yet another stack of local books that we can't bring out while non-magical tourists visit during our regular hours.

I've been trying to focus for the past hour, but my mind keeps drifting back to karaoke night. To Eli Lancaster channeling his inner Stevie Nicks (okay, fine, Lindsey Buckingham) and absolutely bringing down the house. Who knew Professor Buttoned-Up had *that* hiding under all those pristine oxford shirts? But more than his surprisingly amazing voice, it was watching him transform on stage that got me thinking. One minute he was shy, reserved Eli, and the next... pure magic.

Which might explain why I've spent the last three hours down this rabbit hole of local legends and lore instead of, you know, sleeping like a normal person.

Because watching Eli at karaoke—seeing him really let go,

light up, become someone unexpected—made me realize something. You can read about a person all day, hear their stories, learn the facts. But experiencing them—watching them come alive in a moment you never saw coming—is something else entirely.

And that got me thinking. How many stories are tucked away in these books, waiting for someone to see them, really *see* them, instead of just skimming the surface? How much of history has been left gathering dust when it was meant to be felt?

Not that I've been thinking about Eli specifically. Much. Okay, maybe a little. But in my defense, it's hard not to when he sang that song while looking right at—

"Burning the midnight oil?"

I jump approximately sixteen feet in the air, nearly baptizing my research in cold chamomile tea. Speak of the devil and he shall appear, wearing a navy sweater that makes his eyes look unfairly gorgeous. I swear I'm one accidental smile from real feelings. And that cannot happen.

"Lancaster!" My voice definitely doesn't squeak. "What are you doing here?"

He holds up an ancient-looking book bound in leather that's seen better days. "Reinforcing some of the older magical wards. I saw your light on." His eyes drift to the chaos of papers spread across my desk. "Local folklore?"

"I might have had an idea." I tap my pen against my bottom lip, trying to ignore how his presence makes my skin tingle. "Want to hear something potentially brilliant or possibly insane?"

That's how all my ideas are—dancing on that fine line between genius and disaster. Like my matchmaking service. After weeks of that eye-catching flyer pinned to the library bulletin board, with its perfectly chosen font and just the right amount of glitter, I still haven't had another sign-up beyond

Eli. No one's biting, despite my enthusiasm and the town's usual appetite for anything new and quirky.

It stings more than I want to admit. But I'm not giving up. Not yet.

When plan A falls through, you look for plan B—other ways to spark connection, to bring people together.

Which is how this new idea was born.

Business has been slower than molasses in January, and I've got time on my hands—plus, this might be exactly the thing to make my Library Fellowship application shine.

Eli's lips quirk up in that half-smile that definitely doesn't make my stomach do backflips. It's like one minute I'm dreaming of him, the next I've summoned him in the flesh. And why is he even more handsome in reality while the shadows cut across his sharp jaw. "Those tend to be the best ideas."

"I'm thinking the library should offer evening tours but make them *experiences.*" I wave my hands, probably looking like a crazy person but too excited to care. "Like, performances of local legends!"

Eli's eyes light up like I just admitted that 80s music is better than 70s music. Which, for the record, I will never do. "Like the phantom ship that appears in the harbor during storms?"

"Yes! Or the story about the first settler who learned magic from merfolk, except we can't exactly advertise that part to the tourists..."

I scoot over, patting the chair next to me with probably too much enthusiasm. It's not until after I make the action that I realize what I'm doing—inviting him to join me, implying he should stay later. I mean, surely he planned to leave; it's probably almost midnight and why would he want to spend his sleeping hours—

He settles in beside me before my mind can spiral further,

close enough that I catch the scent of his vanilla and cedarwood cologne. I've imagined that scent since karaoke night. "I've actually been researching similar legends for my current project. Did you know that in nearly every coastal town there's lore around ghost ships? Each one has their own twist—cursed crews, ghostly captains, and the like, but they have a lot of similarities too."

And just like that, we're off. Hours slip by as we pore over volumes, trading stories and completely forgetting that sleep is supposedly a thing humans need. Eli knows *everything* about folklore, and watching him get excited about obscure details makes me want to—

I won't finish that thought, because I'm doing this project to get *the* fellowship. The one that would let me zip between twenty-four different libraries across six continents like some kind of book-loving Carmen Sandiego. During the week, I'd assist the local librarians and help them reach more people in their communities, running the kind of events that make my heart sing and diving into projects that could actually make a difference. And the weekends? Those would be for exploring hidden streets in Paris, getting lost in Bangkok's night markets, maybe even tracking down that theater-turned-bookstore in Buenos Aires that Grandma Ida always said we'd visit.

I'll be gone in six months, and I can't afford to get attached—especially not to someone like Eli Lancaster. He's the opposite of a casual fling: thoughtful, precise, the kind of person who would matter. The kind who could unravel everything I've worked so hard to keep stitched together.

I've been careful these past few years, choosing flings that fizzle out before they can hurt. Eli, though, would leave a crater.

This is why I swore off serious dating. Not because I don't believe in love—but because I've already given everything to someone once, and it still wasn't enough. Some people just ask too much, feel too much. It's easier—for everyone—if we don't go too deep.

Even if my heart flips every time he looks at me like he sees it all.

"We could start here," I say, spreading out my very professional sketch—read: scribbled mess—of the library layout. "Turn the reading room into a moonlit study for the Moonlight Reader legend. You know, the one where the ghost appears after hours to read unfinished stories by candlelight?"

"Yes! Then you could move to the garden for the merfolk legend." His fingers brush mine as he points to different locations on the map, and I pretend my skin doesn't buzz from the contact. "The fountain would make the perfect backdrop. Or if you wanted to go bigger you could even incorporate parts of the town? Like a walking tour?"

It's a good idea. Too good. And the way he says it—like we're already building something together—makes something in my chest tighten.

I should tell him about the fellowship—about how whatever buzzes between us can't go anywhere. Maybe even throw in a disclaimer that I'm allergic to emotional risk. That the idea of letting someone in makes me break out in a cold sweat. How my therapist mother could probably name this behavior, give it a label, and offer three grounding exercises before I even finished blinking—if I ever actually let her try. But he's looking at me with such warmth and enthusiasm, and I'm weak. Sue me.

Plus, I might not get the fellowship. I mean, I'm assuming I will—I'm busting my butt to make it happen. But nothing's guaranteed, and if it doesn't work out... Well, why get everyone excited over something that might not even happen? Yes, this is the excuse I'm using to continue not discussing it with Mom. Yes, I feel guilty about it. No, that guilt isn't enough to make me brave that particular conversation yet.

The hours pass in a blur of quiet conversation and ink-smudged notes, the kind of late-night haze where exhaustion should be setting in—but somehow, I feel *wired*. Maybe it's the steady warmth of his leg pressed against mine, the accidental brush of our arms sending sparks dancing over my skin.

Or maybe it's him.

It doesn't help that he smells amazing—old books and coffee and that cologne I swear I've never smelled on anyone else. Or that every time he gets excited about an idea, he runs a hand through his hair, leaving it a tousled mess that makes my fingers ache to smooth it down. Or maybe it's the way our magic hums in sync—mine all spark and scatter, his steady and sure, like we're dancing to the same song without even trying.

I should be tired. I should be yawning, blinking blearily at the pages in front of me. But the way he looks at me when we stumble onto something interesting? The way his voice shifts when he's caught up in a thought?

Yeah. No chance of sleep now.

I'm supposed to be his matchmaker, not sitting here fantasizing about how his stubble might feel against my palm if I cupped his face and—

Focus, Rhianna. Focus on the project. The fellowship. The dreams that don't include kissing literary professors in dark libraries. And the safety that comes with sticking to the plan—one that doesn't leave room for heartbreak.

"What time is it, anyway?" I ask, stretching arms that definitely don't appreciate my terrible life choices. At least it gives me something else to focus on.

Eli checks his watch and lets out a surprised laugh. "Almost five in the morning."

"What?" I blink at him. "We've been at this all night? How did that happen?"

"Time flies when you're plotting ghostly appearances." His smile is soft in the lamplight.

"Want to grab breakfast?" I hear myself ask before my brain can catch up with my mouth—before I can follow my plan of focusing on something else and ending things before we both get hurt. "I know a place that makes cinnamon rolls that'll change your life."

I waggle my eyebrows to emphasize my point and he laughs. Every drop of resistance I've clung to fades in the warmth of that sound. It's impossible to hold back a smile, too, as I catch his gaze lingering on me just a bit longer than usual.

"The Whisk is open at five?"

"Sure is."

"Hmm." He pretends to consider, running his fingers down his jaw. But when he turns back to me, there's a new seriousness in his eyes. "I don't know. I've heard those cinnamon rolls can make people fall in love. More local lore, perhaps?" He adds the last part with an attempt at casualness, but it feels forced.

My mouth goes dry. Oh. This is the part where I should laugh it off, where I should steer us back to safer ground. Eli and I discussing love, specifically one of us falling into it with the other, is dangerous territory. Because this is how it begins —sweet and easy and full of sparks. But when the storm comes, the boat won't hold. And I have no interest in drowning and gasping for air, wondering how I got pulled under again. I'd rather stay on shore.

The words catch in my throat, and for a moment, all I can do is hold his gaze, feeling my heart thud a little too hard.

"Maybe it's time to branch out, try something new, Lancaster." I'm smiling, but like his words it feels forced. "The cinnamon rolls aren't the only thing Ethan makes that's worth risking your heart over. His chocolate croissants have inspired poetry."

I'm deflecting and we both know it. But to his credit, Eli

just chuckles and offers me a hand like some kind of romance novel hero. Which he's not. Obviously. Even if he's checking a lot of the boxes.

"I'll have to take your word for it. Though I warn you—my poetry is even worse than my conversation skills on random dates."

"I've still yet to see these horrid conversation skills." With myself at least. Topics flow between us like a river.

"Yeah, I guess you haven't."

He catches my eye, and for a moment the air between us crackles with everything we're not saying. I can feel it—our energies swirling together, brushing and sparking like wind against embers. It's soft, magnetic, impossible to ignore. I clear my throat, breaking the spell. We both busy ourselves, gathering our things, but the silence between us feels charged, heavy with the unspoken.

As we walk through the quiet streets, shoulders bumping, trading ideas about costumes and staging for the event, I realize I'm in *way* deeper trouble than I thought. Because this feels real. It feels like something that could matter. With every laugh, every brush of his arm against mine, I can feel the ground shifting beneath me, pulling me toward something I swore would never happen again.

So I focus on the way the streetlights cast long shadows on the cobblestones, on perfecting my terrible ghost impressions (which makes him laugh every time), on anything but the way my heart does backflips when he smiles. Sometimes living in the moment is the only way to keep from thinking too far ahead, especially when you're already bracing for the part where it ends.

I tell myself I'm getting better at it. At not thinking. At pretending this is simple. Maybe if I lie to myself enough, I'll start to believe it.

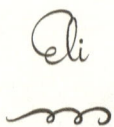

Eli

Crisp night air nips at my face as I make the walk back from the forest's edge. The last of our tour group disappears back toward the town, their excited chatter fading into the distance.

It's hard to believe it's only been three weeks since Rhianna and I stood in the library, half-joking about planning this event. Two weeks of late nights, tangled research, and more coffee than I care to admit—and somehow, we pulled it off.

Rhianna walks ahead, her laughter carrying on the breeze, her energy still buzzing from the night's success. I should be focused on that—on what we pulled off, on how incredible it was to see weeks of research turn into something real. Instead, my mind keeps drifting back to breakfast at The Whimsical Whisk—that morning we'd spent bleary-eyed and buzzing on caffeine, riding the high of our all-nighter. Despite the early hour, despite the fog of exhaustion that should have dulled everything, I'd felt more awake, more present than I had in years. It wasn't a date—at least, we hadn't called it one—but it had felt like one. The kind that leaves you checking your phone later, hoping for a message, replaying moments in your head when you should be focusing on something else. Like right now.

For a moment, on that hazy morning at The Whisk, I wanted more. I'd wanted to lean in, to close the space between us, to taste the cinnamon still clinging to her lips. But I saw the hesitation in her eyes—subtle, but unmistakable. She wasn't ready. Not in the way I was.

So I followed her lead. Kept things easy, light. Pretended I didn't feel the current humming beneath every word. Because every time we edge closer, she retreats. There's a wall there— one I can't name, one she's not ready to lower—and I don't know what's behind it.

What scares me most is how quickly my plans are unraveling. How easily I've started picturing a life here, in Magnolia Cove, long after the summer ends. One with cinnamon mornings and late-night laughter, if she'd let me in.

I exhale, refocusing on the night's success instead. The whole town had become a stage—phantom ships projected onto the harbor mist, Mrs. Delehay playing the ghostly widow in the museum, even Tom's elaborate fog effects at the dock. And Rhianna—she'd been in her element. Watching her bring these stories to life, seeing that spark in her eyes, it did something to me.

Even if she never lets me get closer, even if she keeps that part of herself locked away... I still want more.

I can feel myself falling, tumbling toward something that might shatter me in the end. Each step closer to her feels like walking toward an inevitable heartache. I see the signs—her hesitation, the careful distance she maintains—but I can't seem to stop myself. I'm drawn to her brilliance, her energy, her light. And even knowing I might be the only one crossing this bridge between friendship and something deeper, I can't turn back. Not yet.

"That," Rhianna announces, dropping onto a nearby

bench, "was absolutely amazing." Her eyes sparkle with triumph, and there's a streak of ghost makeup smudged near her temple. The silver glitter catches in the streetlight, making her look like she belongs in one of these stories we've been researching.

I resist the urge to reach out and wipe away the smudge. "You're amazing," I say instead, then quickly add, "The way you brought everyone together, made the stories come alive..." Even Head Warlock Dean Markham participated, though he spent most of the evening eyeing the tourists suspiciously and probably watching to see if we slipped up and shared too much. Dean's young for his role, and even more suspicious and tightly wound than most warlocks. Which is saying a lot, coming from a man who alphabetizes his spice rack for fun.

Rhianna beams at me, making me forget all about Dean Markham. These past two weeks have been dangerous—late nights planning at *The Hungry Gull*, research sessions that turned into deep conversations, watching her charm the whole town into helping. I should have been working on my research that's due in the fall semester. Instead, I've been falling harder for this whirlwind of a woman who keeps reminding me she wants nothing serious.

But tonight felt different. The way she kept glancing at me during performances, how her hand brushed mine between stops, how she laughed at my terrible ghost puns that would have made Piper groan.

"Hey Lancaster," she says, standing up and pulling a pair of flashlights from her bag. The lingering ghost makeup is smeared, her hair wild from the evening wind, and she's never looked more beautiful. "One more adventure before the night is over?"

I follow her gaze to the hill looming behind us, dark trees swaying against the starlit sky. I take the flashlight without hesitation—it's become instinct, following wherever Rhianna

Wilder leads. Half of our adventures I would have considered *bold* before meeting her. Now they feel natural, like breathing. Like being pulled into the orbit of a star.

At this point, to achieve my third bold move I'm going to have to do something outrageous. Like confessing my feelings. Or, you know, sing karaoke sober.

"Define 'adventure,'" I say.

She grins, and even in the dim lights I can see the mischief dancing in her eyes. "Oh, come on, where's your sense of spontaneity?"

"I think it might have died on the stage of *The Tipsy Mermaid* a few weeks ago," I shoot back, earning a laugh that makes my heart squeeze.

As we start our trek up the hill, flashlights bobbing, I lift my face. The stars peeking from behind dark tree boughs are stunning. They gleam like crystals. A month ago, I wouldn't have dreamed of traipsing through a forest in the dead of night. But here I am and loving every minute.

"So, are you going to tell me why we're risking life and limb climbing a hill in the dark?" I ask as I duck beneath a low-hanging branch.

"Nope." She swings the light around. "Where's the fun in that? It's good, though. I promise."

I'd previously thought this misery rather than enjoyable. I'd even daydreamed of getting trapped in a broken elevator with her. As long as Rhianna is with me, I think I could define almost anything as fun.

Since I first saw her in the library dancing to music, I've felt more alive than any previous moment in my life.

We continue the climb, our conversation flowing easily from the event to books we've read to bizarre Magnolia Cove traditions to our families. I talk about Piper, about her career as a reading specialist and how much she loves the kids she works with. About how she teases me relentlessly and always beats me in Pac-Man and why she's the reason I took vocal lessons.

"She sounds amazing," Rhianna says softly. Twigs snap beneath our feet and our heaving breaths are the only other sound. "You're lucky to have each other."

"We are," I agree. "What about you? Any siblings?"

"One brother, Gavin. Older. Responsible. Always got straight A's. Grew up to teach history at the local high school. Makes sure baby ducks can cross the road. The whole ten-four." She dips under another low branch. "Our best story together is the Great Pumpkin Caper."

"The Great Pumpkin Caper?" Even before I hear the tale, it already has Rhianna all over it.

We reach the hilltop. All around us stars stretch like a blanket we could reach up and wrap ourselves in. It's breath-taking, but my attention immediately shifts back to Rhianna who launches into the story.

"So, there's this huge pumpkin patch on the outskirts of town, right? And I talked Gavin, when he was sixteen and I was fourteen, into playing the ultimate prank. I'm actually still shocked I convinced him."

I'm not surprised. Rhianna has the personality that could convince a statue to tap dance. Her enthusiasm is infectious, her smile disarming.

"We'll be over here." She lowers on the hill's edge where the forest spreads out until it reaches the dark peaceful expanse of the sea. "This is where I come when I'm feeling too much," she whispers.

I sit beside her, taking in the beauty and the hush around us. It feels like she's just shared a secret, something fragile and shimmering. Speaking into it would be like touching a bubble, bursting what's too gentle to hold. So instead, I let the silence settle, then shift back to the conversation we left behind. "Go on, what was the ultimate prank?"

Rhianna's eyes sparkle in her flashlight before she flicks it off. "Well, I had this brilliant idea to sneak out at midnight and rig all the pumpkins with tiny speakers. Can you imagine? An entire field of pumpkins suddenly comes to life with spooky sounds!"

"From your tone of voice it sounds like that didn't go as planned?"

She bumps her shoulder into mine, and my stomach clenches as I struggle not to lean closer. As she continues the story filled with hijinks and theatrical moments her hands move animatedly, punctuating each part of the story. Watching her, it's no wonder she could create tonight's event with such ease and flair. I feel like a sailor turned toward a siren, drawn in and unable to break away.

"...and there we were, covered in mud, trying to explain to Mr. Johnson why his pumpkin patch had turned into a midnight chorus of 'Monster Mash'!"

I'm laughing down to my stomach. "You're something else, Rhianna Wilder."

She nudges me again. "Oh, come on. Don't tell me you never got into trouble as a kid."

"Me? I was a perfect angel," I deadpan. "Just don't ask Piper about it."

"I'm desperate to meet her now."

As our laughter fades, I become acutely aware of how close we are. In the starlight, Rhianna's eyes seem to hold galaxies of their own. The air between us crackles like a storm is brewing but the skies are perfectly clear.

A light streaks the sky, breaking the moment. Rhianna gasps and points. "It's starting!"

Another gleaming streak of light soars across the heavens, and I release a breath. "Meteors?"

"Yes," she whispers, her face lifted toward the heavens, her skin bathed in moonlight. When another meteor bursts across

NOEL BAILEY

the darkness she reaches for my hand. I embrace her smooth fingers, my pulse racing at the touch.

Over the next fifteen minutes, more follow, painting bright arcs across the dark. But I find my gaze drawn more and more to Rhianna. The wonder on her face, the pure joy in her eyes—it's more breathtaking than any celestial display.

"Eli," she whispers, turning to me as a grin slides up her face. "Have you ever seen anything like this before?"

I look at her—really look at her—illuminated by starlight, eyes shining, a strand of sky-dark hair falling across her cheek. Staring for a moment too long at her mouth, I wonder how she'd taste if I closed the distance between us—if she'd lean in, if she'd let me. My pulse quickens at the thought. But even if she wouldn't, I'd still choose to be here watching joy spread over her face as stars streak the skies above us. Suddenly I know with absolute certainty that I've fallen for her. It's not a maybe anymore. It's a definite, irrefutable fact.

"No," I whisper back, my eyes never leaving her face. "I haven't."

Something in my tone must give me away because her smile falters, replaced by a look of... anticipation? Fear? Hope? I'm not sure.

Slowly, giving her every chance to pull away, I lean in. Her eyes flutter closed as our lips meet. The world falls away. Maybe a thousand more lights rush above us, but I see none of them. There's only Rhianna—the softness of her mouth, the warmth of her hand in mine, the faint scent of her perfume, and the taste of cherry ChapStick.

When we finally part, we're both a little breathless. Rhianna's eyes open slowly and her brows pull together. "Eli," she whispers, "what are we doing?"

I take a deep breath, my heart pounding. The words I want to say—about how watching her tonight made me realize I'm already rethinking my plans—stick in my throat.

I've seen her hesitation, heard her jokes about avoiding serious relationships, and watched her careful dance away from commitment. And maybe I'm careening toward heart-break, but I'd take it if it means even another day with Rhianna Wilder. So, I offer what I hope she can accept. "We don't have to define it," I whisper, my voice barely carrying over the rustling leaves. "No pressure, no expectations. What if we just... explore whatever this is? Like another adventure?"

There's a pause of time where the wind howls and an owl hoots. I'm terrified Rhianna is going to say no. Terrified that even this carefully casual suggestion will send her running.

The thought of her rejection makes my chest ache. Three weeks of late nights planning this tour, of shared meals and stolen glances, of watching her step into rooms and gather everyone's attention—it's changed something in me.

I've never been the type for casual relationships. The Type A in me wants everything catalogued, organized, defined. But for Rhianna... for the chance to be with her, even temporarily, I'd rewrite every rule I've ever lived by. Maybe it's foolish to hope that 'exploring things' could grow into something more, but after tonight—after seeing how she brings magic into everything she touches—I can't help but hope.

"I'm not a serious-relationship person, Eli." Her voice is quiet but firm. "I like you too much to lead you along and make you believe this could go somewhere. And you don't exactly strike me as the casual type."

I nod, heart still pounding, but keep my tone light. "I'm not usually." A beat passes and I chuckle. "But I'm trying new things, remember?"

She hesitates, and I can see the war waging behind her eyes —the fear of hurting me or perhaps of getting too close. And maybe I'm a fool, but I'd risk it all for Rhianna. Even just for a few more weeks of holding her hands and listening to her dreams. My heart is already hers. Risking it feels inevitable. Almost easy.

So I lean in, just enough that my whispered words barely rise above the hush of the breeze. "If you're even considering this, just know—if or when you're ready to call it quits, I'll respect it. No guilt. No pressure. You say you're done, then we're done." I give her a small smile. "Until then... maybe we just explore this. See where it goes? Just for now?"

There's another long pause. Rhianna doesn't look away, but something shifts in her expression. Her lips pinch, just slightly. Her eyes flicker, like she's replaying every reason she's told herself this is a bad idea. Like she's weighing the risk, counting the cost.

I want to tell her it's okay. That she doesn't owe me anything. But I can't make myself say it because if she turns me down right now, I think it might break something in me.

My stomach churns, every second stretching out like it's trying to teach me patience. Or humility. Or the precursor work for heartbreak.

This is so miserable it could almost count as bold move number three. If only it didn't also feel so terrifyingly natural.

Then slowly, Rhianna's lips curve into a smile. "You know what, I'd like that."

Relief floods through me, so sharp and sudden it almost makes me feel dizzy. She said yes. Not to forever, not to something defined. But to this. To me. Hope unfurls in my chest like a lit match, fragile and flickering but real.

This time, she's the one who leans in, her soft hands grazing down my jaw then sliding down my neck. Her mouth is warm and sweet and I'm pretty sure the entire purpose of my three bold choices was this moment, this woman.

When we finally break apart, we're both grinning like fools. Her hair is wild in the wind, dancing with the stars. I reach over as I've longed to do a hundred times and tuck strands back. She smiles up at me, glitter still clinging to her cheeks from her ghost makeup, and it nearly undoes me. I know what we agreed to. This isn't forever. I made that clear. The moment it stops feeling right, she'll walk, and I'll honor what I said. No pressure. No expectations.

But right now, under the meteor-streaked sky, with her eyes shining like I'm the only thing she sees, I decide some things are still worth the risk.

"So," I say, "does this mean you'll be my Blue Moon Festival date?"

She huffs a laugh. "Well, I gave you a scout's honor, so I guess I'm committed. Besides, my matchmaking service hasn't exactly been flooded with clients. You're still the only brave soul who signed up."

Signing up for that might have been the most important decision I've ever made in my life. I'd wanted to throw up. I wanted to run away. But I didn't. And now I sit beside the most beautiful, charismatic, magical woman I've ever met in my life... someone who makes me feel as explosively alive as the stars streaking the sky. But I somehow know those words are too much. So I reply to her joke about giving a scout's honor instead.

"I'd hate for you to break the years of scouting and commitment behind those words." My smile feels ridiculous. Piper would tease me until next year if she saw it. "Should we head back?"

Rhianna stands with me and takes my hand, intertwining our fingers. "Lead the way, Lancaster."

We make our way down the slope, hand in hand, stealing glances and sharing soft laughs. It feels surreal, like a dream I don't want to wake up from.

As we reach the bottom, Rhianna's steps slow. She turns to me, her expression shifting to something more serious, more deliberate. She reaches into her bag and carefully pulls out two books, handling them over with reverence.

"These are for you," she says softly, extending them toward me. "I've been waiting for the right moment tonight to give them to you. They're yours to keep."

There's a weight to her words, a significance that tells me this isn't some casual offering. The way her fingers linger on the covers before fully releasing them to me speaks volumes about what these books must mean to her.

I take them. The first is a colorful paperback that gleams in Rhianna's flashlight beam. A woman builds a snowman on the cover and a scowling man leans against his snow shovel. "A man-written-by-a-woman romance novel, I presume?"

"There's no elevator in that one, but I think you'll like it."

"If I remember correctly, I'm supposed to read it as my manual on how women like to be treated, no?"

She blushes. Even in the low light the color is visible. I want to reach out and feel her skin's warmth under my fingers but it feels like too much.

"I was exaggerating a bit," she says.

"Seagulls do not a romantic date make. I remember that much, at least."

She laughs. "That's right. Okay, next book."

I slide the paperback behind the second. My breath catches. It's a beautifully bound copy of Cyrus Whitlock's *Welsh Gods and Goddesses*. By the weight and material's feel it's a first edition, too—one I don't even own. It was such a limited print run that few copies remain.

I blink, stunned.

I trace my fingers over the embossed title, the gold still vibrant against the worn spine. It's perfect. So perfect it doesn't feel real. Mark would've lost his mind over even getting to hold this book and Rhianna just handed it to me.

Tonight has felt like all the magic in Magnolia Cove has

gathered just for us. It seems possible that this enchantment could extend to finding a long-lost signed copy. My fingers tremble slightly as I pull back the cover.

No signature greets me. Instead there's floral fabric paper for bookends which significantly drops the value. Perhaps it's not a first edition after all. Maybe someone found a cheaper print and rebound it. It's been known to happen. I'm not disappointed, though. Instead, my attention shifts to a delicate bookmark peeking out from the pages. I flip to the marked section. *Rhiannon: The Enigmatic Goddess of the Moon.*

As I scan the pages, I notice delicate handwriting in the margins—elegant script with little drawings, hearts, and notations. I run my fingers over the ink, feeling the slight indentation where someone pressed their thoughts into permanence. I've always loved books with character like this—the ones that carry traces of their previous owners. There's something magical about a well-loved book, how it becomes more than just the text between its covers but a collection of memories, a catalog of all the readers who came before, their thoughts and reactions preserved alongside the author's words. Each note, each dog-eared page, each smudge or stain tells a story of its own.

I look up at Rhianna who's biting her lip. "Did I match you with the right book?"

I look down at the beautifully preserved copy of my favorite author's work. I smile. It's not just any mythology chapter she's marked, but the one about Rhiannon—the goddess she shares a name with, the very topic that sparked our first real conversation that day in the library. The coincidence seems too perfect to be accidental, like the universe or something older and quieter is nudging our stories into alignment. I'm not one to believe in fate. But holding this book in my hands after everything that's led me here... It makes me wonder. Maybe this risk won't end the way I expect. Maybe, just this once, something uncertain could still turn into something true. "You couldn't have chosen a more perfect copy."

She jumps up and down on her toes, her flashlight bobbing with the motion. I want to laugh. I want to pull her into my arms and kiss her again. I want to tell her how much her joy seeps into me and I think it's changing me. Filling me up like coffee spreading its warmth into a thermos. Making me want to say big things she's not ready to hear—things like, "Maybe I shouldn't move back" and "How does forever sound?"

But I know better. Agreeing to a 'no commitments' exploration does not a promise of the future make—no matter how hopeful I'm feeling. So I tuck those dangerous thoughts away, file them somewhere between *wishful thinking* and *maybe someday*.

I close the book gently, already knowing it's going on the shelf for my most treasured editions. "Thank you, Rhianna. This is... incredible. You're incredible."

She steps closer. "I mean, maybe I'm not as incredible as a moon goddess or a song by the world's best *soft-rock* band?"

"You're never going to let me live that one down, huh?"

She takes another step then presses up on tiptoe to whisper against my lips. "Never."

I chuckle and wrap my arms around her waist. "Rhianna Wilder, you're better than any genre-defying band I've ever heard."

Her laughter vibrates through me as she presses her lips to mine. For the first time in my life, I'm not thinking about a to-do list or scholarly pursuits. I'm thinking about the future, about possibilities, about the adventure of falling for this woman who turned an entire town into a stage tonight, who makes everything feel magical. For the moment, I couldn't be happier.

However there's a whisper in the back of my mind.

Only a few months left.

I shiver at the realization. A few months to explore whatever this is, a few months until I have to return to my real life, my career, my carefully planned future. A few months to convince her that maybe some adventures are worth staying for. But then I push those thoughts away—tonight is about meteors and folklore and first kisses. Tomorrow can worry about itself.

I give myself over to Rhianna's kiss, the taste of sweet ChapStick, and the quiet promise of possibilities lingering between us.

Rhianna

I'm halfway through sorting through a stack of new releases at the library when Mom drops by my desk, radiating that special brand of maternal concern that means she's about to analyze my life choices. Again.

Though she has a Whimsical Whisk bag in hand which means she's bringing a delicious treat. I'm weighing out whether the payoff will be worth the conversation as she approaches.

"So," she says, drawing out the word like taffy. "The Blue Moon Festival?"

"Yep." I scan a barcode and slide another book into the shelf-ready pile. "That is a thing that happens every year."

"Rhi." She grins and thrusts the bag with the peace offering out to me. I accept and when the smell of chocolate chip cookies hits, I've already forgiven the first part of this interrogation. Hand-delivering desserts at work? She's definitely up to something. "I've heard you're going. That's different for you. Usually you avoid the festival claiming it"— she adds air quotes—"goes beyond kitschy and straight into cheese-ville."

I can't help but smile, because I do say that. And also because Ethan and Zoe's cookies are basically the love child of magic and joy wrapped in chocolatey perfection and I'm daydreaming of escaping this conversation, making it to the break room, and stuffing one into my mouth.

"Change is healthy, right? Isn't that what you tell your clients?"

I flash her a saccharine smile and hope it distracts her from the emotional panic attack happening behind my eyeballs. I keep replaying that moment beneath the meteor shower with Eli. How calm he was, how gently he laid it all out. No pressure. No promises. Just the chance to explore without strings attached.

I almost said no. The word was *right there.* But I couldn't make myself say it. I know this is probably a terrible idea. He's steady and thoughtful and actually seems to like me for who I am, big ideas and all. Which is exactly what makes it terrifying.

Maybe I'm trying to be brave. Or maybe I'm just being selfish and wanting something I'm not built to keep. Either way, the idea of dishing all this out with Mom within hearing distance of regular library patrons makes me want to throw my body into the nearest book drop.

Mom's eyes sparkle with a dangerous mix of professional insight and maternal intuition. "Interesting that you'd bring up my work. Are we perhaps deflecting from something? Or should I say... someone?"

"And there it is." I point with the hand holding the cookie bag at her accusingly. "You promised no psychoanalysis before noon."

"Darling, it's 12:15." She grins, completely unrepentant. "And Grammie Rae told me you and the charming new professor had sparks flying at that folklore event you two put on—practically lit up the whole town, she said."

I scowl. Once, I'd admired Grammie Rae—figured I'd

turn into her, even. The single, older lady the entire town considered themselves vaguely related to. The quirky one with big opinions and a bit of magic up her sleeve at all times. Now, though? I'm thinking being on the receiving end of her attention isn't as charming.

My mind drifts to the previous night. To Eli bathed in starlight, the way his gaze had remained on me rather than the celestial display exploding above us.

The kiss wasn't part of the plan. Neither was catching feelings for someone with forever in his eyes.

But Eli makes me want to be brave again—even if I have no idea how.

And deep down, I know how this ends. He likes the polished version of me. The real mess? That's the part people leave.

Just like Jacob did.

"Eli's just working at the library," I say with a shrug that feels too stiff to appear casual. "He's a professor and amazing with protection wards. Very professional. Very... scholarly."

"Mhmm." Mom draws out the sound like she's savoring it. "And does this scholarly gentleman happen to be joining you at the festival, by chance?"

I groan and move an entire pile of books that don't need to be moved. Mom only smirks at me, willing to accept defeat in the conversation although the twinkle in her eye says it's not over—not close. But she pulls an envelope out of her bag. "My real reason for dropping by is that this came in the mail today and I thought you'd like to see it sooner than later."

As I accept the envelope, I read the sender information. The *World Library Tour Fellowship* logo makes my heart stutter. Someone shuffles by, a woman pushing a toddler in a stroller, but I barely notice them. My gaze is glued to the envelope in her hands.

"You knew I applied?"

Mom's expression softens into something that makes my throat tight. "Of course I knew, honey. I was waiting for you to share when you were ready. I see how hard you've worked, how carefully you've saved." She pauses and her gaze goes distant like she's weighing her words. "Maybe I've pushed too hard sometimes, tried to shape your path because I'm so content with mine. But this isn't about my dreams for you anymore."

She reaches across the desk and takes my hand. "I just want to see you happy and successful, Rhianna. And maybe that means you can't go through life my way, or process things my way. Maybe you have to go your own way."

Go your own way.

The words slam into me, sending me straight back to *The Tipsy Mermaid*, to Eli on that stage, his voice raw and beautiful as the words to that song poured from him. To the way his eyes found mine, like maybe the lyrics weren't random.

So much for keeping things simple.

Eli has infused himself into my bloodstream, sunk into my bones. Last night the stars seemed to rain when his lips met mine. The world narrowed to just that moment—his hands gentle on my face, the soft brush of his thumb across my cheek, the expert way he molded our mouths together.

It's casual. That's what we agreed. A little adventure, no strings attached. But there's nothing casual about the way my heart does backflips when he walks into the room, or how I've begun reading through Cyrus Whitlock's works just to see his eyes brighten when I discuss them. There's nothing casual about the way I catch myself memorizing the sound of his laugh, or how I think about him even when I shouldn't.

My stomach's been in knots all day. I couldn't even finish breakfast. Because I know myself. And this isn't casual anymore. Not for me.

I keep thinking about how easy it is to say yes to him.

Yes to dinner.

Yes to staying later after work to chat.

Yes to letting him in, inch by inch, even when I swore I'd never do that again.

After Jacob I swore to myself to never give someone the ability to break me again. Eli is like a too-rich wine I shouldn't have sipped. Now I can't stop. I keep going back for more, even though I know how this ends. Because I've lived it.

Jacob not only left me when I needed him most, he made it feel like it was my fault. Eli doesn't know that version of me yet. The cracked, unraveling girl beneath all the magic and charm and good intentions.

But when he does—when it stops being light and flirty and starts getting messy and *real*—he'll do what Jacob did. He'll leave.

And the worst part? I'm already hoping he won't. And that's what terrifies me the most.

My fingers trace the envelope's edge. Inside could be everything I've worked for. Six months of adventure and, with my savings, possibly more.

So why am I hesitating to open this letter?

This is my escape plan. The one I've clung to since Jacob left. I should tell Eli about the fellowship and my travel plans. Lay it all out. Let him know clearly and simply that this thing between us can be only for the summer. That it's casual, just like we agreed.

But something is stopping me.

Some quiet, persistent beat of hope that doesn't want to say the words out loud. Because somewhere between the gentle kisses, enthusiastic conversation, and the way his magic tangles with mine, I started wondering if this could be something more.

Maybe this envelope will make the choice for me. Maybe it'll let me keep pretending I'm not already halfway in. I slide open the envelope's flap. My hands are trembling and Mom is watching me in a way that says she isn't breathing and I'm pretty sure I'm about to throw up all over a book return cart when I read the words that don't seem real:

Dear Ms. Wilder,

We are pleased to inform you that you have been selected as a semifinalist for the World Library Tour Fellowship...

"Oh, my god." The words come out as a whisper. "Oh, my god."

Mom peers over my shoulder, then squeals loudly enough that it echoes around the library and draws the attention of Claire and a few patrons. "Rhianna!" she says. "This is incredible!"

It is incredible. It's everything I've dreamed of. Half a year of exploring the world while doing work I genuinely love. The kind of adventure Grandma Ida and I used to stay up late planning, tracing our fingers across maps and imagining the stories we'd collect. And maybe... a break. From Magnolia Cove and Jacob and the memories that seem to huddle at every corner.

I'm pretty sure I can convince my boss of the program's merits—she'll likely hold my position while I'm gone.

The excitement bubbling in my chest meets something else—something that feels suspiciously like regret. Because I told myself this envelope would decide everything. Now that it has, my stomach swoops with the kind of sinking feeling you only get when you realize, too late, that maybe you wanted a different answer.

Last night, under a sky full of shooting stars, Eli Lancaster kissed me like I was something precious. Like I was worth discovering.

I thought I never wanted to be seen again, not really. But now? Now I'm terrifyingly starting to consider that being seen, by the right person, could be a good thing.

Maybe.

"Do you want to tell your dad, or can I?" Mom is beaming, color flushing her cheeks. I should be in awe of her support, should be matching her enthusiasm watt for watt. This is what I've wanted. What I promised. What I literally backtracked adult steps and moved in with my parents to achieve.

All I can think about is the way Eli's voice gets soft when he talks about reading the same folklore someone else shared around a fire a thousand years ago. About the way he bows his head when he laughs at my silly puns. About the warmth and strength of his hand in mine at the meteor shower.

"You can tell him," I manage, trying to sound normal. Trying not to think about how Dad will absolutely want to help me research every library I'll visit, how he'll probably start sending me articles about each country's literary history. How Eli would love that about him.

Mom plants a kiss on my cheek then glides toward the exit. I'm left standing, stunned, the future I've worked and planned and hoped for in my hands. But I don't look at the letter again. Instead, I fish out my cell phone (a foolish thing to keep on me as service never works around the Cove anyway) and open the message Eli sent me last night.

Sweet dreams, fellow stargazer.

Four words shouldn't be able to raise my body temperature a dozen degrees. Shouldn't be able to conjure up the taste of his kiss, the rumble of his laughter.

I slide the letter into my bag, but not before running my fingers over the *World Library Tour Fellowship* logo one more time. This is my dream. My plan. Everything I've worked for.

It's just... Now there's this other feeling too, taking up space in my heart right next to my wanderlust. This warm, dizzy, terrifying feeling that has everything to do with the way Eli looks at me like I'm his favorite undiscovered story.

I take a deep breath and let reality settle into my bones. This thing with Eli is just a feeling, not my future. I won't tell him about the fellowship. Not yet. I'm only a semi-finalist and we're just... exploring.

No need to weigh down a summer adventure with long-term plans.

Not when everything's still so beautifully, terrifyingly uncertain.

Eli

A sharp knock on my office door startles me from the massive tome I've been cataloging all morning. It's a medieval manuscript on Celtic tree deities that I unearthed from the dustiest corner of the library's archives—fascinating stuff about druids and their belief that certain trees housed specific magical properties. Before I can rise to answer, the knock sounds again.

"Yes?" I call out, carefully marking my place with an acid-free bookmark.

The door swings open, and in walks Alex Sinclair. Even though we only exchanged a few words during karaoke night at *The Tipsy Mermaid*, she left an impression—poised, self-assured, and somehow managing to look effortlessly in charge even while sipping something pink and fizzy from a fishtail-shaped glass. Today, she's dressed more professionally—polished blonde waves, a sharp linen blazer—but the confidence is exactly the same.

"Hi, Eli," she says. "Alex Sinclair. We met a few weeks back."

"Oh—oh, yes. Of course. Karaoke night." I jump up,

nearly knocking over my stack of research notes. "I never got the chance to say—I had an amazing espresso blend at *Sinclair's* my first day in town. It might've convinced me to stay permanently."

Her smile widens. "Rhianna loves the blends we make as well, actually." She steps further into the room, casually scanning the chaotic sprawl of books and notes. "And she's actually the reason I'm here today."

My heart gives a quiet stutter at the mention of Rhianna's name, immediately followed by a rush of anxiety. Is something wrong? Did I miss a message from Rhianna? Did I somehow inadvertently offend her at our last meeting? She had book club last night, so I didn't see her. But she seemed okay when we texted goodnight. My mind races through our last conversation, searching for any missteps. Or worse—is this some kind of friend reconnaissance mission?

I clear my throat, attempting to appear calm despite the sudden spike in my pulse rate. "Oh? Is everything alright with Rhianna?"

Alex smirks, and I realize I've probably revealed more than I intended with my concerned expression. "Everything's perfect. She actually speaks very highly of you, which is part of why I'm here."

It's been days since the meteor shower, but I can still feel the press of her lips against mine, the way everything else slipped away as the stars streaked across the sky. She kissed me like we were writing our own story—one neither of us had planned but both of us felt coming.

"Please, feel free to have a seat," I say, bringing myself back to the present as I gesture to the chair across from my desk while trying to look like a man who hasn't spent most of his morning daydreaming about her friend instead of tackling the overwhelming workload still waiting on his desk.

"Thanks for letting me drop in," Alex says as she sits. "I

know Rhianna mentioned you prefer scheduled appointments."

I feel my face warm. "She did?"

But of course she did. Rhianna seems to see straight through me—like she already understands that unstructured social events are mildly excruciating and that I need to be coaxed out of my head like a wary animal. That I lose track of time when I'm deep in focus, and the last thing I want is to be interrupted mid-stream. It's equal parts unsettling and... oddly comforting. Like maybe she understands me in a way I never expected to be understood.

"Don't worry, it was said with affection." Alex laughs, a warm, genuine sound. "She also said you were the best person to talk to about protection wards, which brings me to why I'm here."

"Oh?" I straighten in my chair, curiosity piqued.

"Ethan is catering a wedding this weekend on Heron Island. Small affair, but important. The couple wants his three-tier vanilla bean cake with these delicate sugar flowers he's known for."

I nod. If his decorating is even half as good as the cinnamon rolls he makes, I'm sure it's spectacular.

"The problem," Alex continues, "is transportation. Tom Bryson is taking the wedding party out by boat, but the water's been choppy lately." She grimaces. "The last time Ethan tried to transport a tiered cake by boat without magical intervention, it arrived looking like it had survived an earthquake."

I can picture it—the cake swaying precariously with each swell, those intricate sugar flowers snapping off like brittle leaves in a storm. "That's unfortunate, but I'm not sure how I can help. I don't know anything about baking."

"No, but you do know protection wards." Her eyes sparkle with something like mischief. "And from what Rhianna tells me, you're quite good at them."

Ah. Now I understand. "You want me to place a protection ward on the cake."

"Exactly. Something to keep it stable during transport." She presses her manicured fingers together and presses her chin against them. "The only other person around here who can pull off wards like that with finesse is Dean Markham—and Ethan would rather swim the cake over himself than ask Dean for help... That's why when Rhianna mentioned your brilliance with protective wards that I had a brilliant idea for a trade."

My heart does that strange little jump again at the thought of Rhianna talking about me to her friends. I adjust my glasses. "What kind of trade?"

Alex reaches into her bag and pulls out an envelope. "Rhianna mentioned your interest in folklore books. Ethan has an extensive personal library at his cottage. Books passed down through his family, many about mythology—and many with wards that are starting to fade."

My interest immediately spikes. Access to a private collection? That kind of opportunity is rare, even in a place like Magnolia Cove.

"You add the ward to the cake, and Ethan will be happy to let you poke around his shelves. He thinks there might be something in there worth your while—maybe even useful for your work."

Or perhaps even a signed Whitlock. I pull in a sharp breath and redirect the sudden surge of energy by fussing with the alignment of my pens. The chances are slim, but still—an unexplored collection of magically warded books? It's academically irresistible.

"When would he need the ward placed?" I try to sound casual, but I can hear the eagerness in my own voice.

"Tomorrow afternoon? The wedding is the day after." Alex smiles, clearly sensing she's got me. "You can come by the cottage afterward to look at the books. He'll be home around four."

I nod, already running through the logistics. "That's ideal. Wards on organic material—especially something as delicate as a cake—work best when applied within twenty-four hours. The magic feeds off the carbon structure, and since a cake's, well, perishable, the ward starts to degrade as the sugar and flour do. There's actually a whole study on the half-life decay rate of magically treated food items—"

I catch myself mid-ramble and clear my throat. "Sorry. That was probably more than you needed."

Alex just laughs. "No worries. Ethan once gave me a ten-minute explanation that I still don't understand of why they infuse magic into food here fresh instead of ahead of time. You're in good company."

I pull out my planner—a reflex I haven't quite broken despite how Rhianna teases me about it, always laughing when I check it before agreeing to her impromptu picnics because "books will still be dusty tomorrow, Lancaster." The memory makes me smile despite myself. Tomorrow afternoon is clear except for some archival work that could easily be postponed.

"That should be fine," I say, closing the planner. "Just let me know where and when."

Alex stands, looking pleased. "Perfect. I'll email you the details. And thank you, Eli. This means a lot to Ethan."

"Happy to help." I rise as well, walking her to the door. "Though I should warn you, if I find anything particularly interesting in his collection, I might lose track of time."

"Warned and noted." She grins as she pauses at the threshold. "How are things with Rhianna, by the way? She hasn't stopped smiling here lately."

The question catches me off guard, and I feel heat rise to my face. "Things are... good. Really good."

That's an understatement. Since our kiss under the stars, I've been in a constant state of wonderment. Every moment with Rhianna feels like discovering a rare first edition—thrilling, precious, slightly overwhelming. I keep waiting for the logical part of my brain to panic about how she only agreed to this when I made it clear it was temporary—something she could walk away from any time. No strings. No promises.

That part of my brain should be waving a red flag right now, warning me to not get attached. Not to sink into this. But instead, I find myself craving the disruption. Leaning into it. Looking forward to the way she turns my carefully ordered life upside down—how she somehow makes me feel both grounded and weightless at once.

And besides, isn't that why I came to Magnolia Cove in the first place? To shake myself out of the rut. To disrupt the structure I've clung to for too long and actually live for once—not just follow a neatly color-coded calendar from one safe, predictable decision to the next. Losing Mark didn't just rattle me—it shocked me.

One day he was there, buried in his work just like I was. The next, he was gone. But now, here with Rhianna's laughter still echoing in my mind and the warmth of something real starting to take root in my chest... it makes me feel like maybe that shock has led to something meaningful.

That aches in a painful, beautiful way.

But I think Mark would approve.

He'd like Rhianna Wilder too. With her glitter and chaos and sharp insight, she didn't just knock me off balance—she made me want to stay unbalanced. To see what happens if I stop holding so tightly to the plan.

Alex gives me a knowing smile. "Good. You two are good together. It's nice to see her so happy."

The door clicks shut behind her, but her words linger—

settling into the quiet like dust motes in sunlight. I sit there for a long moment, letting them echo in the space she's left behind.

Eventually, I try to return to my research, but my thoughts keep drifting to tomorrow, to Ethan's mysterious collection, and inevitably back to Rhianna. I trace my thumb over the binding of the aged book before me. Life has a way of surprising you.

I came to Magnolia Cove to play my field's version of the ultimate Where's Waldo—tracking down a signed Cyrus Whitlock, the holy grail of obscure folklore texts. To shake up my routine with my—let's be honest—mildly ridiculous three-bold-moves challenge, and experience something different before returning to my neatly ordered existence. And maybe... to try and find some meaning in Mark's loss.

I close the book and lean back in my chair, staring at the ceiling. Three months ago, if someone had told me I'd be placing protection wards on wedding cakes and falling for a librarian with a penchant for glitter, I would have thought they were confusing me with someone else entirely.

I thought finding a signed Whitlock would be the pinnacle of this little adventure—the scholarly equivalent of climbing Everest. Instead, I find myself caring less about rare books and more about rare people. About a woman whose laugh makes my heart race. About a community that, despite its eccentricities (or perhaps because of them), feels increasingly like home.

My second bold move was signing up for Rhianna's matchmaking service, and that led me to the most unexpected discovery of all—not a book, but the possibility of a future I never planned for. A future that feels both terrifying and more right than anything I've meticulously plotted on my five-year plans.

Yet here I am. And strangely, wonderfully, it feels exactly right.

* * *

Ethan's cottage sits at the far edge of the beach, its navy exterior with worn ivory shutters standing apart from the other homes. It looks like something from a postcard—the kind of place that embodies coastal living without trying too hard. Two rocking chairs face the ocean on the small porch, a chessboard positioned between them as if waiting for players.

I approach the door, carefully balancing a worn 19th-century baking book I'd brought as a thank-you gift—its margin notes from the original owner were too charming to part with easily, even if the book never quite fit into my research.

After successfully warding the wedding cake this afternoon—a relatively simple spell that will keep it stable no matter how much the boat rocks—I'm more excited about this visit than I probably should be. But academic passion has always been my weakness, and the prospect of unexplored magical texts has me practically vibrating with anticipation.

Before I can knock, the door swings open, revealing Ethan in a henley and jeans. It's the first time I've seen him outside his professional attire—apron off, shoulders relaxed. He looks effortlessly at home here.

There's something about the people who live in Magnolia Cove long term—no matter how different they are. They all carry this quiet confidence, like they've found their place and settled into it without hesitation. And lately, I'm starting to wonder if I've found mine too.

"You must have magic footsteps," he says with an easy smile. "I didn't hear you until you made it to the walkway."

I offer a polite shrug, but my mind flickers back to the first time we shook hands—the telltale flicker of his magic coursing through me. Ethan's a shifter, a powerful one from what I've gathered, though he doesn't carry himself with any need to prove it. His senses, though, are still sharp—especially his hearing. He could probably hear most people the moment they stepped onto the beach in front of his cottage. Some people find that kind of magic intimidating. But Ethan Hart is the kind of person who puts others at ease the moment he enters a room—like gravity, but gentler.

"I can't help it, I'm afraid," I say, adjusting my glasses. "Occupational hazard of working in libraries and ancient university buildings. We're trained to move silently."

He chuckles and steps aside. "Come on in. Thanks again for helping with the cake. You saved me from begging a favor off the council."

The inside of the cottage is every bit as inviting as the outside—cozy, lived-in, effortlessly warm. A leather couch faces a small stone fireplace, a quilt draped across the back. But it's the far wall that draws my attention. Floor-to-ceiling bookshelves dominate the space, packed with volumes of every size and subject. Some are arranged in tidy rows, others piled sideways or crammed in wherever they fit. Loose papers and worn bookmarks protrude from their pages.

"Alex wasn't exaggerating," I say, nodding toward the bookshelves. "That's quite a collection."

Ethan follows my gaze. "They've been in the family for generations. My dad used to read to me from these when I was a kid—mostly adventures and old folktales. We both got hooked early. I guess letting them go just never felt like an option." He gestures to the book in my hands. "What's that?"

"Oh." I'd almost forgotten I was holding it. "Just a small token of appreciation. It's a nineteenth-century baking book I picked up years ago—nothing rare, but the original owner scribbled detailed notes in the margins. I thought it might interest you."

Ethan takes the book, his eyes widening slightly as he flips through the pages. He pauses at a recipe near the center, tracing one of the handwritten notes in the margin. "This is incredible. Look at this butter layering technique—way ahead of its time. I'll lose hours testing something like this." He pauses and offers a sheepish smile. "Alex calls it my 'science project phase' whenever I start tweaking recipes at three AM."

I chuckle, more in recognition than amusement. "I once spent an entire weekend cross-referencing an obscure Welsh legend across five different translations just to prove a footnote wrong."

Ethan quirks an eyebrow. "Now that's commitment."

"Commitment should be my middle name," I say and we both laugh. Then I nod toward the bookshelves. "Alex mentioned some of them have magical wards that are fading?"

"Yeah, about a hundred or so. They've been in the family for ages. Warding doesn't run in my line. Can't do it, no matter how many times I've tried." He sets my gift on the coffee table. "Before we dive into that, how about some coffee? I grind the beans fresh—can't start anything without the good stuff."

"That would be great. And I couldn't agree more. Life's too short for mediocre coffee."

"Coming up," he says as he moves to the kitchen. I can't help but advance toward the bookshelves, drawn like a moth to flame. Even from a few feet away, I can sense the subtle hum of magical energy emanating from certain volumes. Some wards are still strong—a low, steady pulse that speaks of skilled spellwork. Others flicker weakly, like a candle about to be extinguished.

Warding has always fascinated me—technically demanding and heavily rooted in magical mathematics, it's one of the more intricate branches of magic. Even among those who have the magical ability, not all enjoy the precision it requires, but I've always found comfort in its structure.

"Cream or sugar?" Ethan calls from the kitchen.

"Black is fine, thank you."

He returns moments later with two steaming mugs, handing one to me. "Go ahead and explore. I know that look —you're itching to get your hands on them."

I take a sip of the coffee and nearly sigh aloud. It's exceptional—rich and complex with notes of chocolate and something else I can't quite place.

"This is excellent," I say, taking another drink.

Ethan smiles. "Coffee's my other passion. I roast the beans myself."

"I can tell." I set the mug on a nearby table on a coaster and turn back to the books. "Mind if I...?"

"Have at it. That's why you're here."

I approach the shelves with the reverence they deserve, automatically falling into my cataloging mindset. First, a visual assessment—I scan the titles, mentally sorting them into rough categories: culinary texts (approximately 30% of the collection), fiction (perhaps another 25%), historical references, philosophy, poetry, and—most interestingly—a solid section on folklore and mythology.

Next, I evaluate the physical condition. Many volumes show signs of regular use—softened spines, minor foxing on pages, small imperfections that speak to books that have been read and loved rather than merely collected. Others appear remarkably well-preserved despite their obvious age.

Then, I move to magical assessment, focusing on the volumes emanating magical energy. I categorize these by ward type: preservation spells (the most common), anti-deterioration charms (slightly different magical signature, more focused on paper stability than overall preservation), and enhancement wards (designed to make the reading experience more immersive).

I pull out my small notebook and jot down quick observations—which books need immediate ward reinforcement versus which can wait. Some texts appear to have multilayered wards, suggesting they've been maintained by different wardens over time. Then my fingers brush across a familiar binding—a deep green leather with gilt lettering that makes my heart skip a beat.

I carefully slide it out, hardly daring to hope. The title confirms it: *The Forgotten Heroes: Tales from the Welsh Borderlands* by Cyrus Whitlock.

"Find something interesting?" Ethan asks from where he's settled into an armchair with his coffee.

"Very," I breathe, carefully opening the cover. It's a first edition—I'd recognize the typesetting anywhere. My heart races as I flip to the title page, half-expecting to see Whitlock's looping signature scrawled in ink.

But the space beneath the author's name is blank.

Still, the pages are in remarkable condition, with only minimal foxing. A first edition Whitlock in this state is a rare find—signature or not.

"This is..." I struggle to find words that won't reveal how desperately I'd love to have a copy like this in my collection. "It's quite valuable. Did you know that?"

Ethan shrugs. "I figured it might be. It was my great-grandfather's. He used to say Whitlock himself gave it to him, but I always thought that was just a good story."

I nearly drop the book. "Whitlock gave it to him? Directly?"

"That's the family legend." Ethan takes a sip of his coffee. "My great-grandfather traveled to Magnolia Cove often for work. Supposedly, he and Whitlock stayed at the same boarding house whenever they were in town."

This new information sends my mind racing. If Whitlock personally gave this book to Ethan's great-grandfather, then the chances of other signed copies being in Magnolia Cove increase exponentially. Maybe my quest isn't as quixotic as my colleagues suggested.

I carefully set the book on the table and take a steadying breath. "Ethan, I hope this isn't inappropriate, but would you consider selling this? I'd pay well above market value."

Ethan studies me for a moment, then smiles. "Consider it payment for the protection wards."

I stare at him, certain I've misheard. "I'm sorry?"

"The book. It's yours." He nods toward it. "For helping with the cake."

"But—" I sputter, shocked by his generosity. "That's far too much. The ward was a simple spell, hardly worth—"

"It's worth it to me," Ethan interrupts gently. "That cake represents a lot more than just food to the couple getting married. It's a centerpiece of their celebration, something they'll remember their whole lives." He shrugs. "Besides, the book would mean more to you than it does to me. I'd rather see it with someone who appreciates its value instead of gathering dust on my shelves."

I'm momentarily speechless. In academic circles, there would be fierce competition for a first edition Whitlock. People would call in favors, pull strings, perhaps even engage in some ethical corner-cutting to acquire it. Yet here's Ethan, casually giving it away because he thinks I'd appreciate it more.

"I don't know what to say," I finally manage. "Thank you seems inadequate."

Ethan laughs. "It's just a book, man."

I glance down at the book again, its worn leather cover warm beneath my fingertips. *Just* a book? Maybe to someone else. But to me, it means so much more.

"Besides," he adds, "Alex tells me you've made quite an

impression on Rhianna. Anyone who can make her smile like that is good in my book. No pun intended."

At the mention of Rhianna, warmth spreads through my chest. "She's... remarkable."

"She is," Ethan agrees. "I've known her since shortly after I met Zoe. Never seen her this happy."

I take another sip of coffee to hide my smile. "I'm still trying to figure out what she sees in me, to be honest."

"That's usually how it goes." Ethan's eyes crinkle at the corners. "When I met Alex, I couldn't believe someone like her would give someone like me a second look. But sometimes life just works out, you know?"

"Yeah," I say. "I think I'm starting to understand that."

We fall into an easy rhythm after that. Ethan's laid-back energy makes it hard not to feel comfortable—he doesn't rush the conversation or fill every silence. Instead he just lets things unfold naturally. It's rare, being around someone who doesn't expect quick answers or constant chatter. And for someone like me, who typically rehearses responses and analyzes social cues with academic precision, that's... unexpectedly comforting.

When I mention I'd be happy to help restore the wards on his most deteriorated volumes, he simply nods and says, "Whenever you get around to it. No rush." No scheduling, no deadlines, no formal arrangement—just a casual understanding. A month ago, such vagueness would have sent me into a mild panic. Now, I find myself nodding back, accepting the unstructured nature of the offer.

We discover a shared interest in chess—the board on his porch isn't just for show—though our approaches couldn't be more different. While I've memorized dozens of opening sequences and strategic patterns, Ethan admits he plays purely by intuition.

"I just move the pieces where they feel right," he says with a shrug when I ask about his strategy.

"But how do you plan several moves ahead?" I can't help but ask.

Ethan laughs. "I don't, and that's kind of the fun—just seeing where it leads. I take some things seriously, like baking, but it's nice to be laid-back somewhere else." It's such a foreign concept—approaching something without mapping out every possible outcome—yet I find myself oddly drawn to it. Perhaps there's something to be said for letting things unfold naturally, for finding the balance between careful planning and spontaneous joy. Isn't that what Rhianna has been showing me?

"I should get going," I say later as I gather my things. "Thanks again for the book. And the coffee."

"Anytime." Ethan walks me to the door. "You know, when I first moved here, I planned to leave the first chance I got. It felt too small, too quiet—nothing like the cities where I'd trained."

I pause on the threshold, curious. "What changed your mind?"

"The people," he says simply. "There's something special about this place—the way everyone knows each other, looks out for each other. It grounds you. And then there was Alex..." He smiles. "Sometimes you find yourself in places you never expected to be, with people you never expected to meet, and it just... feels right."

His words strike a chord within me. I came to Magnolia Cove seeking adventure, a departure from my meticulously planned life, something to shake me out of my routine before I returned to the academic world I know so well. After losing Mark, I realize how quickly life can end. I didn't just want change. I want to live a little before I miss the chance entirely.

And this adventure is doing that. It's making me feel awake for the first time in my life.

But what if this isn't just a temporary adventure? What if this small, magical island with its quirky residents and impossible beauty is where I'm meant to be? What if Rhianna Wilder, with her boundless enthusiasm and uncanny ability to make me forget all my careful plans, is who I'm meant to be with?

The thought should terrify me. Three months ago, it would have. And maybe it still should—especially knowing how guarded Rhianna is, how she flinches at the thought of anything permanent. She's made it clear she's not looking for something long term. Not now. Maybe not ever.

But my heart won't let it go. Not yet.

So I'll respect her boundaries, give her the space she needs. And maybe—just maybe—she'll find room for me in whatever future she's building. Because I already know I'd love for her to be part of mine.

Clutching a book I've only dreamed of finding in this condition—one I've read before, sure, but never like this—I think about the woman who makes my heart race with a single smile, and I feel something entirely different.

I feel like I've found home.

"I know exactly what you mean," I tell Ethan, and for perhaps the first time in my life, I truly do.

Rhianna

The Blue Moon Festival is in full swing, and I can't help but grin as Eli and I make our way through the crowd, hand in hand. It's been a couple of weeks since our meteor shower and kiss, and every day since has been a whirlwind of stolen lunch breaks at the library, laughter-filled dinners at various restaurants around the Cove, and late-night conversations that leave me daydreaming at work like a lovesick teenager. Which is ridiculous, because this isn't supposed to be serious. This can't be serious. It's casual—no strings attached, no expectations, no complications.

Except I'm falling for Eli Lancaster, hard and fast, and the thought both thrills and terrifies me. Every logical part of me is screaming to stop, to turn back, to protect my heart before it's too late. But I don't think I can.

The fellowship letter burns a hole in my cardigan pocket. I should tell him about it. About the six months (*or more*, my traitorous brain whispers) I'll be gone. But bringing it up now feels like opening a door I'm not ready to walk through. Like saying, "Hey, just so you know, I'm planning a future you're not in." Or worse—like admitting I want him in it.

Eli's only seen the fun side of me, though. The glitter and charm and half-baked plans. Apparently he finds that kind of thing entertaining. Some people do until they get the flip side of that coin. The part that's still chaotic, but in a hard way. The kind that feels like too much. Then they run.

As much as I want to believe Eli could be an exception, he already told me he left his last relationship when it stopped being interesting.

So yeah. That hope? Dangerous.

This is my season for gallivanting across Europe and chasing joy and possibility and whatever version of freedom still exists after heartbreak. Not for a second round of devastation.

So, I won't be telling him. We'll have a fun summer together like we've agreed. And if I get accepted into the program, I'll end things with him. That was the deal. No commitments. Just two people enjoying the in-between.

Even if part of me already knows I'm lying to myself. Even if part of me knows this already means more to him than he was willing to admit. And if I'm being honest? It means more to me, too.

I push the guilt down and focus on his hand in mine as we make our way through the crowd.

The town square is decked out in a bizarre mix of Elvis memorabilia and celestial decorations. Cardboard cutouts of The King pose next to papier mâché moons. A group of kids run by in sequined jumpsuits and fairy wings.

"So," Eli says, leaning close so his voice carries over a speaker blaring 'Blue Suede Shoes'. "Is it just me or is there a lack of promised rhinestones?"

I bat my eyelashes at him. "Why, Lancaster, are you implying that I oversold the majesty of our Blue Moon Festival?"

He chuckles, the sound warm and rich even amidst the chaos. "I'll let you know by the time the night's over."

"Rhianna! Eli!" A familiar voice cuts through the crowd. Alex waves at us, her other arm looped through Ethan's as they weave through the throng of festival-goers.

I navigate us close enough to speak with them as a couple passes us who are decked out in outfits studded in rhinestones from brimmed hats down to their heeled boots.

I give Eli a look. *Hmm, is that a lack of rhinestones?*

He rolls his eyes, conceding. *Fine.*

I'm smirking as we approach Alex and Ethan. "Enjoying the festival?"

Alex grins but her gaze drops to Eli's hand in mine. "Oh, absolutely. Ethan was just telling me about the time he entered the Elvis impersonation contest as a kid when his family visited on vacation one year."

Ethan groans good-naturedly. "I thought we agreed not to share that with others."

"Hang on," Eli says. "*You* entered the Elvis contest?"

The two of them have hit it off since Eli helped ward a wedding cake and spent an afternoon geeking out over rare books and perfectly brewed coffee. Ethan rolls his eyes but dives into the story of how he eagerly wore pomade and cat-eye glasses while singing his heart out.

Alex is half-listening to the story, but her focus remains on me. Or more specifically, on my hand twined with Eli's. She gives me one of her knowing looks. Dang city journalists and their ability to communicate without speaking.

"There's honey candy, Rhianna. Want to get some?" Alex asks when the conversation breaks.

"Sure." I give Eli's fingers a squeeze before joining her. We push through the crowd and get in line for the treat.

Alex tucks her hands into her pockets. "You two seem cozy."

My fingers graze the edge of my cardigan pocket, where the fellowship letter sits folded like a reminder. A promise. There's a whole world waiting out there—twenty-four libraries, twenty-four chances to experience something new without the risk of losing what I love. I've started carrying the letter with me like a shield. A reminder that I can't let myself get too deep. That getting too close to someone like Eli was never part of the plan. "We're... exploring things."

"Exploring things, huh? Is that what the kids are calling it these days?"

The line moves forward, and I roll my eyes as we move up. "It's very casual. We're just having fun and haven't felt the need to make any kind of announcement about it. It's not... a thing."

My heart gives a warning thud in my chest. Because something is shifting. I can feel it. In the way I scan rooms for him without thinking. In the way his laugh finds its way into the quiet space of my day. But every time I get close to naming it —whatever *this* is—fear flares. Like admitting it would make it real. And real means risk.

Letting someone in, really in, feels like reaching for something fragile with soap-slippery hands. I'm not the kind of person who gets to hold on to something this good. I've tried before. And the moment my hands trembled, it shattered.

"Where do you want it to go?" Alex asks.

A kid with smeared face paint and a half-eaten stick of cotton candy runs by us shrieking with laughter. I shrug. I'm going to pretend this is casual. Not even my friends get to see the icky, insecure parts of me. "It really can't go anywhere. I mean, I have the fellowship coming up—assuming I get accepted, fingers crossed."

Alex gives me a long, knowing look. Not pushy. Just.... Present. The kind of look that says she's not buying it, but she's not going to call me out either. Which somehow makes me feel both seen and exposed. We reach the front of the line and Alex throws up two fingers then pays. The attendant hands us cones of the candy that reflects the festival's colorful lights.

Alex loops her arm into mine and leans in to whisper as she walks us back through the crowd again. "For what my opinion is worth, I think you're going to get in. But maybe don't write off Eli so quickly... he seems great. Maybe don't assume this is something that can't work."

"Isn't that exactly the problem?" My hands crunch around the honey candy cone. "That he *is* great? It terrifies me, the idea of falling for someone."

Alex stops walking. The festival roars around us, colorful lights flashing, kids shrieking, fair rides blaring. But between us it feels quiet.

She studies me. "Why does that scare you so much?"

I exhale slowly, "I've told you about Jacob before."

Her nod is small, careful.

"Some things like that... they leave scars. He saw me at my lowest and decided it was too much. And ever since, I've just assumed that if anyone gets too close, they'll do the same." I pause, struggling to find words for something I almost never speak about—especially not with carousel music blaring behind me and the scent of fried Oreos clouding what little dignity I have left. "The idea of letting someone in again, especially someone who's actually kind, and thoughtful, and makes me feel seen in this impossible, terrifying way? That's not just scary. It's risky."

Alex's expression softens. She squeezes my arm. "Yes," she finally says, her voice barely above a whisper. "Sometimes the best people are the ones who make it a little terrifying. Because you know they're different. And maybe... that's worth risking your heart for."

The words settle over me like a truth I've been avoiding.

Because Eli is different. Not just because he's kind or thoughtful or beautiful in that unassuming, old-books-and-soft-eyes kind of way. But because he doesn't make me feel like I have to be anything but myself. He doesn't flinch at my chaos. He leans in.

And that's... new.

Jacob laughed off my biggest ideas, gently steered me away from the parts of my ideas that didn't fit into his picture of stability. At the time, it made sense. I told myself compromise was part of love, that healthy relationships included balancing each other.

But then I met Eli.

Someone who doesn't just tolerate the wild ramblings of how my brain works—he embraces it. Listens like it's poetry. Like there's something beautiful in my mess.

Being seen like that—really seen—and loved not despite the chaos but because of it, should feel like a gift. But instead, it feels like a risk I don't know how to take. Because love that true, that steady, only means it'll hurt that much more when it ends.

And how could it not end?

Eli is grounded in a way I've never been. He builds his life with quiet intention, with roots and structure and long-term thinking.

And me? I have a travel goal chart taped to my wall and an ever-growing list of cities I want to disappear into. I chase change like it's oxygen.

We want different things.

We live at different speeds.

The ending feels inevitable. Like something we're both pretending not to see because we like the way the beginning feels too much to stop now.

We walk the last stretch toward the guys in silence, my thoughts still tangled around that truth. Eli's dark bangs have fallen over his forehead, and he's caught in conversation, his mouth wide in a grin. His gaze shifts to me automatically, like he can sense me. My breath catches. Our magical energies reach for each other without any hesitation, intertwining like they've always belonged together. Like they've made the decision my heart's too scared to embrace.

Alex walks back over to Ethan and bats her eyes at him. "Ethan has promised me a ride on the Ferris Wheel. I'm forcing him to take me up on that."

Ethan laughs but claps Eli's hand and gives me a nod before the two of them disappear into the crowd. Alex and Ethan seem so in sync—something that seemed impossible with their backgrounds. Alex gave up living in New York City —one of the coolest cities on the planet—to come live here. She had a whole life there, a career on the rise, and she chose something else instead. She chose Magnolia Cove. She chose love.

Nope. Not going there right now. Not while I'm standing in the middle of a corny festival with gum stuck to my shoe and Elvis crooning *Suspicious Minds* in the background. These are not thoughts for tonight. Tonight is for fun and sparkles and maybe stealing kisses behind the Ferris Wheel. I can freak out about potentially life-altering feelings tomorrow.

"So," I say, looking up at Eli and smiling when I discover he's already looking down at me. "Ready to experience more of the Elvis extravaganza?"

He moves closer. "Lead the way, Wilder. I'm all shook up with anticipation."

I groan but take his hand and pull him through the crowd. We pass a variety of cheesy stands. *The Hound Dog Ring Toss.* A pink and white striped *Love Me Tender* kissing booth. And the local soup kitchen's stand where Grammie Rae is decked out in a rhinestone-studded jumpsuit and cries out, "Try your luck at the *Jail House Rock Escape Room*!"

We spend the next half hour hamming it up in the photo booth, trying on various Elvis wigs, and striking ridiculous poses with plastic guitars. Eli's laugh is like coffee on a cold morning—rich and warming and somehow essential. I want to bottle that sound and keep it forever, which is exactly the kind of thought I'm trying to drown in kettle corn and festival chaos.

But between the sugar rush, the swirling lights, and the way Eli keeps looking at me like I'm something precious, my heart feels too full, too raw. I need a minute. Just one moment away from the sparkle and noise to catch my breath.

As the sun sets and darkness falls, I tug on his hand. "Come on, I want to show you something."

I lead him away from the rhinestone-filled chaos to a quiet spot near the water, where wooden benches overlook the bay. The moon rises in the distance, painting a silver path across the waves.

We settle onto a weathered bench, our shoulders touching. In this moment, with the festival a distant hum and the water lapping gently against the shore as the moon rises in the sky, everything feels right. Easy. Natural. Like we've done this a hundred times before. Like we could do it a hundred times more. His warmth beside me, the rhythm of his breathing matching the waves, the comfortable silence—it all fits like the ending of a story I didn't know I was writing.

But that makes me think of someone else.

"I used to come here with my grandmother," I say. "She taught me to canoe right over there."

Eli's breath warms my cheeks. "Something tells me there's a story there."

I laugh. "Oh, there is. Picture this: me, age twelve, convinced I knew everything about everything. Figuring out my magic one disaster after another. Grandma Ida, who never met a challenge she didn't like, decided we should race across the bay. We made it about twenty feet before I got cocky, tried to show off, and flipped us both into the water."

Eli's gasp echoes across the water. "What did she do?"

"Came up sputtering and laughing so hard she could barely swim. Then she dunked me again for good measure." I smile at the memory. "That was Grandma Ida—she believed life was an adventure, even if that meant getting soaked in your Sunday best. She told me to always live life to the fullest."

"She sounds amazing."

"She was." I trace patterns in the condensation forming on the bench. "I know it probably sounds odd that my grand-mother was one of my best friends... but it's true." My voice drops to a whisper. "I grieved hard when she passed. Too hard."

Maybe it's better to let him see the bitter truth now. We're clearly falling into something neither of us has dared to name, and if it's going to unravel, I'd rather it happen before I start hoping too much. Better he see the mess early than fall for the edited version and feel surprised later.

Eli turns to face me more fully. "Why do you say that? *Too* hard?"

"Because I sank into this pit I couldn't claw my way out of. I couldn't pretend to be okay and it got... ugly. And some people—people I loved—thought I was being ridiculous. That I was overreacting. That I was just being..." My voice falters. "Too much."

Eli reaches for my hand, his grip warm and steady. "Grief, in my experience, doesn't have a timeline or logic," he says gently. "You just told me she was one of your best friends. Of *course* you grieved hard."

A lump rises in my throat, but I manage a nod. "She was... she was the only person who never tried to make me be some-thing I wasn't."

Eli is quiet for a moment, then says, "I would have loved

her, because there's not a single thing I'd change about you. And she'd be proud because you're already following her advice."

"What do you mean?"

He squeezes my hand, his thumb brushing across my knuckles. "I came here afraid. I'd just lost someone as well, my coworker, Mark. His death made me realize how easy it is to let your life slip by in routines and caution. I was afraid of looking back and wondering if I'd ever really lived." He clears his throat. "But being here... meeting you... it's the most alive I've ever felt. You're teaching me how to live in color instead of grayscale. How to not let fear call the shots." He looks at me then, his breath warming my cheek. "You're not just following her advice, you're showing others how to do it too."

His hazel eyes, darkened in the low light, make me feel like I see what he sees in me. Like maybe, just maybe, I am someone worth staying for. But the letter in my pocket presses against my side like a secret. A truth I haven't shared.

And despite these moonlight confessions, despite the way he's looking at me like he could weather the storm with a smile, it's not enough to make me brave. Not enough to open my mouth and start talking about timelines and futures.

If anything, it swallows the words. They feel too massive, like they'd echo across the bay and carve themselves into the future in a way I'm just not ready for.

From the festival, music plays—slower now, strings and gentle percussion playing 'Can't Help Falling in Love'. The announcement comes over the speakers: "Ladies and gentlemen, grab your partners for our moonlight slow dance."

Eli stands and holds out his hand, his smile soft in the gathering dusk. "What do you say? Want to dance with me? I know that if it's with you, I'll actually feel this moment, every bit."

I look at his extended hand, then up at his face—this

wonderful man who somehow makes me feel both grounded and free. Taking his hand feels like stepping off a cliff and coming home all at once.

And maybe that's why I keep trying not to look too closely at what this is—because if I let myself really feel it, I'll have to face what it means to walk away.

"With you?" I place my hand in his. "Lead the way, Lancaster."

Rhianna

The string quartet plays slow and sweet, their instruments glowing with a soft blue shimmer of magic that matches the enormous moon hanging above us. Eli's hand is warm against my lower back, and I try not to think about how perfectly we fit together, how natural it feels to rest my head against his chest. The sweet scent of his cologne mingles with the salty breeze coming off the water.

"You're quiet," he murmurs, his breath tickling my ear.

"Just feeling the music." It's not entirely a lie. The violins are weaving actual magic through the air—the shimmer of it falls like stardust around us. But mostly I'm feeling him. The steady rhythm of his heartbeat. The way his thumb traces small circles on my back.

"Liar." His tone is teasing, but there's something else there too. Something that makes my breath catch. "You're thinking so loud I can almost hear it, Wilder."

I laugh softly. "That's rich coming from the guy who probably catalogues his thoughts alphabetically."

"How did you know?" He chuckles but pulls back just

enough to look at me, and the intensity in his eyes makes my stomach flip. "Though I have to admit, you've been throwing off my organizational system lately."

"Oh?" I try to keep my voice light, playful, but it comes out breathier than intended. "How so?"

"Well, for starters, you've filed yourself under every letter of the alphabet." His hand slides up my spine, leaving a trail of warmth. "Remarkable. Intriguing. Hilarious. Addictive. Noteworthy. Alluring..."

Each word sends a shiver through me. "You forgot 'Impeccable Music Taste.'"

"That's under 'I,' along with 'Ingenious' and 'Irresistible.'"

My breath catches. It's one thing to flirt, it's another to be seen like this. My usual defenses stutter and all I can do is look up at him, heart thudding so loud I'm sure he can hear it.

God, I'm in trouble.

The music swells around us, and I close my eyes, letting myself sink into this moment. Into him. Having someone I loved walk away from me when I needed him most forced walls up around me—fortresses I didn't even realize I was building until they were too high to climb down from. I thought they'd keep me safe. Untouchable. But maybe it's not force that brings those walls down. Maybe it's gentleness. Eli never pushes. Never asks for more than I can give. He just... shows up. Listens. Laughs at my terrible puns and remembers the little things. And somehow, without demanding anything in return, he's made me want to sit by the gate I swore I'd never open—wondering if, maybe, it's safe to unlatch it after all.

His hand glides lower, and suddenly I'm hyper-aware of every point where our bodies meet. The steady pressure of his fingers. The warmth of his chest against mine. The way his breath hitches when I shift closer, eliminating what little space remains between us. The distant murmur of the crowds fades and the music wraps us up like silk. I swear I can feel his heartbeat pick up to match mine. When I tilt my head back to look at him, his eyes are dark behind his glasses, intense in a way that makes heat pool in my stomach. I've spent months studying his careful movements, his precise habits, but there's nothing careful about the way he's looking at me now.

The song ends, but neither of us moves to break apart. The moon bathes everything in an ethereal blue light, making the ordinary magical—or maybe just revealing the magic that was always there.

"Come home with me?" Eli's voice is soft but certain.

My heart stutters. There are a dozen reasons to say no. My future plans he doesn't know about. My promises. My fears. But looking up into his eyes, I can't remember a single one of them.

"Yes."

We leave the festival behind, stepping onto the winding path that leads back toward town. The distant hum of the crowd still lingers in the air, laughter and music carrying over the water as we walk. The path curves through the trees before spilling us onto Main Street, where the glow of twinkling shop windows and lantern-lit flower boxes makes everything feel impossibly warm, even at this late hour.

Our hands are linked, and every few steps he brings my fingers to his lips, pressing gentle kisses to my knuckles like he can't quite help himself. Each one sends sparks of warmth through my entire body.

I've always prided myself on being able to read people, to sense the thread of connections. But this—this is different. This feels like standing in the center of a storm, like being struck by lightning and discovering you've been waiting for it your whole life. Magic hums beneath my skin where his lips touch, and I wonder if he can feel it too, this electric current running between us.

The town I've known my whole life looks different tonight. Or maybe I'm the one who's different. Every familiar sight feels new when seen through the lens of this feeling, this possibility —the old brick buildings with their weather-worn signs, the cobblestone streets that have guided me home a thousand times. I'm holding my breath in my attempts to memorize this moment, save it. Each landmark seems to whisper *stay* even as my dreams pull me toward distant horizons. And now there's an anchor that's warm against my hand, holding me here.

This trip I planned to escape Magnolia Cove after the wreckage Jacob left behind lands in my lap at the same time as this beautiful, kind man. A man who somehow makes the mundane feel magical, who treats my quirks like something rare and wonderful. And now I'm torn—standing at the edge of a path unfurled in the woods, unsure which direction is the one that will change everything.

Ugh. Dad's poetry always sneaks up on me when I'm feeling things. Big things.

And that's the problem. I'm starting to feel *BIG* things.

So that's going to get stuffed into the box of all-the-things-I-refuse-to-think-about-tonight. Taped up, labeled 'emotional crisis—do not open,' and shoved into the deepest corner of my mental storage closet. I can't afford to unpack that—not now. Not with Eli smiling at me like I've just handed him the moon.

His apartment, when we reach it, is exactly what I'd expect. Spare but thoughtful, like he carefully chose each item. A record player sits in the corner, its needle locked precisely in place because of course it is. He's arranged his shoes with mathematical precision by the door. But it's the books that catch my eye.

They're everywhere, protected by shimmering wards that

make the air around them ripple like heat waves. Ancient leather-bound tomes and rare books share space with well-loved paperbacks, all treated with the same reverence. And there, on his dresser, warded just as carefully as what I'm sure are priceless volumes, are the books I gave him. The romance novel I insisted he read. And the Cyrus Whitlock book that once belonged to Grandma Ida—the one I nearly couldn't part with.

I remember the way my fingers hovered over the cover that night, the weight of it almost too much to let go. But something in me had known—it was meant for him.

Seeing it here now, nestled among his treasures and guarded by a protection spell as if it were priceless, I feel that knowing settle deeper. I made the right choice.

I trail my finger down the spine and think about the mythological Rhiannon on her white horse, how many suitors tried to catch her but she couldn't be caught. It was the man who called out to her she stopped for. That she fell in love with.

I've spent so long guarding myself. But here, in this moment, with the blue moon's magic still tingling on my skin and Eli's eyes on me, I understand why Rhiannon chose to stop. And that terrifies me more than any adventure ever could.

My hand lands with a soft thunk against the dresser. When I turn to Eli, his eyes are soft, watching me explore his space.

"It's not much," he says, running a hand through his hair. "Still getting settled."

But that's not quite right. The apartment might just be a place, but Eli—Eli feels like coming home. I step closer to him and slide my hands up his chest and feel his heartbeat pick up pace. "It's perfect."

His breath catches, and then his lips are on mine, and I stop thinking about anything else at all.

Eli's kiss is gentle at first. It reminds me of his uncertainty, his one-word answers, and how he ducks his head when he blushes. Then it changes, gaining a heat that makes my pulse race. His hands slide up my arms, every point of contact electric, like the air hums with magic we've stirred between us.

When his fingers tangle in my hair and he lets his other hand drift to the small of my back and pull me closer, I stop thinking. Instead, I lose myself to the pressure of his fingertips on my spine, the soft embrace of his lips, the warmth of his body where it touches mine.

The world narrows to this—to soft sighs, to hands that move like they want to memorize the feel of me, to breath that mingles with mine in the apartment's quiet. Outside, the festival continues, a dim hum of music and magic and laughter.

He pulls back just enough to rest his forehead against mine, his breath warm against my lips. "Are you sure?"

I track my thumb along his jaw, over the six o'clock shadow and the sharp lines. "I've never been more sure of anything."

This is what every romance novel in the world tries to convey. This feeling like your heart is too big for your chest, like every love song suddenly makes sense, like you've found some piece of yourself you didn't know was missing.

And suddenly, nothing about this feels like a mistake or a detour or something I need to guard myself against.

It just feels right. Like every step I've taken, every book I've read, every song I've listened to, has been leading me here. To this moment. To him.

Eli kisses me again, slow and soft this time. It's so tender it makes my chest ache in the best way. He grabs my hand like he did on the night of the meteor shower, and leads me across the studio apartment toward the bed.

He pauses as we reach it and looks down. I grab his jaw with both of my hands and lift his face until his gaze meets mine. "Hey, Lancaster, now you're the quiet one."

Eli's lips curve into a small smile. "Guess I'm feeling the moment," he whispers, echoing my words from earlier, but there's a hint of vulnerability there, something uncertain.

I brush my thumb across his lips then loop my hands behind his neck and draw his face closer to mine again. "Good. Someone told me that's what it means to really live." I smile and he returns it. "You make me feel alive too, Eli."

His smile fades, replaced by something deeper, and when he kisses me this time, it's different from any we've shared before—slower, more deliberate. It's like he's savoring the moment, every touch and taste. And I do the same. My fingers tangle in his hair, my other hand gliding under his shirt and skimming along the warmth of his flesh.

We sink onto the bed together. His weight feels grounding, solid, like an anchor that holds me steady. Moonlight spills past the slanted blinds, painting everything in a silver-blue casting shadows that flicker like whispers. Our heartbeats thunder together in rhythm, like they've created the beat of a song together.

His hands move slowly as he finds my dress' hem. "Still sure?" he murmurs against my ear.

"More than ever."

The words feel like both truth and lie—I am sure about this, about him, about us. What I'm not sure about is what comes after. Not tomorrow, not next week, not the moment when this stops being a summer fling and asks to become something more.

But when his mouth meets mine once more, when his hands find bare skin and his body moves in perfect rhythm with mine, I let myself forget all of that. Just for tonight, I push away thoughts of the fellowship and choices and all the ways this could break me.

All that exists is the heat between us, the way his touch feels like being seen and not turned away, and the terrifying, beautiful sense that maybe, for once, I'm exactly where I'm meant to be.

Eli

"Brubba, you're actually giggling." Piper's voice carries that mix of amusement and disbelief that only little sisters can perfect. "I didn't even know you could make that sound."

"I am not giggling." I adjust my phone, trying to sound dignified while I sort through the stack of research notes I should have worked on last night. Instead, Rhianna had asked me if I wanted to go for a moonlit swim in the ocean and I spent the evening memorizing the way starlight glistened in her hair and the warmth of her body against mine. "I'm... expressing measured enthusiasm."

"Right. And I'm the Queen of England." She snorts. Something clinks and I imagine her dropping her coffee mug to the table. "Come on, tell me everything. Have you kissed her yet? Has she stayed over? Oh my gosh, if so did you make her breakfast? Please tell me you made breakfast—you know that fancy French toast thing you do."

Heat creeps up my neck and I refuse to glance at the kitchen where the pan I use for French toast still rests on the counter, washed but not put away. Because I got distracted by more pleasurable things. "That's none of your business."

"OH MY GOD YOU DID!" Her squeal makes me hold the phone away from my ear. "Look at you, living your best romance novel life! I'm so proud. My unchangeable, perfectly organized brother, falling head over—" She pauses, then laughs. "You went to Magnolia Cove to find some dusty signed book and instead you found love."

"Can we change the subject?" But I'm smiling so wide my face hurts. The truth is, Piper's not wrong. I came here chasing Cyrus Whitlock's signature, searching for meaning through bold choices in a life that suddenly felt fragile, convinced both would change my life and the former might become the crowning achievement of my academic career. Now that feels almost trivial compared to finding Rhianna. "It's just... Piper, she's incredible. She has this way of making the most mundane things fascinating. Did you know there are nine different ways to categorize romance novels based on the protagonist's journey? She spent an hour explaining it to me last night and never in my life would I imagine me even thinking about the topic but... I don't know, Pipes. Man, and when she laughs—"

"Wow. You've got it so bad." Her voice softens. "I haven't heard you this happy in... maybe ever."

"I know." I sink into my desk chair and run a hand through my hair. "It's just, I can't stop thinking about her. Everything reminds me of her. It's irritatingly distracting. My department head is going to be so displeased with the lack of work I've done this summer."

"Oh, so you plan to come back home?"

The question lands like a physical blow, as if someone's yanked away my chair. My stomach drops and the warm, floaty feeling that's carried me through the morning vanishes. Suddenly I'm acutely aware of my surroundings—the stack of untouched notes, the grant proposal I haven't even started, the rare book inquiries I should have sent weeks ago.

"I... well. That was always the plan."

"Eli?" Piper's voice is soft. "You went quiet on me."

I thumb through papers, trying to find words that won't make this feel more real. "I did, didn't I?" A weak laugh escapes me. "Sorry, Pipes. I just... I haven't thought about leaving. At all. Which is bizarre. My old life is waiting just around the corner for me. The old me would have a countdown calendar on the wall."

"And the new you?"

"The new me is a ridiculous sap who sings at karaoke bars and watches meteor showers in the middle of the night and is getting an unhealthily low amount of sleep."

"Sounds like the new you is actually living a little." Piper's smile carries through her voice. "Who knew all it would take was a cute librarian to get you out of your head."

"She's not just—" I stop speaking. What I wanted to say was that she's not just a librarian. Not just some cute girl. She's Rhianna Wilder. She's the moon itself, magic embodied.

But we haven't even had a real conversation about the future yet.

"Eli?"

"Sorry, I think the connection isn't very good. Magnolia Cove's internet service is this side of non-existent." I try to laugh and make it sound like a joke but it's pitiful even to my ears. "Can I call you back later?"

"Okay, Brubba." Her tone is low, doubtful. She doesn't buy my excuses, but she doesn't push it either. We hang up, and I stand there for a moment, then release a breath that echoes around the apartment.

The walk to the library feels longer than usual, the quiet streets giving me too much space to think. Two and a half months. Ten and a half weeks. Seventy-five days. How is that possible? It feels like I just got here, like I just met her. Like we're just getting started.

I pause at the corner where Main Street meets Seabreeze Avenue, watching the morning crowd filter into The Whimsical Whisk. The thought of returning to my old life, to endless faculty meetings and rigid schedules, feels wrong now. Like trying to squeeze back into clothes I've outgrown.

Maybe.... Maybe I don't have to go back, not completely. I could apply to teach virtually next semester. The internet here is abysmal—I'd probably have to rent an office space in town just to hold lectures—but it's possible. The thought settles something in my chest, making it easier to breathe.

The truth is, my priorities have shifted. I came here seeking academic glory and a chance to live life differently for a season. Instead, I found something better. Someone better. And for the first time in my life, I want to be reckless enough to choose love over logic.

I need another bold move. Something to keep this feeling alive, to distract from the countdown ticking in my head. To push away the fact that Rhianna still flinches away from anything permanent, hiding behind library facts and folklore stories whenever we edge too close to talking about the future. I enter the library's foyer and smile at the bulletin board that led me to Rhianna. That's when I see it—a bright yellow flyer that ripples with the breeze as the door closes.

Experience the Ultimate Adventure! Slanted, dark words splash across the top. *Skydiving this Tuesday Evening!*

The irony almost makes me laugh. When I first came to Magnolia Cove, this was exactly the thing I thought I'd do. Jump out of planes. Learn to surf. Climb mountains. Instead, I've been free-falling completely differently, terrified and exhilarated and unable to stop.

Oh god.

I'm in love with her.

A breath rushes out of me. I'm in love with Rhianna Wilder. I'm in love with her book pun pins, with the way she plays Fleetwood Mac every single morning in her AirPods to *set a positive tone for the day.* I'm in love with how she insists on carrying extra bookmarks in her bag *just in case* and the way she sings off-key when she thinks no one's around. I'm in love with the way she looks at me—like maybe, just maybe, I'm the best plot twist she's ever read.

My hands tremble as I snatch the flyer and stride into the library, my heart pounding. Rhianna is at her desk, sorting through returns, bopping to whatever Stevie Nicks' song will set the right tone for this morning. She's pulled her hair back into a messy bun secured with a pencil and she's wearing a cardigan covered in tiny embroidered books.

She's the most beautiful thing I've ever seen.

I slap the flyer down on the circulation desk.

She taps her headphones to pause the music, lifts the flyer, then looks up at me. "Skydiving?" Her nose wrinkles adorably. I want to kiss it until she laughs, until she clenches her fingers into my hair. "The Council doesn't really trust these human-run attractions and—"

"Life's an adventure, right?" I'm practically bouncing on my feet. "It terrifies me. Which is exactly why we should do it."

She stares at me for a long moment, and I can see the exact second my enthusiasm infects her. A slow smile spreads across her face. "You know what? You're right. Let's do it."

* * *

"I am never, ever doing that again," I declare, still shaking slightly as we walk along the beach. My toes sink deep into the sand as if I need to remind myself that I made it safely back on land and survived. I'm not sure my brain has received the memo yet. "Ever."

Rhianna laughs, her eyes bright and her braided hair wind-blown. "Are you kidding? That was amazing! The way everything looked so small, like we were on top of the world! We have to do it again."

"Absolutely not." But I'm laughing too. Her excitement and joy has enraptured me from the moment we met. "Once was enough to prove I'm not completely set in my ways."

"Oh, I don't know about that." She bumps her shoulder into mine then twines our hands together. "You filled out those liability forms like they were going to be archived in the Library of Congress."

"Maybe they will be. Future historians could study them as evidence of my temporary insanity." I squeeze her hand. Everything about our bodies touching feels natural. "Exhibit A: The day Professor Eli Lancaster willingly jumped out of a perfectly sound, functioning airplane."

The sun sets over the water, painting everything in soft gold. Rhianna's skin glows in the light and I want to kiss the freckles that follow her cheekbone. She's changed everything. Less than three months ago, I was living life according to a carefully plotted schedule. Now I'm jumping out of planes and falling in love and...

And I need to decide whether I'm leaving or staying before the next semester begins.

I need to tell her. We need to talk about what this means, what we want, what's possible. I know she's still hesitant and I remember the terms we set. No strings. She can walk away any time she wants. Maybe bringing this up means risking that she will. But I don't want just a few more weeks with Rhianna Wilder. I want forever. I want skydiving in the sunshine and holding her through the storms. I want every bit of glitter and laughter, every twist and turn in between.

"There's something I need to tell you," I start, my heart thundering against my ribs. "Being with you has made me realize—"

"Come to dinner with my parents?" she blurts, too fast, like the words escaped before she could think them through.

I blink. There's a pause—half confusion, half trying to remember how to breathe. She's cutting me off. She's cutting off the conversation I've been building toward for days.

Then it hits me. She's inviting me to meet her parents.

She misreads the silence and barrels ahead. "I mean, you don't have to. My parents can be a lot. My mom will definitely psychoanalyze you, and my dad will quiz you on obscure Romantic poets before you even get a bite of bread, and—"

"I want to," I say, my voice coming out softer than I expect. "I want that, Rhianna."

She goes still, and for a moment, the air between us tightens—not with tension, but with understanding. A shift. Something is changing.

Her fingers tremble slightly, but then she smiles, tentative and real. "Yeah," she whispers. "I think I want that too. Let's.... Let's save our big, probably-too-much-for-a-Tuesday conversation for after." She lifts her chin like she's joking, but her voice wobbles just a little. "I've got things to tell you too. And I need time to prepare. Maybe make some glittery posters. Possibly a tri-fold. So... y'know, brace yourself, Lancaster." Then, more softly, "How does Saturday sound?"

I nod too fast and too eager because my throat suddenly feels tight with everything I don't know how to say. "Saturday sounds perfect."

She beams, and the lightness returns to her eyes, but I can still feel the weight of what just passed between us. I don't need to wait for Saturday's conversation to know where we stand. She's letting me meet her parents. She's giving me a piece of her future—even if she's too scared to name it yet. And for me, that's enough.

The decision is made before I even realize I'm making it.

I'm staying.

I'll email the university tomorrow and tell them I'm transitioning to remote work through the fall. Maybe longer. Maybe for good.

This is it. The risk I took—hell, maybe bold move one, two, and three all wrapped into one—landed me here. Here in Magnolia Cove. Here with Rhianna Wilder.

And in four days, we'll have that conversation. The big one. Possibly accompanied by glitter.

And I'm so excited, I can hardly stand it.

"Come on." I tug her forward. "Let's get ice cream?"

The tension in her expression washes away, her shoulders dropping. "I know the best place. How do you feel about jazz?"

I let her lead me up the beach, the setting sun glistening over her windblown curls. And as the waves roll in behind us, all I can think is: let it all come. I'm ready.

Rhianna

I'm balancing on a stepladder, trying to attach sparkly vines to our *Enchanted Reading Forest* display for next week's Library Comes Alive night, when my fingers brush against the thick envelope in my cardigan pocket. The one with the World Library Tour Fellowship's golden seal Dad handed me this morning. The one I've been too nervous to open because somehow holding onto the possibility feels safer than knowing for sure.

My mind wanders back to the beach. To Eli's almost-confession. To the way my heart had nearly burst through my chest because I knew—*I knew*—what he was going to say.

I'm terrified and wobbly and mentally all over the place, but I'm also... strangely ready.

Eli isn't Jacob.

Even if my heart has been living in my throat ever since I blurted out that invitation to meet my parents, I think—maybe—I'm finally ready to try again. Who knew my failed matchmaking plan would result in me finding love? My mom would absolutely *love* that line of thought. Unfortunately.

"Miss Wilder!" Jasper calls from below, where he's sorting

through the costume box I'd dragged out of storage that morning. "Can I be the Lorax? I already practiced twitching my mustache!"

"Only if you promise to speak for the books," I tell him as I step down and pull a measuring tape from my cardigan pocket. I've been carrying it around to get the dimensions perfect for my Mary Poppins costume. Somehow, I thought designing my own was a good idea. I stretch the tape out before Jasper who has his shoulders rolled back and is nearly on his toes to stand as tall as possible. "And according to my calculations, you're exactly the right height for a Lorax. Practically perfect, in fact."

Jasper beams and starts practicing his grumpy voice while I adjust my daisy-decorated hat—a trial run for the one I'll wear that evening. Claire's going as the White Witch (complete with Turkish Delight samples) and Michael from acquisitions is planning an impressive Mad Hatter ensemble. I've got my carpet bag all ready to go, and maybe—just maybe—I'll speak with the Council and see if someone will add a bit of actual magic to make it seem bottomless. What's the point of being a librarian in a magical pocket town if you can't have a little fun with it?

I climb the ladder and begin decorating again but a vine slips from my fingers and bops me on the nose. "Most unsatisfactory," I tell it in my best Mary Poppins voice.

I pin the final vine in place then hop down from the ladder and push my fists onto my hips to survey my handiwork. The display glitters under the library's soft lighting, constellations of books arranged in spiraling patterns. A council member has already worked a bit of subtle magic to keep it from toppling. It's exactly the kind of whimsy that makes kids' eyes light up when they walk in.

Just like the way his eyes light up when he looks at you, my brain offers in an annoyingly sincere voice.

I groan and press my palms against my heated cheeks. Because I've made up my mind.

I've spent summer convincing myself this was temporary. That we'd agreed on no strings. Just a summer of stolen moments and soft laughter and pretending the future wasn't coming fast. But now? Now I want something more. A chance, maybe.

I think I'm going to ask him to wait for me.

And I can't believe I'm even entertaining the idea. But I am. I'm going to try.

Six months. That's all I'm asking. Time for me to finish what I started—to honor the dream Grandma Ida and I shared. To see the world, to grow, to come back knowing not just what I want, but who I want.

And maybe that's what I need anyway—space to choose him without fear, to let the wanting stretch into something real.

I almost laugh. I've never been the girl who asks someone to wait. I've always been the one left behind. But maybe this time, I'll be the one who comes back.

Maybe—

"Rhianna!"

I spin around to find Eli himself hurrying toward me, looking adorably flustered. His glasses are slightly askew and his dark hair ruffled like he's run his hands through it. My heart does its ridiculous jig it's taken up whenever he's in my presence.

"I just got a call about a potential first edition Cyrus Whitlock." He waves a folder frantically. "A private collector on the mainland is considering selling. I wanted you to know I'll be out of town just for the night. These opportunities disappear in hours. Oh shoot. I need to take these research papers back to my office before I leave, and I have to grab my authentication kit from my apartment and—"

"I can take it for you," I offer, trying not to smile at his scattered state. It's so unlike his usual composed self, but his eyes sparkle with that gleam he gets when talking about unique editions of rare books. It's unfairly attractive.

"You're a lifesaver." His shoulders sag, though he's practically vibrating with excitement. I get it—Cyrus Whitlock is his literary white whale. A smile tugs at my lips. I gave him a Whitlock book weeks before I even knew about the depth of his obsession. My magical intuition strikes again, though this time it feels less like magic and more like proof that some part of me just *gets* him, right down to his bookish soul. And that maybe this person is someone I can actually risk trusting my heart with again.

"No problem."

He goes completely still despite his rush, and something in his expression makes my breath catch. Like what he's about to say matters. "I'll be back in plenty of time for dinner tomorrow." His voice is low and sure. "I'm really looking forward to it."

My stomach flips—nerves and excitement mingling in a way that makes me feel sixteen again. "Yeah. Me too."

He lingers just a moment longer, looking at me like he sees all of it—my hope, my fear, the thousand emotions I'm still learning how to name. Then he leans in and presses a quick kiss to my cheek before heading out the door.

Maybe telling my parents about him wasn't a mistake after all. Maybe Mom's knowing smiles and Dad's not-so-subtle hints about having plenty of space at the dinner table weren't premature. Maybe having the talk—the one where I tell Eli about the fellowship, ask if he'll wait, admit I'm hoping for something more—isn't the wrong move after all. Maybe it's all coming together as it should.

After he rushes off, I head toward the stairs to his office with the folder tucked against my chest.

"Hey, Rhianna, wait up!"

I freeze, clutching Eli's folder to my chest. Claire's heels click against the floor as she hurries over, and my stomach twists. Things have been awkward since her date with Eli—the one I basically pushed them into, back when I was trying to be a proper matchmaker instead of falling for my client. The date went absolutely nowhere but Claire had seemed excited about it.

When she reaches me, she's smiling. "I just wanted to say... I'm really happy for you two."

"Oh." I blink. "I... thanks?"

"Seriously." She smooths her hand down her dress—a silky navy blue one, exactly the kind of understated elegance I could never pull off. "The way he looks at you? That's the real deal. I knew it even when we went out. He spent half the history tour talking about you."

A warm flush creeps up my neck. "He did?"

"Mhmm. It was actually kind of adorable. Annoying at the time, obviously, but adorable in retrospect." She touches my arm. "You deserve something real, Rhianna. I'm glad you've found it."

She graces me with another smile, then turns and walks back through the shelves. I stand there, Claire's words echoing in my head. The real deal.

My heart feels too big for my chest as I climb the stairs, like it's trying to expand to hold all this joy. For once since Jacob shattered me, I'm not thinking about escape routes or keeping one foot out the door. I'm just stupidly, wonderfully, romance-novel-level happy.

Eli's scent—old books and luxuriously rich coffee and the unique cologne he wears—lingers in the air as I approach his desk. His planner lies open, and I can't help but smile when I spot my name doodled in the corner, surrounded by tiny stars.

The man can't draw. The stars look more like spiky blobs,

but something about their earnest wonkiness makes my heart squeeze. Because of course perfectionist Eli Lancaster, who color codes his notes and has his desk arranged like a museum display, would have adorably awful doodles.

I stack the folder with others and turn to leave but my gaze catches on an underlined note in the planner.

2 PM - Department Meeting @Zoom (return timeline/fall schedule)

Return timeline? My brain stutters over the words, trying to make them mean something else. Return to what? He moved here. He's starting fresh here. That's what he said. That's what everyone said. Unless...

Unless he didn't.

I'm frantically thinking back to our early conversations. Had he ever said he was moving here permanently? Or had I just assumed? He'd talked about needing a change, about wanting an adventure, about starting fresh... but had he ever used the word 'permanent'?

My fingers grip the edge of the desk as possibility after possibility crashes through my mind. Maybe it's about returning to teach a guest lecture. Maybe it's about returning library books (okay, that's desperate even for me). Maybe—

I sink into his chair, the leather still warm from where he sat this morning. His scent permeates my next breath, and it feels like a betrayal that it still makes my heart flutter even as my stomach twists with dread.

I shouldn't look. I shouldn't flip through his journal and invade his privacy. But Jacob had secrets and signs he was slipping away too—and I ignored them until they exploded. I can't make that mistake again.

I look.

A month from now another entry. *Moving day.*

The pages flip forward under my trembling fingers.

Faculty meetings. Class schedules. Office hours. An entire life mapped out.

Without me.

A sob builds in my throat, pressing against my ribcage like a trapped bird. The hat feels stupid now. Everything does. And still, his scent lingers—coffee and old books and comfort —and it guts me that it still makes me feel safe.

I thought... God, I thought this was it. The real thing. The kind of love story I stay up late reading most nights—sacrificing sleep for another happily ever after. A story worth risking heartbreak for. And I really believed... this time, it would be different.

But then I stop myself. *Wait. Deep breath, Rhianna.*

I press my palms against the cool wood of his desk and force myself to breathe. In through the nose, out through the mouth.

Eli is reliable. Steady. Thoughtful. He's the kind of man who underlines important dates and folds his socks in that joy-sparking, possibly cult-like way people were doing a few years ago. This isn't some secret he's been hiding—it's right there in plain sight in a planner he keeps on his desk.

This is worth a conversation, not a meltdown. He'll explain. Maybe 'return timeline' means something else entirely.

But as my heartbeat slows, another realization hits. I think back to the beach—Eli's face lit by the amber sunset, his voice low and serious.

There's something I need to tell you, he'd said.

And I'd dodged it. Smiled too brightly, invited him to dinner, bought myself time instead of just saying what I needed to. Like a grown-up. Like someone ready to be honest.

God, this is what I always do. I leap. I chase big, glittering ideas before I've figured out where they'll land. Just like the matchmaking service. Where I've had one client. Who I am now dating.

Once again, I'm being the definition of too much—too intense, too guarded, too emotional, too spontaneous, too *everything*.

Regardless of what Eli's plans are moving forward, I know he wasn't slinking back to his life in secret. That conversation yesterday was something. I knew it then, and I know it now.

But knowing doesn't stop the fear welling up in my chest. It doesn't quiet the voice in my head whispering that I'm the problem. That I always have been.

Now, seeing this planner has only confirmed the thing I've tried not to believe—that even when someone says they love you, they can still leave. Just like Jacob did. It hurts so badly to see that Eli might leave too. What would happen if I let myself fall completely, if I let him become as essential as oxygen, and then lost him?

No, I'm not doing this again. Not setting myself up for that kind of devastation. Better to end it before the inevitable happens.

My fingers find the envelope in my pocket—the one I've avoided all morning. I'd said before I'd let the envelope decide. If I got the fellowship, I'd focus on my future travels. If not, maybe I'd let myself believe in something here. In him. But then I promptly ignored it and shoved it to the back of my mind like so many other inconvenient truths. It's time to stop pretending. I tear the envelope open, the golden seal breaking with a soft snap.

Dear Ms. Wilder, we are pleased to inform you...

Somehow I can't even force a smile to my lips. I got in. My dreams are actually coming true. And the universe isn't being subtle about it. This is my direction. Maybe Eli and I have come to two paths in the woods, and he's supposed to travel one, and me another. Maybe it's better to let it end now, while it's still golden and beautiful—before I ruin it with all my too-much-ness. Before he sees the whole of me and realizes he was never meant to stay.

The thought should bring relief—validation that I'm on the right track—but instead it feels like swallowing glass. This hollow ache in my chest is the exact reason I've guarded my heart. Because even the possibility of losing him hurts more than I expected.

So I'll do what I've always done. Pull away. Smile through dinner. Pretend I'm not already broken wide open.

And when it's finally over, I'll let myself fall apart where no one can see me—where no one can look at me and remind me that I'm always too much to love.

Eli

I pause at the corner of Main Street and Oak, checking my reflection in the window of *A Novel Idea*. My collar sits slightly crooked, and my fingers tremble as I adjust it. The butterflies in my stomach are doing aerial acrobatics that would put circus performers to shame. Meeting the parents. It's a big deal, right? Has to be. Especially since Rhianna's barely dated anyone in years, according to pretty much everyone in town.

The evening air is thick with the scent of salt and blooming jasmine as I make my way down the brick sidewalk, past the warmly lit shop windows and the usual evening crowd heading to *The Hungry Gull*. The bottle of wine from The Market Basket & Vine's surprisingly excellent collection grows slick in my palm. I've walked this street a hundred times since moving here, but tonight every step feels weighted with possibility.

Piper would laugh if she could see me now—her always logical big brother, the one who plans every detail of his life down to color-coded semester schedules, now following his heart like the protagonist in one of Rhianna's beloved romance novels. But here's the thing: for the first time in my life throwing logic to the wind feels absolutely right. When I think about teaching virtually this upcoming semester, about maybe looking for a permanent position at a college here, about building a life in Magnolia Cove... my usual anxiety about major changes doesn't surface. Instead, I feel that same thrill of rightness I got the first time Rhianna laughed at my terrible puns.

I'm even going to have to buy a new planner—something that would normally set me into a tailspin of anxiety. I've filled the current one out through December with my return time-lines and teaching schedule back in Misty Pines, all written in different colored inks for various commitments. The idea of crossing all that out when I wrote it would have been unthinkable. Now? Now I'm actually excited about it. About rewriting my future, even if it means using white-out on my carefully laid plans.

Yesterday's eight-hour round trip to examine what was supposed to be a first-edition Cyrus Whitlock turned out to be a clever reproduction—something that would have devastated me a month ago. Today, though, I barely care. Knowing that Rhianna's smile—and the way she lights up when she sees me—is waiting for me matters more than any book ever could.

My whole life, I've approached every decision with care. Pros and cons lists. Five-year plans. Risk assessments. But Rhianna? She makes me want to skip all that and just leap. Maybe that's what real love is supposed to feel like—like all your carefully constructed rules don't matter anymore because you've found something better than being right. Something real. Something Mark never got the chance to find. His death was the push that set everything in motion, the move, the bold choices. I'd like to think he'd be proud of that.

I reach the end of the street and take a deep breath before walking up the pathway. The Wilder house is exactly what I pictured—a beautiful Victorian painted in shades of sage green and cream, with a wraparound porch that practically begs for summer evenings with lemonade and books. Flower boxes overflow with vibrant blooms, and wind chimes tinkle softly in the evening breeze. It's the kind of house that would make you believe in magic even if you didn't know it was real.

I head up the steps. Before I can knock, the door swings open to reveal Rhianna, stunning in a flowing dress covered in tiny yellow flowers. Her smile seems a bit too large, forced. Her eyes twinkle but not with happiness. It hits me in the gut, that flicker of something off. Before I can analyze it, she's pulling me inside.

"Mom! Dad! Gavin! The book nerd has arrived!" she calls out, her voice echoing through the house. The interior is even more magical than the outside—every surface seems to tell a story. Colorful rugs with patterns from around the world layer over the hardwood floors, and an eclectic mix of artwork covers the walls. Books are everywhere, which makes my heart sing. This is what happens when generations of professors and artists live in one place.

"Finally!" A tall man with dark hair and a cleft chin, who can only be Rhianna's brother, Gavin, emerges from what I assume is the kitchen. "I was starting to think she'd made you up. It's been what, four years since you've brought anyone home, Rhi?"

My heart warms until it fills my entire chest. This *is* significant. Four years. She's been so careful with her heart, just like me, and yet here I am, standing in her family home, about to share a meal with the people she loves most. Maybe we're both ready to stop being so careful. Maybe sometimes the most terrifying, emotionally driven choices are actually the correct ones.

I've heard the whispers around town—about the man who left her when she was already grieving. I don't know his name. But some small, uncharitable part of me would very much like to find him, hand him a copy of *How Not to Be A Coward*, and throw it at his face.

I don't claim to be an expert on love, but I'm pretty sure the '*in sickness and in health*' part isn't just for wedding vows —it's the whole point. Being there when your partner is hurting... that's the line between loving someone and just enjoying their light.

And now, Rhianna's invited me in—to her family, her history, her heart. She's giving me a chance to be the one who stays.

"Ignore him," Rhianna says, but there's something forced in her laugh. I want to pause the moment, reach for her, and ask what's wrong. Because something is. Maybe it's just the fear of going this deep again—of letting someone all the way in. But before I can, she smirks at her brother. "He thinks being the older sibling gives him teasing rights."

"It absolutely does," Gavin grins, extending his hand. "Welcome to the madhouse."

Dinner is... perfect. Almost too perfect. Mr. Wilder— "Please, call me Richard"—keeps me engaged in a fascinating discussion about the evolution of poetry through the ages, from ancient oral traditions to modern experimental forms. His eyes light up the same way Rhianna's do when she's passionate about something. Mrs. Wilder—Alma—is quieter but razor-sharp, offering occasional insights that make everyone laugh.

Even Gavin and I click instantly when he mentions his current reading obsession with Norse mythology. Sure, I spend most of my time with Celtic and Arthurian texts, but soon we're deep in a friendly debate about the parallels between Odin's sacrifice on Yggdrasil and other mythological trees of knowledge, while Rhianna rolls her eyes fondly.

This feels like home. Like family. Like forever.

I can already picture Piper here, trading quips with Gavin and commiserating with Alma about their shared concern and love of the children they work with. Mom would absolutely adore Richard—they'd probably spend hours debating poetry while Dad and Alma bond over their shared love of abstract art.

I can see summer barbecues on the back patio, lazy Sunday brunches, Christmas mornings with the banister wrapped in garland, stockings hung by the fireplace. It would be chaos with Piper trying to organize everyone into her infamous family photo shoots while our parents compete to plan the most elaborate family vacations. The thought makes my chest ache with how much I want it.

"Eli?" Richard's voice pulls me from my reverie. "Would you like to see my study? I have a few older books you might appreciate."

I follow him down a hallway lined with black and white photographs—generations of Wilders, I assume. His study is everything I dreamed of having someday: floor-to-ceiling bookshelves, a well-worn leather chair, the smell of aged paper and wisdom.

"I have to say..." Richard chuckles, running his fingers along a shelf of poetry collections, "It's nice to finally have someone over who appreciates these old things. Rhianna loves books, of course, but she's more interested in where they can take her than where they've been. Gavin tolerates my collecting habit, but you"—he gives me a knowing look—"you understand the magic in the binding itself, don't you?"

I can't help but grin. It's exactly how I tried to explain it to Piper last week when she called my collection *fancy dust-gatherers*. "There's something about holding a piece of history in your hands. Each crack in the spine, each dog-eared page tells its own story. And part of me—sacrilegious as it feels to admit —wants to peek beneath those covers, to touch wooden book boards from trees growing during the Renaissance. To imagine connecting with a tree that could have been a sapling when Shakespeare penned his plays."

"Now that's poetry," Richard says. "The way you talk about books—it reminds me of how my students react when they first discover Wordsworth isn't as stuffy as they assumed. When they really *feel* the words for the first time."

"That is exactly what drew me to teaching."

Richard nods, then reaches for a book off a shelf. "You know, Rhianna's been different lately. More content, even with all her big plans brewing. Usually she's moving from one thing to another at a pace I can't keep up with, but these past few weeks..." He smiles. "It's nice to see her happy again, like she's finally finding the perfect balance."

My heart swells at his words. Rhianna had seemed off since I arrived—her smile tight, her usual effervescence dimmed, like she's holding herself back. But of course she's nervous. According to Gavin, it's been years since she's brought anyone home. This is a big step for her, probably bigger than I realized.

I can see the fear hiding behind her smile, the careful way she's moving around me tonight. Letting me into her family, into this level of her life, is probably terrifying for her. I understand—I've read enough of her story to know she guards her heart fiercely. I can wait until she's ready. My call to request teaching virtually for the upcoming semester was the right one. I won't tell Rhianna yet—I won't push her. She needs time, and I can give her that. Some books are worth savoring slowly, page by page, and what we're building feels too precious to rush.

But before I can dwell on that thought or respond,

Richard pulls another book down. "Speaking of Rhianna, here's her favorite of my collection. Limited edition of 'Around the World in 90 Days.' She begged for this one when she was younger. Said it would be her planning guide for her own big adventure around the world. I can't believe that's coming up so soon."

He says it fondly if with a bit of wistfulness. The way parents do when they're proud of their children's dreams but wish those dreams didn't take them so far away. I barely register his tone though, because my brain has snagged on one phrase: *around the world.*

My heart stutters, but I keep my voice casual. "She's talked about traveling, but I don't think we've discussed the details." I'm amazed at my ability to speak with so much calm. If I wasn't living inside my head where I'm mentally screaming, I'd believe myself relaxed. "When is she thinking of going?"

"Oh, she's saved for years." Richard hands me another book. High-quality leather, but second edition lacking any inscription. The kind of copy a true collector would admire but not covet. And I can't believe my brain is able to even process this considering the continued internal screaming. "Following her Grandma Ida's dreams." He sighs but smiles. "My mother had a wanderer's heart her whole life—picked Rhianna's name, in fact. Those two were like twin spirits from the moment Rhi was born. Always planning adventures, mapping out far-off places they'd visit together someday." His voice softens. "And now with this fellowship acceptance— twenty-four libraries in six months! And she thinks with her savings she can extend the trip to a year. That's my girl, doing it in true librarian style. I can't believe she'll be gone in a couple of months."

The room tilts slightly. A year. And she's leaving in *a couple of months.* A fellowship she hasn't even told me about. And if it's anything like the ones through the university, she's been working on this since we met or earlier. Planning it. Dreaming about it. Never discussing it with me.

While I've been imagining a future here... with her.

Everything crashes into place—her reluctance when I tried to talk about feelings at the beach, the way she deflects whenever I mention the future, her saying she had plans that inhibited her wanting anything serious. God, I've been such a fool.

I've been planning holidays that will never happen. Imagining our mothers' mingled laughter which will never exist. Standing in this study, surrounded by generations of Wilder family photos, dreaming about where our children's pictures might hang one day—while she's been counting down the days until she leaves. Until she leaves me.

I've already made the call to teach remotely next year, started looking at the long-term lease options for my apartment, even begun the paperwork to transfer my research grant to the Magnolia Cove archives—all to build a life around a woman who never planned to stay.

This is exactly what happens when you abandon logic for feelings. When you throw away carefully crafted plans for the wild beat of your heart. I've spent my entire life making calculated decisions, weighing every option, considering every outcome. Then Rhianna Wilder walks into my life with her bright smiles and quirky book pins and strong opinions, and suddenly I'm restructuring my life around a woman who never saw anything serious with me. Who probably hasn't thought twice about who she's leaving behind, because I was never meant to be anything but temporary.

When we rejoin the others, I see her differently. Her laughter sounds lighter because it *is* lighter—unburdened by the weight of attachment I've been feeling. Every smile, every touch, every moment we've shared... was I the only one building castles in the air?

"Walk you out?" Rhianna asks later, already moving

toward the door. Her voice holds that same warmth it always does, but now I hear what's missing—any hint of reluctance to see me go, any suggestion that this evening meant as much to her as it did to me.

On the porch, the salt air that usually invigorates me now stings. The stars that usually promise possibility now mock my naivety. She rocks back on her heels, hands tucked into the pockets of her dress—a gesture I once found endearing but now recognize as an action that creates distance.

"Thanks for coming," she says, and I search her face for any sign that she means more than just tonight. Any hint that she's about to bring up the conversation we said we'd have. That I'm not the only one holding space for it. Her eyes don't even meet mine as she speaks. "My family really liked you."

"They're wonderful," I manage. *They could have been mine too*, I think, but push the thought away. "I can see why you love them so much."

She steps forward for a quick hug. Her arms brush mine, light and brief, like the memory of touch rather than the thing itself. It's the kind of hug you give an acquaintance, not someone you've kissed beneath meteor showers and woken up bare and warm and wrapped in their arms—and I breathe in the scent of her shampoo. "Night, Eli," she murmurs, already pulling away.

I wait for a word, a pause, a glance that might signal she's about to say more. That she hasn't forgotten. But nothing comes. And by the time I realize *this is it*—that she's not going to start the conversation—we've already passed the moment. I open my mouth, but the words catch behind my teeth, tangled in the shock of it. She's gone before I can untangle even one.

"Night, Rhianna," I whisper to the empty porch as I watch her disappear inside, taking all my dreams of forever with her.

Standing alone outside, surrounded by the gentle glow of

Magnolia Cove's evening lights, I realize two things: I need to have an honest conversation with her, even if it breaks both our hearts, and maybe leaving Misty Pines was a mistake after all.

When I'd planned my three bold moves to shake up my life, I'd imagined transformation—not heartbreak written in ink I can't erase.

Rhianna

The acceptance letter sits on my desk like a ticking time bomb, its crisp edges mocking me with possibility. I've read it so many times I could recite it in my sleep: *Dear Ms. Wilder, We are pleased to inform you that you have been selected for the World Library Tour Fellowship...*

Mom's humming floats up from the kitchen downstairs, the scent of her famous sweet and spicy apple pie following close behind. It's her third pie this week, which means she's worried about me. Stress baking is hereditary in our family.

"Honey?" she calls up. "Dinner's almost ready. Your father's bringing home that wine Eli brought the other night."

My heart does that annoying flutter thing at his name. Stupid heart. Stupid Eli with his perfect book recommendations and his ability to charm my parents in exactly one dinner. Dad hasn't stopped talking about their hour-long discussion over the importance of poetry and spoken word in folklore.

"The pie smells amazing!" I shout back, buying myself another moment alone with my thoughts.

"Eli told me apple is his favorite!"

Of course it is. Because the universe hates me.

I smash my palms against my eyes until I see stars, trying to push back the ache in my chest. This is exactly why I need to accept this fellowship. Maybe even leave sooner than later. Because Eli Lancaster isn't just clicking with my family—he's fitting into every corner of my life like he belongs there. Like he's always been there.

That hurts more than any breakup I've ever had, because this isn't even an actual relationship ending—it's me running away before it can truly begin. I'm the one who insisted on "no strings attached" from the start. I'm the one who's been holding back, deflecting whenever things got too real. Which was fine—manageable, even—until I had to watch him bond with my dad over books and make my mom laugh with his terrible puns and generally be... perfect.

I want to keep him. Just for a little while longer. Want to pretend I'm brave enough to build something real with him, even though I know I'll eventually panic and flee. But seeing him here, in my childhood home, talking about vintage wines with my brother and complimenting my mom's art collection... It's like watching a reality I both desperately want and am terrified to claim. A reality where someone sees me—all the messy, disorganized, passionate, over-the-top versions of me—and loves me anyway.

But to face that means opening the parts of me I've spent years keeping locked away. It means risking the kind of heartbreak that would leave me gutted, hollowed out in place that never quite fills back in.

Eli isn't Jacob.

He's better.

Which means when it ends, it will cut that much deeper.

The faster I leave, the less it'll hurt. That's just math. Or science. Or whatever branch of knowledge that deals with hearts that don't know how to follow simple instructions like 'don't fall for the cute professor who's just passing through.'

I pull out my travel planning journal. Twenty-four libraries. Twenty-four adventures. Twenty-four chances to finally take the trip Grandma Ida and I always dreamed about. Twenty-four degrees of separation between me and the kind of love that could break me. The fellowship even includes a stop in Edinburgh, where Grandma once said we would drink strong tea, hunt down obscure poetry collections, and pretend we were scholars-in-residence for the summer.

"Did you respond yet?" Mom appears in my doorway, wiping flour from her hands onto her apron. "The deadline's tomorrow, isn't it?"

I nod, my throat tight. "Just... double-checking some details."

Mom lingers in the doorway, her eyes soft with that knowing look she gets when she's trying to read between my lines. "Sometimes when we hesitate, it's our heart trying to tell us something." She glances meaningfully at the photos of Eli and me from the Blue Moon Festival that I stupidly haven't taken down. "Or someone."

I don't answer, but something must show on my face because she gives me a more gentle mom-smile and takes a step back. "Dinner is in twenty, sweetheart."

When she leaves, I stare at my reflection in the mirror. I've been so focused on protecting myself, I didn't even notice how deeply I've fallen for him despite all my carefully constructed boundaries. But falling doesn't mean I'm ready to stay grounded.

Eli is steady and thoughtful and good. He's the kind of man who makes his bed every morning and actually folds the corners of the fitted sheet. The kind of man who remembers to send birthday cards with actual stamps.

And me? I'm a train wreck barreling toward him at full

speed. Maybe I'm some divine punishment for a transgression he committed in a past life. Like forgetting to return a library book. Or saying he didn't really like *Pride and Prejudice*. Or using Comic Sans in a syllabus just once.

Jokes aside, he deserves someone who sees forever as a gift. Someone who loves him fully and without fear.

And I don't have that in me anymore. All I want to do is run. Even if it breaks me. Even if he's the best thing that ever happened to me. Because loving someone like Eli takes more bravery than I have left—and if I stay, I'm afraid I'll only end up proving myself right: that I *am* too much. That people like me don't get chosen. Not for keeps.

I open my laptop, the screen illuminating with painful brightness and start typing:

Dear World Library Tour Fellowship Committee,
I am honored to accept...

The words blur as I type, but I keep going. Sometimes being brave means walking away from something that could be beautiful, toward something that could be extraordinary. At least, that's what I tell myself as I hit send, ignoring my thoughts screaming internally. My stomach twists. My heart aches like I've pulled the muscle.

Dad's voice carries up the stairs, along with the pop of a wine cork. He's telling Mom about his lunch date with Eli, his voice warm with pride over a new acquisition Eli's found as if he's already part of the family.

I stare at the sent email confirmation, waiting for the rush of excitement, the soaring euphoria of dreams coming true. That's how this moment was supposed to feel.

Instead, I feel like a balloon that's had all its helium let out —deflated and earthbound when I should be floating. My grand adventure, my perfect escape, and all I can think about is how Eli's bangs fall across his forehead, and how his skin smells like coffee, and how he argues about mid bands just to be contrary, and how he... *No, Rhianna. Stop it.*

I close my laptop and head downstairs, the weight of my decision settling around my shoulders like a heavy cloak. Two dozen libraries. Two dozen adventures. And one heart left behind in Magnolia Cove, tucked between the pages of a book in Eli's carefully curated collection.

At least I'll have plenty of material for my own story. Even if it's not quite the happy ending I didn't know I wanted.

Rhianna

The Library Comes Alive event is a roaring success. So many kids fill the library's main area that I can't even count them all. We've transformed each section into a different storybook world, complete with twinkling lights and more than a little magical enhancement (though the tourists just think we're great at special effects).

Claire's White Witch holds court in the winter wonderland we've created in the Reference section, complete with fluffy snow we'll have to vacuum up for weeks. She's also arrived with her promised Turkish Delight. (I'm so curious to see if any kids actually eat the stuff.)

In Fantasy, Michael's Mad Hatter leads tea parties every half hour with delicacies purchased from The Whimsical Whisk. The Mystery section has become a Victorian London street where kids can follow clues to solve cases with a certain consulting detective who looks unfairly handsome in his deerstalker cap—no, I'm not thinking about that right now.

I've transformed the circulation desk into Number Seventeen Cherry Tree Lane, complete with a painted London skyline.

"Spit spot!" I announce in my crispest British accent to my crowd of wide-eyed visitors. "Who's ready to see what's in my carpet bag?"

I reach in, grateful that the Council allowed me this bit of magic for the night. The children gasp as I pull out an impossibly large umbrella, then a potted plant that shouldn't fit through the opening, and finally—for the grand finale—a coat rack that I sit beside me. The children whisper among themselves, trying to figure out how I managed it. To the non-magical parents, it looks like a clever sleight of hand. They're certain I have a hole in the table the bag rests on. To the magical folks, their smirks give away their true understanding.

From the back of the room, Eli watches. He's devastating in his Sherlock Holmes getup—the cap casting shadows across his cheekbones, giving them sharp angles. The fitted coat makes it seem like he stepped straight out of a Victorian novel. The sight of him sends an ache through my chest so fierce I nearly fumble and drop my bag.

"Miss Wilder!" Jasper bounds up, his Lorax mustache slightly askew. "Can you pull a Truffula tree from your bag next?"

I force a smile. This should be one of the best nights of the year. I've spent months planning and organizing it. Yet, here I am, my heart weighing heavier than all the books in my carpet bag combined. I'm trying to focus on the kids but my mind keeps remembering Eli's wonky star doodles, him singing Fleetwood Mac without reserve, him kissing me beneath starlight. His voice getting low and shaky as he—

"I'm afraid Truffula trees are strictly outside my jurisdiction," I tell Jasper as I reach into my bag. "However..." I produce an orange feather boa that matches his costume. "Perhaps this will suffice?"

His eyes double as I drape it around his neck, and for a minute I'm reminded why I love this job, this life, and even this town. Then I notice Eli again, his expression unreadable, and the weight settles back into my chest.

Some things even Mary Poppins can't fix with a spoonful of sugar.

"And now," I announce to my gathered crowd, channeling every ounce of the beloved British nanny that I can muster, "I believe it's time for us to solve a mystery! Inspector Holmes is waiting for you on Baker Street to help our young detective crack a most curious case."

I usher the children toward the Mystery section. Gaslight-style lamps cast a warm glow over cobblestone paths crafted from carefully painted cardboard. Eli stands beneath a light, his tall frame casting long shadows across the fake street.

"Gather round young detectives," he greets them, his voice dropping into a perfect British accent that makes my treacherous heart skip.

It's strange how he can fumble over small talk and get flustered ordering coffee when they don't have his usual, but put him on a karaoke stage or in front of these kids and he transforms. Like he knows exactly who he's supposed to be in those moments. I wish I had that confidence.

"We have a most peculiar case before us," he continues. "The library's rarest book has gone missing, and only the keenest observers among you can help locate it."

He kneels down to the children's level, and I try not to notice how the motion pulls his coat across his shoulders, how his eyes spark with enthusiasm behind his glasses. I try not to think about how I've seen those shoulders bare beneath moonlight, or how those eyes lit up in different ways when we were alone—softer, darker, full of promises I'm too afraid to embrace.

I feel like I've betrayed him. We had a deal based on no commitments, just an exploration. A summer of fun and possibilities. And when I said it's over, it's over. No strings. No regrets.

But all week, I've avoided him. All week, I've been quietly pulling away while telling myself it's for his own good. Telling myself he deserves better than a girl who can't bear the vulnerability. And that's the whole problem. He does deserve better. He deserves someone who won't flinch at 'I love you's' and long to run the moment serious conversations begin.

Instead, he got me.

And now I'm going to break his heart. Not because I want to, but because I was too selfish to act sooner. Too scared to tell the truth. Too cowardly to face the conversation we said we'd have. I've told myself I was sparing him. But really? I think I was just sparing myself. And somehow, that makes me feel worse than if he'd been the one to leave.

Eli explains the clues the children need to look for, then before setting them off he says, "Remember, in every mystery, the truth is often hiding in plain sight. We just have to know where to look."

A lump forms in my throat. Because he's right. And maybe the truth about us has been right there all along. He's a man brimming with love to give, with a steady heart and a hunger for commitment. And I'm a woman whose heart didn't heal right after it shattered, someone too afraid to try again, too unsure she can ever do justice to love as big and generous as his.

The children scatter like autumn leaves in a breeze, their excited squeals echoing around as they begin their hunt. They weave between fake lamp posts, magnifying glasses held close to their faces. Their joy should be infectious—usually it is—but tonight it just reminds me of how temporary everything is. Tomorrow I'll have to clean all of this up and only fleeting memories will remain. Just like this relationship.

I take a step back. I should check on the other stations.

Make sure Claire's snow isn't getting out of control. See if Michael needs more tea cups. I have an entire event to run, after all.

"Rhianna?" Eli steps up beside me, his voice soft but urgent. "Can we talk?"

He's intent, his facade washed away. It's just Eli's haunted expression looking at me from beneath that cap. This isn't how tonight is supposed to go. We're supposed to be Inspector Holmes and Mary Poppins, delighting children with our mysteries and magic. Not... whatever this ache between us has become.

"Right now?" I whisper. The kids are all still distracted, their parents following along behind and helping in the search.

"I've tried to speak with you all week," he says, and the edge of frustration in his voice makes me flinch. "You're always busy, or with a patron, or going out with Alex."

Of course I am. Because I can't bear to do what needs to happen. I can't stand the thought of breaking this man's heart —of watching the light in his eyes dim when I say the words I've been dreading. But I'm also not brave enough to try. Not brave enough to risk everything for a love that might leave me shattered again.

This is my problem, not Eli's. But he's the one who's going to pay the price for it. Like my namesake, I don't know how to let myself be caught. The first man I ever slowed down for left me wounded in a way I've never fully healed from— left me skittish and wary, always scanning for the next escape route.

And I don't think I know how to stop again.

Not without shattering.

"We have to focus on this event right now." I gesture to my Mary Poppins outfit—the navy dress and daisy covered hat. I even added some smudges of makeup across my nose for soot.

"I know." Eli runs a hand through his bangs, dislodging the

deerstalker hat. He looks different tonight—sharp edged and mysterious. He's devastatingly handsome as Sherlock Holmes, which is entirely unfair because it's hard enough dealing with regular Eli breaking my heart. This version of him, all brooding detective with his collar turned up against imaginary London fog, is just cruel and unusual punishment. "But we need to—"

"Miss Wilder!" Jasper bounds up with a pack of other kids brandishing a pocket watch triumphantly. "Look what we found! And it's got weird numbers on it!"

"Excellent work, young detective! Keep searching for another clue."

He nods firmly and runs back onto Baker Street. I'm turning to escape, but before I can Eli's hand catches my elbow. "Please," he whispers. "Just five minutes."

Behind us, a child shrieks with delight at finding another clue. The sound echoes off the library's high ceiling, a stark contrast to the heavy silence between us.

A few parents have lifted their faces in our direction. One woman frowns, probably wondering why we're having a lover's quarrel in the middle of a children's event.

"Follow me," I whisper, leading him to the shadowy Reference section. The children's gleeful laughter feels distant here, like we're in our own pocket universe of pain.

"You've been avoiding me," he says softly.

My heart cracks at the quiet truth in his voice—at the way he's not angry, just hurt. Because he's right. And I hate that I've made him feel this way.

But better now than later. Better to pull away than commit to something I know I can't fully give. I should've stuck with being his matchmaker instead of falling for him. Should've stayed at a safe distance, nudging him toward someone steadier. Someone ready.

"You're right," I whisper. "I have been avoiding you."

The words land between us with more weight than I expect. What else can I say, though? That I've been hiding because I'm scared? That loving him feels like standing on the edge of something too big and beautiful, and I don't trust myself not to fall? Or worse—he realizes I am too much after all, and he's the one who does the pushing.

The truth swells in my chest, but I can't find the space of it.

So I say nothing.

"I've missed you," he says and the quiet honesty in his voice nearly breaks me.

And I really am a coward after all, because instead of answering, I focus on straightening my white gloves. "It's been a busy week."

"Rhianna." The way he says my name—like its precious and fading—makes me hold my breath. "What's happening here? Ever since dinner with your parents, something's changed. Did I do something wrong?"

"No," I admit, because I can't bear to let him think this is his fault. "You were perfect."

He steps closer, and I can smell the faint scent of his cologne mingled with the comforting smell of old books. "Then what is it?"

The children's laughter rises in a crescendo from the Mystery section, the sound so at odds with the heaviness between us. I draw a shaky breath.

"It's just..." I finally say, my voice barely above a whisper. "We agreed to keep things casual, remember? No expectations. Just... exploring for the summer."

He's quiet for a moment, his eyes searching mine from beneath the brim of his cap. When he speaks, his voice is steady, but there's something raw underneath like he's trying to hold together the edges of something that's already cracking. "And that's what you still want?" he asks softly. "Something casual? Something that ends when summer does?"

A lump rises in my throat. Of course it's not what I want. I want him—his quiet smiles, his steady hand in mine, the way his mind somehow makes sense of my chaos.

But what I want doesn't matter. I've seen how this ends. I'm always too much—too emotional, too messy—and eventually, they leave. Eli would too. Building history with someone only to lose them isn't romantic. It's ruinous.

"I think it's for the best," I say, the words tasting like dirt. "We're different people, Eli. You plan your life in color-coded sections. I spill glitter on everything I touch."

"That's what I love about you." The intensity in his voice makes my breath hitch. He means it. At least for now, he does.

I shake my head. "You say that now. But eventually, you'll get tired of the chaos. Of me being too much."

"Too much?" His brow furrows. "Rhianna, that's ridiculous—"

"No, it's not." My voice rises before I catch myself. "It's what happens. People leave. They always do. And when they leave, it breaks something inside you that never quite heals right." I swallow, my throat tight. "I'm so sorry about this. You deserve someone whole and lovely and just right. But that isn't me."

His gaze softens with something like understanding. "This isn't really about me, is it?" he says gently. "It's about... someone before. Someone who hurt you."

The fact that he knows—that he's pieced together the fragments of my past I've shared over late-night conversations and sun-drenched beach walks—only make this harder.

"It's about me knowing how this story ends," I whisper. "About trying to protect us both before we get in too deep." I take a deep breath that doesn't feel like it reaches my lungs. My voice trembles when I speak. "This was supposed to be a no-commitment summer fling. And I was foolish to ever believe I could keep it that simple. I'm sorry I've hurt you. I never meant to but this has shown me that I'm selfish. That I wanted all the magic without the risk. And you..." I look at him, the man I love and am letting go. "You deserve someone better than me."

He takes my hand, and I let him, because I'm weak and this might be the last time I feel his touch.

"Don't do this," he says, his voice catching on the words. "Don't decide our ending before we've even had a chance to live the story. That's not fair. Not to me. And not to you either."

"Fair?" I pull my hand away. "What's fair about letting you rearrange your entire life around someone who will never fit into your perfect system?"

"Perfect system?" He lets out a short, disbelieving laugh. "Rhianna, have you seen me these past months? I've jumped out of planes. I've sung karaoke with a bunch of strangers. I've made more spontaneous plans than I have in my entire adult life. And I've never been happier or more alive."

For a moment, I almost believe him. Almost let myself hope that maybe, just maybe, he's different. That maybe I could be enough. But then reality crashes back.

"You say that now," I repeat, crossing my arms over my chest. "But what happens when the adventure wears off? When I'm just me—too loud, too messy, too much—and you realize you've upended your carefully planned life for someone who doesn't fit?" I shake my head before he can speak. "You're still caught up in the spark. But one day the glitter settles, and all that's left is the mess underneath. And when that happens, this will end—it'll just hurt a hundred times more for both of us."

Eli looks too stunned to speak. A child's shriek of glee in the distance snaps me back to the present—to the event I'm supposed to be running, to the library filled with laughter and scavenger hunts and carefully arranged book displays that suddenly feel a million miles away.

"You told me once," I say, my voice steadying, "that if I ever said we were done, you'd respect it. Not guilt. Not pressure. You promised." A sheen spreads across his eyes, but I force myself to keep his gaze. "I'm done, Eli."

It's what needed to be said. So why do the words feel like arrows I've plunged into my own heart? Not Cupid's gentle shots—but something fatal. The light in Eli's eyes dims and I hate myself for putting that spark out. But this is necessary. It's short term pain for mercy in the long run.

His jaw tightens. For a moment, I think he might argue, might fight for us. A small, selfish part of me almost wishes he would. Instead, he nods once, his eyes glassy with unshed tears. "I did say that," he whispers. "And I meant it. If that's really what you want... I'll let you go."

"It's what needs to happen," I correct, because it's not about want. If it were about want, I'd be in his arms right now.

The silence stretches between us, thick with unspoken words and possibilities that will never come to pass. A whoop goes up in the distance, followed by the sound of children cheering—they've solved the final clue.

"It sounds like Holmes is needed," I say.

Eli adjusts his deerstalker cap with shaking fingers. "Goodbye, Rhianna," he says, his voice steady but just barely. He turns to walk away, his shoulders rigid like he's holding himself together by sheer force of will.

I smooth down my skirt and fix my hat, willing my own hands to stop trembling. This was the right choice. The responsible choice. The only choice I could live with. The only one that wouldn't hurt worse later. But as I turn to rejoin the festivities, to become Mary Poppins again with her knowing smile and perfect posture, a sob catches in my throat.

I step out of the shadows and a little girl in a Belle costume waves at me. I wave back. Mary Poppins wouldn't let a child see her unhappy. Mary Poppins is practically perfect in every way.

I make it halfway across the library before the tears fall. A little boy tugs at my skirt. "You okay, Ms. Poppins?"

I try to smile, to say something about the rain in London, but the words catch.

"I'm so sorry." I'm not sure if I'm apologizing to the boy or to Eli or to myself. "Forgive me. I'm afraid the wind has changed."

Eli

The hill looks different without stars.

I trace my fingers over the damp grass where we once sat together watching meteors streak across the sky. Everything felt possible then—the world crackling with potential and magic. She'd dragged me up here with no warning, no plan, just a couple flashlights and her infectious enthusiasm.

Trust me, she'd said, and I did. I, Eli Lancaster—who tracks ISBN editions for fun and once timed how long it takes my tea to steep for optimal flavor—followed her into a dark forest without hesitation.

Now there's just darkness, heavy clouds blocking even the faintest glimmer of light. The air is thick, oppressive, nothing like the electric anticipation of that night when everything felt magical because I was sharing the same air as her. The sparkle of possibility. The warmth of her hand finding mine in the shadows, her touch making my carefully constructed world tilt on its axis in the best possible way.

"I'm an idiot," I mumble as I pull out the Cyrus Whitlock book she gave me. After all, everything she said was true. She only agreed to this when I promised it would end. *I set the terms.* I shouldn't feel this broken over it. It followed the ending that was foreshadowed from the very beginning.

The leather shows little wear considering its age. Even in the flashlight's dim beam, the pristine condition is obvious. I trace over the gilt edges and remember her expression when she handed it to me. The way her eyes danced with excitement. How she bit her lower lip trying to contain her smile.

For someone who's spent his life studying stories, you'd think I'd have recognized the story here. The temporary nature of summer romance, the inevitable parting at the season's end. That has to be a romance trope. Or maybe not. Rhianna said romances always end with happily ever afters.

I guess I thought we were writing a love story. Turns out, I was the only one who believed the ending.

The leather is soft beneath my thumb as I brush over the title's raised letters. I can be logical about this. That's what I do, isn't it? Analyze, categorize, make sense of chaos. If I had my notepad with me, I could write it down. As it is, a mental list will have to do.

1. She's planning to leave—has been since before we met.

2. She hinted at it during our first dinner together.

3. She obviously didn't want to talk about the future on the beach.

4. I was the one who said just for the summer. I told her— if she ever said she was done, I'd let her go. And she said she was done.

5. She's afraid. Not just of love, but of being loved—fully, honestly, in a way she doesn't think she deserves. And I can't fight that fear without breaking the promise I made.

6. She believes ending things now will hurt less than ending them later. And maybe she's right.

My hand stills and I close my eyes. Logic isn't working somehow. It feels hollow. Like trying to analyze the technical aspects of a poem while missing its heart entirely.

Because, damn it, logic aside I'm in love with Rhianna Wilder.

Unrequited love.

Talk about a trope.

I came here to shake up my life, to do bold things, to actually live after being reminded how quickly everything could end. I never expected to find someone who made being bold feel natural. Who made me *want* to be spontaneous. Who made color-coding a calendar seem unnecessary because every moment with her was worth rearranging any plan.

I tilt my head back, searching for even one star through the clouds. Just one point of light to prove that magic still exists. That the feeling I had that night wasn't just because of her— her laugh, her soft hand in mine, her smile that seemed brighter than any star. That maybe I can take even a drop of that joy home with me.

The sky remains stubbornly dark, though.

Of course it does.

The light was never the scenery, the meteors, or even the magic.

It was Rhianna, all along. But she streaked by so quickly.

My hands shake as I pull back the book's cover and remove a stack of photos. Each one captures a moment where she illuminated my carefully structured world. When she shined a light that made me realize how dark everything was before.

I smile at the first one. The Blue Moon Festival. We both wear ridiculous Elvis wigs and Rhianna is dramatically strumming an inflated guitar. The photo had caught me mid laugh, and now looking at it, I barely recognize myself. That man isn't thinking about proper citations or comparative literature or book curation checklists. He's just... happy.

I slide it to the back of the stack and reveal the next image. *The Tipsy Mermaid* group shot. The bartender took it at the exact moment Rhianna threw her head back laughing at one of my terrible music puns. Her hand rests on my arm, and I'm looking at her like she's a first edition I've spent my whole life searching for. Except that's not quite right—I'm looking at her like she's something far more precious than any book.

The skydiving photo makes my stomach drop all over again. I remember gripping her hand so tightly before we jumped, but in the photo, we're both beaming. She taught me that fear and joy could coexist, that sometimes the scariest moments lead to the most beautiful ones.

I reveal the last photo—my favorite. It's a selfie I took one morning, the two of us tangled in my sheets, her curled against me in my oversized college sweater. She'd stolen it as soon as she got out of bed, padding around my kitchen while I made French toast. The morning light gleams copper in her ebony hair and I look like a man who just stumbled into his own fairytale.

A tear splashes onto the photo and I quickly wipe it away. My hand shakes so hard I struggle to slide the photos back into place. It's like I'm vibrating with emotions. I've felt that way since the moment I met Rhianna. Up to this point, it was joy rushing through me until it seeped through my pores. Now, it's an altogether different feeling—

My thumb grazes the book's cheap floral endpaper. It's starting to peel at the corner. The academic part of my brain kicks in, the part that can identify binding techniques and paper types at a glance.

When she gave me this book, I'd barely examined it. Just the fact that she knew I'd love Whitlock, that she'd thought of me while finding it—that was enough to make it precious. As soon as I'd seen the cheap end papers, I'd mentally marked it as not financially valuable. It had become the most treasured book in my collection anyway, simply because it came from her.

I should have noticed though. The end pages don't match

the era. With shaking, careful fingers I pull the paper down. It releases from the book easily, like someone had only glued the outline.

Under the decorative paper lies the original end page, pristine despite its age. And there, in the top right corner, is a flourish of faded ink that makes my breath catch. I grab the flashlight, fingers clumsy as I lift it closer.

The signature.

The distinctive 'C', pressed so hard it left an indent. The flowing 'k' at the end of Whitlock. I'll need to authenticate it officially, but I already know. It's real. One of the mythical signed Whitlock's that got me into rare book collecting in the first place, that launched my entire career studying folklore and mythology.

And Rhianna just... gave it to me.

Handed it over beneath a starry night sky with a casual smile, like she wasn't changing my entire world. Like she hadn't found the holy grail of my profession.

The floral paper folds back in place again, revealing the photos. The one of us tangled in my sheets blurs through my tears. I found exactly what I've spent my career hunting for, only to realize it's not what I've been searching for at all.

Or rather, it's not all I've been searching for.

The sobs come without warning, echoing into the empty dark. I don't even try to hold the sound in. There's no one here to see me fall apart.

* * *

"You're what?" Piper's voice crackles through the speaker as I wrap another book in bubble wrap.

The record player hums softly in the background, the crackle of vinyl spinning. It's the only thing I haven't packed yet. I told myself it was because I'd need the box last. But the truth is, I couldn't bring myself to silence the music just yet.

I check the book off my packing list—all categorized, organized, just as it was before Rhianna swept into my life and rearranged everything, including my heart.

"Moving back," I say, keeping my voice steady as I place the wrapped book in Box 7: Office—Reference Materials (Non-Fiction.) I've labeled all the boxes as precisely, each category a desperate attempt at order. Fiction, non-fiction. Reference. Personal. As if putting my life back into the neat little containers will somehow make sense of everything that's happened. As if I could pack away the way she's changed me as easily as I store away these books. But where's the box for the sound of her laugh? Which carefully labeled container holds the way she made my heart race every time she said my name? There's no classification system for the hollow ache in my chest that expands with every item I wrap.

Piper hums sadly before speaking again. "But—what about Rhianna? Did something happen?"

Her name pierces through me. A pain that's as explosive as a lightning strike, sudden and searing. "I'd rather not discuss it."

"Eli..." Her voice is soft and I have to close my eyes against the concern in it. Piper, who's spent years teasing me about how she could set her clocks on my schedule, now sounds worried about my return to the routine. "Talk to me, Brubba."

"There's nothing to talk about." I check another item off my list. The pen makes a satisfying mark against the paper. Clear. Definitive. Final. "Sometimes things just... end."

"Are you sad?" Piper's voice is brutally soft. Not teasing, like when she used to ask me about Sarah, my girlfriend of several years. She'd always said Sarah was as exciting as a library card. Our relationship had ended that way as well. Quiet.

Expected. Like returning a book you never really wanted to check out. We'd gone our separate ways amicably.

But with Rhianna...

"I'm fine." My voice sounds hollow and broken and very not-fine even to my own ears. "It was a summer fling. A temporary adventure. That's all it was."

"Eli..." She lets out a soft sigh. "You don't have to pretend with me. Not about this."

I grip the bridge of my nose. "What do you want me to say, Pipes? That I fell in love? That I forgot who I am and what my life is actually like? That I let myself believe in something magical only to wake up and realize that it's a kind of magic that doesn't exist?"

A long pause. Then Piper says quietly, "Maybe you should say those things to her?"

"I can't," I whisper, then clear my throat. "She ended it. She made it very clear that this was never a good idea."

"Oh, Brubba." Her pity is worse than any teasing she's ever dished out.

"It's fine. I wanted to move away, try something new. I've done that. Now it's time for me to return home and back to my real life."

"Well,"—she says after a moment, her voice carefully light —"I'm at least looking forward to a giant hug and a lunch date. It's your turn to pay."

My lips curve into what might be a smile, though it doesn't feel like one. "I'm looking forward to that too."

"See you soon."

After we end the call, I pick up the Cyrus Whitlock book. My hand moves automatically to open it, to look at the pictures one last time. Instead, I wrap it carefully in bubble wrap and place it in Box 12: Personal Items—Books (Special Collections).

I close the lid. The label is perfect. No wrinkles. No air bubbles. Everything in its ideal place.

Gold Dust Woman plays softly in the background, crackling faintly through the record player's worn speakers. Rhianna had been aghast when she discovered I didn't own the album. She'd changed our entire plan for the evening and bought me a copy.

Now it plays in a room that feels far too quiet.

I cross to the record player and gently lift the needle. The music dies with a sigh. I slide the album back into its sleeve, careful not to crease the cover.

Chapter closed.

Rhianna

I'm sitting in the most hidden corner of Alex's cafe, the one where no one can see your tears. Not that I'm crying. Okay, maybe I am, just a little—the kind of crying where you feel like your heart is leaking out through your eyes no matter how hard you try to hold it in. But I'm trying so hard to keep it together, to look professional. Like my entire world didn't just reshape itself around losing someone. Like I'm not counting the days since I last felt his lips against mine, brushed my hand through his hair, or received one of his soft smiles that made everything inside me feel like warm honey.

This was supposed to be easy. I ended it before it could hurt this much. So why the heck does it feel like I just broke my own heart with a first-edition book and no return policy?

Thankfully the universe has handed me a distraction. I finally have another matchmaking client. My trusty notebook is open in front of me, but the words on the page blur. My brain feels like it tripped and fell into quicksand and my heart aches.

I don't know what happened to Eli. He hasn't come into the library for days. I keep telling myself it's for the best—we were a temporary thing, like the pumpkin spice latte. Deliciously perfect for a season but inevitably going to end. But just like how I pretend I'm totally fine with regular lattes the rest of the year, I'm pretending I'm fine without him. My heart knows better, though. It keeps searching for that particular flavor of joy, that specific blend of warmth and excitement and possibility that only Eli could create.

But my chest feels hollowed out every time I think of him.

I take a shuddering breath and try to shift my focus to Iris, my newest matchmaking client. My first being Eli isn't much of a recommendation for my services if I say so myself, but I'm willing to call myself the issue in that situation and give it another try.

"So," I say, mustering in my *I'm totally fine and not at all heartbroken* voice. "Tell me what you're looking for in a partner." I poise my pen over the paper, ready to take notes even though my fingers tremble.

Iris twines an ivory strand of hair around her finger. She's as pale and ethereal as an orchid in her flower shop, all platinum blonde hair and delicate features. I've known her forever but I don't think I've ever seen her this nervous. "Well, there's actually someone specific..." She grabs her glass and takes a long swallow of water.

Oh boy. I know that feeling all too well. "Unfortunately," —I say gently—"sometimes the whole 'someone specific' doesn't work out." Understatement of the century. "But tell me about him, anyway."

I don't know who Iris is specifically interested in. But maybe if I figure out her type, if option A doesn't work out I can brainstorm some other candidates. That's what I need to do—focus on someone else instead of wallowing in my own heartache. Even if said heartache feels like it's carving a gaping hole in my chest. And worse, it keeps gnawing at me that I'm the one who put it there. That I hurt Eli. That I walked away and left him standing in the wreckage.

At least I ended it now. At least I had the sense to stop this before it became something even deeper—before we got in too far and truly ruined our lives when it inevitably fell apart.

Iris' cheeks flush pink. "Well, he's kind and funny." A genuine smile stretches across her face. "Whenever I'm with him, time flies. And he makes me feel like I can be the real me—the real me no one else sees. Like my ideas aren't completely ridiculous." Her voice gets softer. "The problem is, I'm afraid he's not interested in anything serious. With me or maybe with anyone."

I grab a biscotto and pick at it. I know exactly what she means. Eli made me feel that way too—like I could be unapologetically myself, quirks and all. Like my dreams weren't silly fantasies, but genuine possibilities.

Iris tangles more hair around her finger. Her gaze has gone distant, and it's like she's not talking to me anymore. Which is great news because I'm doing a terrible job of listening.

"He's so good at what he does, too, you know? The way his eyes light up when he's talking about his latest project or helping with the baseball team... It's magnetic. And even though we're really different people, somehow it just... fits. Like two puzzle pieces slotting together."

My brain—the whiny, moaning thing it is—wants to wallow more in my misery over Eli but her words make me realize I probably do know who she is talking about. Tom runs his family's bait and tackle shop and volunteers with the base-ball team.

Tom is one of the sweetest guys I know. Vibrant. Funny. Always has your back.

But when it comes to romantic commitment? His interest level is somewhere between absolute zero and the temperature of a penguin's feet. He's made it clear he's married to his work, taking care of his grandmother, and coaching baseball. Love? Romance? That's strictly the stuff of the stories we discuss at book club.

My heart aches for Iris. I know what it's like to want something that was never meant to last. And sure, Tom is upfront about it, but that doesn't mean feelings listen to logic.

It's so easy to get caught up in the what-ifs, to let yourself roll right down the hill into a bramble bush before you even realize you've fallen.

And once you're in, it doesn't matter that you knew better. The thorns still hurt all the same.

"And you know what's really special?" Iris continues, her voice soft and dreamy. "The way he gets excited about little things. Like when he found a signed baseball card of one of the kids' favorite players, or the time he helped me rescue an injured seagull. His whole face lights up, and it's like... like the sun coming out after a storm."

The tears I've been fighting prick my eyes until they burn. That's exactly how Eli looked when I'd given him the Cyrus Whitlock book on Welsh mythology. How his eyes sparkled when he sang that Fleetwood Mac song to me. The expression he had on the beach when he'd almost said—

And just like that, my carefully constructed *I'm totally fine* facade crumbles faster than Alex's famous coffee cake. A sob burst out of me then never stops. It's the kind of ugly crying that makes your nose run and your mascara turn traitor, the kind you usually save for your pillow at 2AM while googling "how to get over someone you never should have fallen for in the first place." Except I'm doing it right here in Alex's cafe, in front of a client, like a complete jerk.

Iris reaches out like she might help. "Oh! Oh no, are you okay, Rhianna?" Her hands move around frantically for a moment before she settles on patting my arm awkwardly.

I try to speak, but all that comes out is a sort of hiccuping sob. Alex appears like she's summoned by the sound of my emotional distress, her hair catching the light like a halo of hope through my tears. She swoops in with the efficiency of someone who has been through an emotional hurricane and knows how to steady the sails.

"Iris." Alex's tone is gentle but brooks no argument. "Rhianna will have to reschedule with you. If you speak with Kasey at the cash register, she'll provide you with a gift card for a complimentary future drink."

She guides the confused florist away from the table with the same graceful authority she probably once used to manage the most challenging editors. A minute later she's back, sliding a steaming mug in front of me that smells like chamomile and something distinctly... magical. It's Ethan's special "Fix Your Blues" tea, enhanced with just a touch of his magic—basically a hug in a cup.

"Want to tell me what that was about?" She settles into the chair across from me, her expression somewhere between concern and that furrowed brow and fixed stare that says she's already figuring everything out and has opinions.

I wrap my hands around the warm mug, letting the heat seep into my trembling fingers. For a long moment, I just stare into the swirling amber liquid, trying to find the right words. Any words, really. Alex waits with the patience of someone who spends their free time mastering tricky recipes, testing each one over and over until it's just right.

"I'm sorry," I finally manage. "I just... I shouldn't be crying in front of Iris. That's like, Matchmaking 101. Right up there with 'don't fall for your own client' which—" I let out a watery laugh. "Well, I failed that one spectacularly too. Maybe your skepticism on this project was deserved."

"Rhianna." Alex's voice is gentle. "What happened with Eli?"

And there it is. The question I've been avoiding since he

stopped coming to the library, since our last conversation ended with that horrible silence that felt like the ending of a book you weren't ready to finish. When I ended things dressed in a kitschy Mary Poppins costume all while he looked too handsome to be real in his coat and shadows.

"I ended things—before I could get hurt even more." I stare into my tea like it might hold answers. Then my voice drops to a whisper. "Because somewhere along the way, I realized I'd already fallen for him. And that scared me more than anything. I just... I couldn't bear the thought of letting him see all of me—and deciding to leave."

Alex's expression softens. "So you jumped first."

"More like I deployed my emotional parachute." I attempt a smile that probably looks more like a grimace. "Which is ironic considering he's the one who convinced me to actually go skydiving. And with one of those sketchy human-run attractions too. No magic at all! Just trust falling! God, Alex, how did I let myself get so tangled up in someone who was always meant to be temporary?"

Steam rises from my tea like it means to brush my tears away. "You know, the worst part is how he's everywhere. I can't do my job without thinking of him. Half the books in the library have his fingerprints on them. The folklore section? Might as well rename it the 'Subjects Eli Lancaster Waxed Poetic On' collection. And don't even get me started on music."

I sniffle and trace the rim of my mug with a finger. "He's ruined Fleetwood Mac for me, Alex. Fleetwood Mac! Do you know how often 'Go Your Own Way' comes on my playlist? Every. Single. Day. And instead of jamming out like a normal person, I just sit there remembering how his voice powered through the lyrics, how his eyes found mind during the chorus, and—" I swallow hard.

The tea in my hands has cooled just enough to drink, and I

take a sip, letting the warmth spread through my chest. It doesn't fill the Eli-shaped hole there, but it helps. At least I'll leave soon. Leaving this island and the memories and the way they hurt like they're carving me from the inside out.

Alex leans forward slightly. "You know, I almost lost Ethan because I was too afraid of looking for different options for my future. I was terrified of the truth and scared of what staying in Magnolia Cove would do to my career, my life plans." She gives a soft laugh. "Then this bear shifter who bakes magical cinnamon rolls came into my life and scattered all my careful planning and it was the best thing that ever happened to me."

My eyes are doing the leaking thing again, and I dab at them with my sleeve. "But this is different. You and Ethan... you're different." Alex raises an eyebrow, but I barrel on before she can say anything. "I mean, look at you, Alex. You're *actually* practically perfect in every way. And me?" I gesture at myself with a watery laugh. "I'm the one who dressed up as Mary Poppins to distract people from the fact that I'm always falling apart."

"You think Ethan and I are perfect? Rhianna, I'm an anxious overthinker and Ethan didn't reveal to me that he could change into a bear until he just showed up at my apartment and shifted right there in my living room... *after* we'd already broken up." She shakes her head, smiling fondly. "He was so afraid of showing me his true self, we almost missed out on each other entirely." She pauses, then adds, "Unless I've missed something major here, you don't have quite that big of a secret. You're not falling apart, Rhianna. You're just scared."

I force a smile, but my throat is tight. What I don't say is: *But that's the difference, isn't it?* Alex saw Ethan's messy secrets —his fear, his shifting, all of it—and loved him anyway. I showed Jacob mine... and he let me go.

Some people are meant to be loved. I mean, look at Ethan. He's got those twinkly blue eyes and makes cookies that taste like a Hallmark movie. He's completely sincere when he offers to judge the kids pumpkin painting contest at the Harvest Hoopla even if he has to do it at Dean Markham's side.

That's not me.

I talk too fast when I'm nervous. I feel too much, say the wrong thing, get big ideas I can't always pull off. I'm glitter and chaos and half-baked plans.

No one stays for that.

"It doesn't matter," I say. "Some stories don't get happy endings. Some people aren't meant for love that lasts."

"I don't believe that," Alex says softly. "And honestly? I don't think you do either. What about the way you swoon over every romance at book club? Or how seriously you took this matchmaking idea? Rhianna you're a person who *loves* love. You pour it into everyone else. You deserve to have it too."

I set down my mug with a decisive clink. "What I know is that I've seen this movie before. I know how it ends."

My mind drifts to Jacob's expression the night my grand-mother died—how his expression shifted from sympathy to discomfort as the days passed and I couldn't pull myself together. How he started making excuses not to come over.

"You know what Jacob said to me when he finally worked up the courage to end things?" I ask, my voice barely above a whisper. "He said he needed someone more stable. That I was too much, felt things too intensely." I swipe at a tear. "Alex, he was right."

"No, he wasn't," she says too loudly. A couple at the table behind us turns to look. She takes a breath, lowers her voice, but her tone stays razor-sharp. "Eli isn't Jacob, Rhianna. I've seen how he looks at you, like you hung every star in the sky. That's not a man who's going to walk away when things get difficult."

For one dangerous moment, I let myself imagine it—a

future with Eli. Mornings spent in quiet conversation. Evenings filled with laughter. A life where I don't have to hide the messy parts of myself. Where I'm loved not in spite of being too much, but because of it.

But hope is a treacherous thing. He's already making plans to leave Magnolia Cove. And so am I. This story always ends the same, no matter how much I hope it might turn out differently.

"I appreciate what you're trying to do." I press my hands together in my lap. "But not everyone gets a fairy tale, Alex. Some of us are just... too much. And that's okay." I force a smile that doesn't reach my eyes. "I'm fine with being the matchmaker, not the match."

Alex opens her mouth like she wants to argue, but something in my expression must stop her. She presses her lips together before she speaks. "Okay," she says slowly. "Then can I ask you something?"

I nod, wary.

"If someone *were* to fight for you... like really show up, no matter how messy things got—would you let them in?"

"In that romance-book scenario, which will of course never happen in real life, then, yeah, I'd like to think I'd at least try to let them in." I attempt to sound dismissive but there's a wistfulness I can't quite hide. "But that kind of thing doesn't happen in real life."

Alex tilts her head, studying me with an intensity that makes me squirm. There's a calculating look in her eyes I've seen before—the same one she gets when she's troubleshooting a recipe or planning a menu overhaul.

"What?" I ask suddenly, wary.

"Nothing." She smiles too innocently and leans back against her black metal chair. "Just thinking."

"Alex..." I narrow my eyes. "Whatever you're plotting, stop

it. This isn't one of our romance book picks. There's no grand gesture that can change anything."

"I didn't say a word about grand gestures."

I grab my notebook and brush tears from my cheeks. "You didn't have to. That look says everything."

Alex raises her hands in surrender, but there's still that gleam in her eye. "I promise I won't interfere with *your decisions* about your love life."

Something about her wording makes me squint. "That's a very specific promise."

I narrow my eyes, but I'm too emotionally wrung out to press further. "Good. Thanks for the intervention with Iris and the shoulder to cry on. I'll Venmo you for the gift card you gave her." I sling my bag over my shoulder with a sigh. "Now I'm going to go be a mature, responsible adult and cry into a carton of ice cream in my bedroom in private."

Alex snorts. "I suggest the lavender honey one from Sweet Harmony. You deserve premium breakdown fuel."

I roll my eyes, but a laugh slips out anyway.

She reaches for the empty mugs. "Go easy on yourself, Rhi. Just because *you* think your story's over doesn't mean the universe agrees."

I pause pushing my chair under the table and look up at her. "Yeah, sure. See you at book club."

Then I walk past customers laughing and chatting, the smell of espresso and sugar hanging in the air, the clink of spoons on ceramic, and the sound of someone sighing happily as they take a bite of the biscotti Alex bakes by hand in this cozy little haven she built after falling in love.

And I realize—no matter how much I want it, or how much the people who love me want it for me—this isn't for me.

This isn't my life.

I'm supposed to be the fun aunt for my friends' kids. The one who travels and brings back weird souvenirs and stories about charming taxi drivers and mildly illegal adventures in distant cities. I'm the chaos. The glitter. The story starter, not the ending.

I'm not the person who gets the grand gesture.

I'm the one who plans the perfect party when it happens to someone else—and pretends that's enough.

I let the door swing shut behind me, the sound final. Like a chapter closing. Like a heart trying to convince itself it hadn't just missed the biggest chance of its life.

Eli

The ferry's engine hums beneath my feet, a steady vibration that should be comforting in its reliability but somehow only heightens my awareness of everything I'm leaving behind. I stand at the railing, watching Magnolia Cove one last time. The late afternoon sun casts the town in golden light, making the white-painted buildings gleam like polished shells against the verdant backdrop of magnolia and live oak trees. Even from here, I can see the subtle shimmer of magic that hangs over the island like a delicate morning mist—visible to those of us with magic, invisible for everyone else.

Behind me, a young couple argues playfully over which restaurant had the best lobster rolls. An elderly woman clutches a paper bag from A Novel Idea, no doubt filled with beach reads for her trip back to the mainland. A child squeals with delight as he spots a dolphin in the ferry's wake. Normal people. Not the kind of people who've had their heart dismantled and reassembled in the wrong order.

I adjust my glasses and try to focus on my mental checklist. I need to contact the department about resuming in-person lectures. I should email my landlord and see if they ever fixed that broken window screen in the bedroom, and I still haven't canceled the forwarding service at the post office. This is what I do. This is who I am. Dr. Eli Lancaster: organized, analytical, precise.

Except my mind keeps wandering to dark curls escaping from a messy bun. To fingers stained with ink and glitter. To wild, heartfelt laughter echoing through the stacks of the library.

To Rhianna.

A lump forms in my throat as I realize I now have a "before Rhianna" and an "after Rhianna" life. And I'm not sure how to navigate this "after" part where I know what it feels like to be completely, irrevocably alive, and then return to mere existence.

The thought brings an unexpected smile to my lips. In a strange way, this pain is a gift. Mark died without this. He never experienced the exhilarating terror of jumping out of an airplane or the transcendent joy of loving someone so completely that you'd happily rearrange your entire life just to be near them another day.

But I have. I've lived.

I've sung karaoke in a bar full of strangers. I've plunged into the ocean at midnight beneath the light of a full moon. I've fallen in love with a woman who contains more passion in her smallest finger than I'd previously believed possible in an entire person. And yes, I've had my heart broken so thoroughly that I'm not sure it will ever beat quite the same way again.

Isn't that what I wanted, though? To experience life outside the careful boundaries I'd drawn for myself? To be bold? To take risks?

I'll take this back with me, I decide. I'll carry Rhianna's gift— her insistence on experiencing everything fully, her refusal to play it safe—back to my old life and make it new. I'll try dishes I can't pronounce at restaurants I've never visited. I'll attend a concert alone just to feel the music vibrate through my bones. I'll listen to Fleetwood Mac and never, ever call them a soft rock band again.

The thought draws a soft chuckle from me that quickly dissolves into another wave of a heartache.

"ELI! WAIT!"

The shout cuts through the ambient noise of the ferry, and I spin around, scanning the dock. Alex Sinclair is running full-tilt toward the ferry, waving her arms frantically above her head. My heart lurches.

"IS EVERYTHING OKAY?" I cup my hands around my mouth to project my voice over the distance.

"NO!" she shouts back. "YOU CAN'T LEAVE! RHIANNA IS STILL IN LOVE WITH YOU!"

I freeze, suddenly aware of how public this exchange has become. Mrs. Delehay, who always carries her Pomeranian in a custom-made sling, has stopped mid-conversation with Grammie Rae to openly stare. Hazel—the owner of *The Hungry Gull*, where Rhianna and I have eaten multiple times a week all summer—has abandoned any pretense of not eaves-dropping. The entire town is witnessing this spectacle, witnessing me being—

Human.

The realization washes over me like warm sunlight. That's what I am. Human. In love. Messy and heartbroken and glori-ously, painfully alive.

And suddenly, I don't care who's watching.

"I PROMISED HER I'D LET HER GO IF SHE ASKED!" I call back, my voice stronger than I expected. "AND SHE DID!"

Alex cups her hands around her mouth. "I KNOW! BUT SHE ONLY ASKED BECAUSE SHE'S SCARED! AND

SHE DOESN'T THINK SHE'S WORTHY OF A GRAND GESTURE!"

A grand gesture. I've heard Rhianna talk enough about romance tropes to understand what Alex means. And if there's anyone in the world who deserves a dramatic declaration of love, who deserves to be chosen completely and without hesitation. It's Rhianna Wilder—with her boundless enthusiasm, her kindness, her ability to see wonder in even the most ordinary things.

But there's a problem.

"I CAN'T BREAK MY PROMISE TO HER!" I shout.

Even from her place in the crowd, I can see Alex roll her eyes. "PROMISES ARE ABOUT THE HEART OF THE MATTER, DON'T YOU THINK?"

The ferry's engine changes pitch, and I feel the subtle lurch as it pulls away from the dock. Panic flares in my chest. I'm leaving. The dock is slowly inching away with each passing second.

With a gasp, I sprint toward the railing and vault over it, propelling myself toward the dock in a leap that is neither graceful nor well-calculated. For a terrifying moment, I'm suspended in the air. Then Marcus Blackwood—owner of A Novel Idea—lunges forward and catches me just before I would have tumbled into the water.

"Your luggage is still below deck!" calls a crewmember from the ferry.

Another flash of panic. My rare books. My research materials. My color-coded file system. "I've already paid!" I call back, straightening my glasses. "I'll get it from you later!"

"It might get lost!" The crewmember warns.

Six months ago, this would have sent me into a tailspin of anxiety. But now I find myself shrugging. Right now there's only one thing I can't afford to lose. "I'll figure it out! I have something more important to handle!"

I thank Marcus then weave through the small crowd that's gathered, hearing snippets of gossip already forming in my wake.

"I just love living in Magnolia Cove don't you?" Grammie Rae says to Mrs. Delehay with a delighted grin.

"Wait until bridge club hears about this," Mrs. Delehay replies, already reaching for her phone—and then holding it up in the air like an antenna, trying to find a signal.

Alex meets me halfway down the dock, and I'm slightly out of breath as I reach her. "Okay," I say, "what's next? Where's Rhianna?"

Alex suddenly looks sheepish. "Well, that's the thing. I kind of promised Rhianna I wouldn't get involved with her decisions around her love life. I didn't think that applies to your decisions... but still, my involvement should probably end here."

I stare at her in disbelief for a moment before a laugh escapes me. "I'm not sure you're the person I should be taking advice from about what promises mean, then."

Alex grins. "Maybe not. But good luck." She starts to turn, then looks back with a raised eyebrow. "Oh, and Eli? Just... be gentle with her. She acts like she's allergic to being loved, but it's really just fear with good PR." Her voice softens. "She loves you, she doesn't believe she gets to have you loving her back."

Her words land like a stone. God, if only Rhianna knew. If she only knew how easy it is. How inevitable it's become. I nod, not trusting my voice, and turn toward the path that leads to her.

Because I've seen Rhianna Wilder at her worst. And I still want her. Every messy, magnificent piece. Now I just need to let her know it.

What follows is a whirlwind tour of Magnolia Cove. I try the library first, but Claire tells me Rhianna called out sick.

Her home yields nothing but Mrs. Wilder offering me a slice of apple pie that smells divine but which I reluctantly decline. I stop by A Novel Idea where Mia gently shakes her head from behind the cash register. I check the gazebos and benches around the town square and park. I walk along the shoreline. I even go as far as the stretch of rocky beach beyond the resident's area, where the wind whips hard and cool—each location emptier than the last.

By the time I approach The Whimsical Whisk, the sun is lowering in the sky, and I'm disheveled and sweaty. Note to self: loafers and a button-down are not built for summer sprints. Discouragement weighs heavy in my chest. My luggage is somewhere docked in Charleston by now, containing nearly all my possessions, including my rare book collection. And still no sign of Rhianna.

The bell above the door jingles as I step inside, and Zoe pops up from behind the counter, her purple-streaked hair twisted into a messy bun. "Well, hey there, Sugar," she drawls, eyebrows lifting. "I thought you were on the last train out of this popsicle stand." Her expression softens as she takes in my disheveled state. "You okay, Eli?"

"Tell me you've seen Rhianna here today," I say, not able to muster enough energy for pleasantries.

Zoe leans against the counter. "Can't say I have. But if I were the betting type..." Her grin widens. "And I am. I'd guess she's somewhere trying real hard to convince herself she doesn't miss you."

I run a hand through my hair, which is now hopelessly disheveled. "That doesn't exactly narrow it down."

"True." She taps a neon-green painted fingernail against her chin. "You know, Mia's got her comfort spots when she's down—usually the bookstore loft or that cliff path near the old lighthouse. Magnolia Cove may be small, but people still have their hidey-holes. You ever figure out where Rhianna goes when she needs to disappear?"

A memory surfaces: Rhianna guiding me up a forest path by moonlight, her voice soft in the darkness. *This is where I go when I'm feeling too much.*

The hill. Of course.

Zoe tilts her head, watching my expression shift. Then she grins. "Bingo." She points at me with a wink. "I can see the lightbulb. Give the man a prize."

"What if I'm guessing wrong?"

She shrugs. "Look, I've known Rhianna since we were setting off illegal magic-infused fireworks behind the elementary school. That girl's got more layers than a wedding cake, but she's also predictable in her unpredictability if that makes any sense. I'd bet good money that whatever place just popped into your mind? That's exactly where she is."

I release a heavy breath. I know she's right. I know exactly where to find Rhianna. But marching up that hill sweaty, disheveled, and not even remotely pulled together doesn't exactly scream *grand romantic gesture*. It doesn't feel romance-novel-worthy at all. It's not even a mid-tier made-for-streaming kind of moment.

Unfortunately, I don't have days to come up with something better. I'm currently homeless, all my possessions are—hopefully—on a ferry docked in Charleston, and Rhianna's leaving soon.

I must act now.

Still... there has to be something. Something small that says to Rhianna that I know her. That I love her. No matter how messy or chaotic life may get.

That's when I see them—the lingering chocolate chip cookies behind the bakery glass, edges golden and glistening with magic that feels like a warm hug.

Not exactly the same as hiring a skywriter or penning an

epic of our own mythology, but she once said that Ethan and Zoe's chocolate chip cookies tasted like childhood dreams. So maybe it's close enough.

And maybe, just maybe, that's enough to begin.

I exhale slowly, hope rekindling. "Do you have any more of those chocolate chip cookies?"

Zoe grimaces. "We're about to close and only have the two left..." My face must fall visibly because she quickly adds, "But we always have time for a love-mergency. Boss?" she calls out louder.

Ethan emerges from the back room, flour dusting his apron. "What's up, Zoe?" His eyes widen when he spots me. "Hey, Eli. I thought you were leaving."

Zoe grins, and a mischievous twinkle sparkles in her eye. "We have a cookie catastrophe. Fire back up the ovens."

Ethan chuckles and pulls out his phone. "Let me see if I can get enough service to text Alex and tell her I'll be late." He gestures toward the kitchen. "Eli, grab an apron if you want and come on back."

As I follow him toward the kitchen, I feel a strange sense of calm settling over me. I don't know if this will work. I don't know if Rhianna will even want to see me. But for the first time in my orderly, carefully planned life, I'm completely fine with not knowing what happens next.

The same calm somehow stays with me as I stand alone, a box of freshly baked cookies under one arm, a flashlight in the other hand, staring at the darkening path that leads to the hill. The evening air is heavy with the scent of salt water and blooming crepe myrtle and the first stars are just beginning to appear in the twilight sky. Crickets chorus in the underbrush as if urging me forward.

For a man who spent his life charting every step, I now find myself stepping into the unknown with nothing but hope and cookies. And somehow, that feels like the boldest move of all.

Rhianna

I'm wrapped in Grandma Ida's scarf, its once-vibrant colors muted with age and tears. My stomach grumbles, reminding me that I haven't eaten since... yesterday? The day before? Time has become fuzzy, measured only in tissues and tears.

I look down at my sweatpants and oversized Fleetwood Mac t-shirt, both rumpled and tear-stained. My hair is a disaster, pulled back in the world's messiest bun, complete with a pencil stuck through it that I don't even remember putting there. Objectively, I know I'm disgusting. But somehow, I can't bring myself to care.

The hilltop is quiet except for the distant rhythm of waves, and the occasional rustle of leaves. Below, Magnolia Cove glitters in the gathering dusk, its lights turning on one by one like earthbound stars. It's beautiful—heart-wrenchingly so—and I almost hate it for continuing to be magical when I feel so utterly broken.

I twist another tissue between my fingers, then tuck it into my bag alongside its dozen crumpled siblings. I'm already becoming the island's eccentric tissue-hoarding grandmother, skipping right over my actual life phase. Great.

The realization has been creeping up on me all day, settling into my bones with a certainty that makes my chest ache: I messed up. I made the wrong choice. I let fear end something beautiful before it had a chance to fully bloom.

And then my boss told me that Eli had moved back to Misty Pines.

Gone. Just like that. The thought makes me pull Grandma's scarf tighter around my shoulders, as if it could somehow shield me from the cold reality of what I've done.

I won't reach out to him, though. That would be selfish. Because what if he answered? What if he came rushing back with that big, steady heart of his, ready to forgive me? I'd only break him again. I'm still scared. Still unsure. Still a mess in all the ways that make me terrible at relationships. I don't know how to love someone without eventually unraveling everything good between us.

As bad as this hurts, it's better this way. He escaped with memories of the best version of me—the fun, adventurous, magical side. Not the mess who cries into decade-old scarves and hoards tissues like they're rare books.

A beam of light dances between the trees, weaving as someone ascends the path. My heart leaps into my throat as I scramble to my feet, squinting into the darkness. A flashlight's glow brightens, growing steadily closer, until finally—

"Eli?"

He steps into the clearing, slightly out of breath. His hair's wild, his button-down wrinkled, and he's... holding a Whisk bakery box?

I swipe frantically at my face, as if I could somehow erase hours of crying in seconds. I look like a swamp monster. Or worse—like Miss Viola Swamp. I'm haggard with a swollen nose and ratty t-shirt, and I'm pretty sure there's an ice-cream stain somewhere on my sleeve. If I hadn't already convinced him ending things was a good idea, this will do it.

"You can't see me like this," I choke out, turning away.

"Rhianna," he says, and just the sound of my name in his voice makes fresh tears spring to my eyes. "Please look at me."

Reluctantly, I turn back. He's closer now, close enough that I can see his hazel eyes behind his glasses.

"You're supposed to be gone," I whisper.

"I know." He takes another step forward. "And I promised I would leave if you asked me to. I'm sorry, but I'm breaking that promise." His voice softens. "But if you say one word—just one—that you don't want me here, I'll go. You won't hear from me again."

I should say something. I should tell him to go and protect the shaky scaffolding of self-preservation I've spent years building. But I can't. Because deep down—down to the smallest, most insecure bones in my body—I want him here. Desperately. The wind tangles through my hair, whipping strands across my face like it's trying to hide me, but it's too late. My eyes betray me first, tears spilling before I can blink them back. The truth is already written across my face—raw, unguarded, impossible to hide: *please don't go.*

He sees it. I know he does. Something in his expression softens.

"If you want me to stay, though," he says gently, "then know this—I'd always stand by you, Rhianna." He sighs and brushes his messy hair back, the flashlight beam wobbling with the motion. "Alex told me promises are about the heart of them, not just the words." He glances down, sheepish. "Well, actually she shouted that to me across the ferry dock in front of about three dozen Magnolia Cove residents."

Despite everything, a laugh bubbles up. "Of course she did. That's what I get for befriending a normie. No survival instincts when it comes to small-town gossip."

He smiles, but then his expression turns serious. "I think I might owe her, though. Because she helped me realize that even though I promised to let you go if you asked... I think what you were really asking for was to be safe. And if you let me, Rhianna—I think you'd find your heart would be so safe with me."

My breath catches in my throat. "Eli—"

"Please, let me finish." He sets down the bakery box onto the grass, then takes both my hands in his. "I came to Magnolia Cove looking for a chance to live. I wanted adventure, bold moves, and new experiences. I wanted to shake up my perfectly ordered life because I was afraid of becoming someone who lived without really experiencing life." His voice softens. "Then I met you. And suddenly, it wasn't about checking items off a list anymore. You made me understand a language I didn't even know I was missing. The language of feeling. Of living fully. Of love that doesn't follow logic but still feels like the truest thing I've ever known."

A tear slips down my cheek, and he reaches up to brush it away, his touch achingly gentle.

"I love you, Rhianna Wilder. I love your wild ideas and your passionate heart. I love the way you see magic in everyday things." His fingers trace along my jawline. "I love how you've turned my perfectly organized world upside down and shown me that the best stories are the ones you don't see coming." He tucks a sticky curl behind my ear. "And I love this too—the messy, real, vulnerable you. The one who feels everything so deeply, who cares so much it hurts. If you'd let me in, I'd protect that version of you too. She'd be safe with me."

A choked sound escapes my throat, and I'm sobbing—messy, shaking, tears spilling faster than I can wipe them back. "You don't understand," I manage between hiccups. "I pushed you away because I was scared. Because the truth is... I've never cared for someone the way I care for you. And if you left—" My voice breaks. "I wouldn't recover. I know that makes me selfish, but I'm terrified." I look up at him, tears blurring the stars behind him. "Because I love you. So much it terrifies me."

His sharp intake of breath makes me look up. The warmth in his eyes is almost too much to bear.

"I love you too," he says, his voice thick with emotion. "And if you give me a chance, Rhianna, I'll prove it to you."

The wind whips free strands of my hair forward and he curls his hands around mine—steady and warm, like he's anchoring me in place. Hope blossoms in my chest, fragile and tentative. I want to believe him. I want it more than I've wanted anything. But there's still one insurmountable problem.

"Eli," I say softly, "I'm leaving Magnolia Cove."

"I know." To my surprise, he smiles. "Your father told me."

"He did?" I blink in confusion.

"Yes, the night I had dinner with your family. He told me about your plans." The smile widens. "It's an amazing opportunity. I'm so happy for you."

I stare at him, trying to process this. "But... doesn't that ruin this? I mean, how could we make it work? Long distance after a messy breakup isn't exactly love by the book."

"I don't want a 'by the book' love story." He moves closer, his hands finding mine again. "I want you, Rhianna Wilder. I want sparkly disco lights, and change of plans, and dancing in crowds together. And I want the hard days too. I don't want you sitting on this hill crying alone. I want to be here beside you, hold you when you cry, listen to whatever is hurting you."

My nose flares as I take a deep breath. "You don't know how big my feelings get, Eli. People walk away."

His expression hardens slightly, the shadows deepening across his features in the shifting light. "I've heard some gossip around town about your ex. And I think he was an asshole."

A startled laugh breaks through my tears. "No, I mean—yeah, he was... but I was also in a really dark place for a year, and it got to be too much, and—"

"I wish I could have had that year," Eli says, his voice quiet but fierce.

The wind tugs through his hair as I stare at him, stunned into silence.

"I wish I'd known you then," he continues, voice low and unwavering. "I wish I could've loved you through it. I wish you'd had someone by your side who showed you that you never had to earn love by being okay. That you were worthy of it in every single moment, even the messy, painful ones."

He cups my face in his hands, his thumbs gently brushing my cheeks.

"I would love that chance, Rhianna. To walk through the chaos and the quiet with you. To stand by you through the highs and the heartbreaks. To build a life that feels real and true, because with you that's exactly what life would be for me."

My heart feels too big for my chest, like it might burst through ribs at any moment. "But... I'm leaving. Is that what you want? Postcards and text messages for six months?"

"Yes!" His response is so enthusiastic it makes me jump and he grabs my hand again. "Yes, I'll take it. I'll write you a letter every day if you like. I'll call you in whatever time zone you're in. I'll rearrange my class schedule—whatever it takes. I'm in, Rhianna. All the way."

"But I want you to be happy too," I protest weakly. "You deserve more than me."

"Rhianna." His voice is soft but steady. "There's no such thing as 'more than you.' You're magic itself. When we met, I honestly thought you'd never look twice at someone like me—a buttoned-up, routine-driven professor who has an unhealthy relationship with his planner. I've been amazed you've let me into your life. The question was never whether you're enough. It's if you could accept someone like me."

"Like you?" I whisper, taking him in. The flashlight's glow throws soft shadows over his face, but the stars have finally come out above us, silver pinpricks in the sky behind his dark hair. His eyes—so warm, so steady—hold my gaze without flinching. His hands, confident and sure, cradle mine like something precious.

"You're thoughtful," I say softly, "and steady, and brilliant in a way that never makes anyone feel small. You remember people's favorite books even if you've only met them once. You notice the details that matter. You make the best French toast I've ever had. And you always make space for other people."

My throat tightens. "Eli, you are the best thing that's ever happened to me. You make me feel safe and seen and entirely, terrifyingly known. And I don't know how to be someone who deserves that... but I want to try. I want to try with you."

Then he's kissing me, and I'm kissing him back, and it feels like coming home after the longest journey. His hands tangle in my disaster of a bun, and I don't even care how gross I must look because he's here. He sees the worst of me and still wants me.

When we finally break apart, both breathless, he reaches for the bakery box. "I brought your favorite cookies."

I accept the package and open the lid to find what once were chocolate chip cookies, now reduced to a pile of delicious crumbs.

Eli's face falls. "Oh no, my grand gesture is decidedly sub-optimal in presentation."

"Grand gesture?" I tilt my head.

"I guess it's not a very good one." He rubs his neck. "Our story has gone off the rails."

"You're the one who said you didn't want a 'by the book' romance. I think this solidly deserves a check mark." My voice drops. "Besides, I couldn't imagine a better grand gesture. Eli, you showed up for me when I didn't deserve it. Crumbled cookies and all."

"You always deserve it, Rhianna."

The next kiss is softer, slower. Then we sit side by side, passing the box between us as we eat cookie crumbs with our fingers, watching as stars appear one by one in the darkening sky above Magnolia Cove. And for the first time in days, I feel like I can breathe again.

"So," I say, leaning my head against his shoulder. "What happens next?"

His arm wraps around me, pulling me closer. "I have absolutely no idea." The wonder in his voice makes me smile. "And I'm perfectly fine with that."

Eli

The box of rare books sits unopened in my living room, exactly where I placed it a week ago. Under normal circumstances, this would be unthinkable—these volumes need proper shelving, climate control, careful handling. But nothing feels normal anymore.

"You haven't even unpacked your Whitlock collection?" Piper's voice carries from my kitchen, where she's perched on my counter despite my many lectures about germs. She does it just to irritate me. I'm currently so far above trivial annoyances that her antics barely register. She seems to realize this and frowns at me. "Who are you and what have you done with my brother?"

I glance at the box, then at my sister, who's swirling a glass of wine with an expression that's far too knowing. "I've been busy."

"Busy staring at your phone waiting for Rhianna to text?"

"I do not stare at my phone." My hand stills where it's slipped into my pocket to remove my phone. "I merely check it at regular intervals."

Piper snorts. "Right. Because that's so much better." She

takes a sip of wine, her dark eyes studying me over the rim of her glass. "You know, Brubba, for someone who just found the love of his life, you look miserable."

"I'm not miserable." The protest sounds weak even to my ears. "I'm just... adjusting."

The truth is more complicated than I can explain to Piper, even though she's been my confidante since we were children. How do I describe the constant push and pull in my chest? The joy that bubbles up every time my phone buzzes with a message from Rhianna, followed by the ache of not being able to see her smile in person. The way I keep turning to share something with her—a passage in a book, a thought about Welsh mythology, even just a terrible pun—only to remember she's not here.

A week ago, I thought I'd lost her completely. I was resigned to returning to my carefully ordered life, trying to forget the way she'd turned everything upside down in the best possible way. Then Alex reminded me that promises are about the heart of them—not just the words. And suddenly, I saw it clearly. Rhianna hadn't been asking me to leave; she'd been afraid no one would love her enough to stay.

So I did.

I ran through town like a man possessed. And when I'd found her, hair wild from the wind, eyes red from crying—I knew. I knew I would never stop choosing her. When she said she wanted to try with me, my heart soared. I've been floating ever since.

I'd already closed the lease on my apartment in Magnolia Cove. I had to chase down my boxes—they were thankfully still being held on the ferry in Charleston—and I didn't have a resident's permit anymore. And with Rhianna leaving on her fellowship in a matter of weeks, it made logical sense to return home for a while to the apartment I already own.

So I did the sensible thing. I went back to Misty Pines.

But nothing feels like home anymore. These rooms feel emptier than they ever did before, because now I know what it's like to have her in a space. Her laughter echoing off the walls. Her wild book theories mid-sentence. The faint scent of lemon and sea breeze clinging to my clothes. It's already faded. I frown at the thought.

I miss her all the time.

It's just six months, though. I'll stick with my plan. Teach my virtual classes. I'll fall asleep to her voice describing the cities she's exploring. I'll live in this in-between space where we're apart but still tethered. And when she's ready—when she's home again—we'll talk about what forever looks like.

"You're doing it again," Piper interrupts my thoughts. "That thing where you get lost in your head thinking about her."

She's right, of course. But how can I not? Rhianna Wilder crashed into my life like a shooting star, and now everything that once felt sufficient feels like a pale substitute for the life I could have—the life I want—with her.

I'm saved from having to explain any of this to Piper by her typical rapid-fire subject changes. She hops off the counter and starts wandering my apartment, poking at my precisely arranged belongings like she's conducting an investigation.

"Besides, what are you adjusting to? Being back in your perfectly organized apartment that you clearly don't want to be in anymore?"

I run a hand through my hair, aware that every unpacked box is only proof to her point. "It's just six months."

"And you'll spend all six of them counting the minutes until you can go back to her." She sets down her wine glass with more force than necessary. "Why did you even come back?"

"I have responsibilities, Pipes. My teaching—"

"Aren't you still teaching virtually this year?"

"Yes, but..." I trail off.

"But what?" Piper prompts.

"But I have a job, a life here."

Piper rolls her eyes so hard I'm worried she might strain something. "A job you can currently do from anywhere, and a life you're clearly not invested in anymore. When's the last time you checked your work email?"

"Last Tuesday," I answer automatically, then wince at her triumphant expression.

"Exactly! The old Eli would never let an email go unanswered for over twenty-four hours. You're still trying to live by your old rules even though they don't fit anymore."

Her words hit me with unexpected force. I think about my inbox, filled with unanswered messages from colleagues, questions about next semester's syllabus, requests for peer reviews. A month ago, letting them sit would have felt like a personal failure. Now they seem... insignificant.

Because every morning, I wake up to a message from Rhianna. Sometimes it's a picture of a sunrise over Magnolia Cove's harbor, sometimes it's a terrible pun about books that makes me laugh out loud in my empty apartment. Yesterday, she sent me a link to a song along with the text: *Still better than Bread.* I'd laughed out loud in the grocery store. People looked over at me and I didn't care.

This lack of focus would have horrified the old Eli. He would have seen it as a disruption to carefully laid plans, a deviation from the proper path.

But I remember something Rhianna said to me once, curled up in my sweater at my apartment. *Sometimes the best stories are the ones that don't follow an outline.* She'd been talking about books, but maybe she was talking about life too. About how the most meaningful chapters aren't the ones we carefully plot out, but the ones that surprise us.

I look around my apartment—at the neat stacks of papers,

the carefully arranged books, the life I built with such precision—and realize it doesn't fit anymore. I've gone back to my old routines, but they don't match the shape of my heart now. With a gasp, I realize what I need to do. "Remember when I told you about my three bold moves plan?"

Piper grins. "You mean your absolutely adorable attempt to be spontaneous that involved making a detailed list of how to be spontaneous? Yeah, that was peak you."

"Moving to Magnolia Cove was the first one," I say, ignoring her teasing. "Signing up for Rhianna's matchmaking service was the second."

"What about skydiving?"

I shake my head. "After moving spontaneously and falling in love with a woman who has more magic in her smile than most people have in their whole being? Jumping out of a plane doesn't feel that bold anymore."

Or jumping off a moving ferry to pursue her, for that matter. Actually, it seems like I've been doing a whole lot of jumping since I met Rhianna Wilder. But I realize there's one jump left.

Piper sets down her wine glass, her expression softening. "So what's the third bold move going to be?"

A smile tugs at my lips as I reach for my laptop. "I think I finally know."

* * *

"Piper, please try to contain yourself," I mutter as we approach *Sinclair's Sips & Savories*. My sister practically vibrates with excitement, clutching my arm like she's afraid I might change my mind and run.

"I can't help it! I can't wait to meet her. She's going to say yes. This is perfect!"

"She might not say yes. Let's not count on that yet."

"Let's count on it!" Piper's grin is infectious. "Let's count on all of it."

The bell chimes as we walk in, and my heart pounds. This idea is wild, completely outside my carefully constructed comfort zone. But that's what Rhianna has taught me—sometimes the boldest moves are the ones that terrify you the most. And this move is bold. No matter what happens, I've fulfilled my promise to myself.

But dear god, I really hope she says yes.

The book club is gathered at their usual table, deep in what appears to be a heated debate. Tom is gesturing with biscotti, Mia is shaking her head, and Violet appears to be taking detailed notes. But my eyes find Rhianna immediately.

She laughs at something Alex says then her gaze catches mine. There's a moment of pause before she jumps out of her seat. "Eli?"

For a moment, I forget how to breathe. She's wearing an emerald green dress that contrasts with her dark eyes, and her hair is doing that thing where it's escaping from her bun in wild, perfect curls. A pen is stuck through the knot, because of course it is. She's absolutely beautiful, and absolutely Rhianna.

Piper elbows me in the ribs. Right. Moving. Walking. Basic human functions.

"Hi." I cross to their table. The book club members stare at us with varying degrees of curiosity and knowing smiles. Tom's got biscotti frozen halfway to his mouth. Alex, for her part, wears the serene, self-satisfied smile of someone who knew this would happen all along.

"Hi," Rhianna echoes, then her eyes shift to Piper. "Oh! You must be the famous sister! I've heard so much about you."

"All terrible things, I hope." Piper grins and shoots me a look that clearly says *get on with it already*.

My hands shake slightly as I pull out the folder I've

prepared. Inside is a map marked with careful annotations, a series of meticulously organized files, and more hope than I've ever dared to carry before.

"I spoke with your father,"—I begin, my voice steadier than I feel—"and he told me all the locations you're traveling to. You'll have weekends free. I already plan to teach remotely." I spread the papers out across an empty table, smoothing the edges with my fingertips. Each one represents a different adventure we could share, a different future waiting to be chosen. "So I looked at all the details and I've made an itinerary for every weekend that will help you get the most out of your time. And"—I swallow hard—"if you'll have me, I'd love to go with you."

The table erupts in noise and motion. Tom whoops, Mia claps her hands together, and Violet mutters something that sounds suspiciously like "finally!"

But I only have eyes for Rhianna, whose expression has transformed from shock to something that makes my heart stop and restart all at once.

When she launches herself into my arms, the force of her embrace nearly knocks me over. The entire restaurant breaks into applause, but I barely notice. I'm too busy memorizing the feeling of her in my arms, the sound of her laughter against my neck. Imagining experiencing those every day from now on.

She pulls back slightly, her eyes dancing. "Okay, not to be dramatic but I think my heart just exploded."

I chuckle, then reach up to tuck a strand of hair behind her ear. "Rhianna Wilder, a few months ago on the beach I wanted to tell you something, but if you remember correctly, you asked me to wait. To put that conversation off until later." Her forehead furrows, but her eyes fill with hope and maybe trust. A trust I'll always protect. I take a steadying breath. "I love you. I love your wild heart and your brilliant mind. I love how you see magic in everything, how you make me brave enough to chase my own dreams. I love that you've completely destroyed my organizational system and I don't even care. I love—"

She kisses me, and the restaurant erupts in cheers again. When we break apart, she's crying and laughing at the same time. "I love you too, you ridiculous, wonderful man."

And that is how my third bold move becomes the beginning of our greatest adventure.

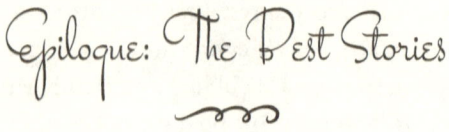

Epilogue: The Best Stories

RHIANNA

I'm spinning in a circle, humming Fleetwood Mac's 'Dreams' in the middle of a tiny bookshop in Edinburgh, flipping through books, when someone taps my shoulder. When I turn, I already know who I'll find.

Eli Lancaster stands there in his navy sweater with leather patches on the elbows (which should look pretentious but somehow just looks adorable on him), holding what appears to be the most touristy guidebook I've ever seen. His hazel eyes dance with amusement behind the black-rimmed glasses I've grown to love.

"Are you the Rhianna who's supposed to be on vacation?" he asks, and my heart does that funny little flip it's done since the first time I saw him.

"The very one." I grin, pulling out my earbuds. "Can't keep me away from books, you know."

He smirks. "Well, good to know. Otherwise, I might've mistaken you for the Rhiannon from Welsh mythology—the one our tour covers in less than an hour."

"Only the very best mythological figure that's ever existed." I say this part with extra dramatic flair.

"I could make a few arguments of mythological figures you'd approve of even more." His eyes are twinkling now, and I want to kiss him senseless right here between the Celtic mythology and Scottish folklore sections.

"Please." I roll my eyes playfully. "Fine, name one that's better."

"What about Athena? Goddess of wisdom, war strategy, and crafts. Patron of heroes. Born fully formed from Zeus's head. Plus"—he taps my nose—"she was often depicted with an owl, which is basically the librarian of the bird world."

I pause, letting my mouth drop open in mock horror. "Oh my god, you might be right. But don't tell Rhiannon I agreed with you."

He laughs then kisses my nose. These past six months have been more than just a dream come true. I've helped librarians in over a dozen different libraries across the globe, hosted glitter-drenched story hours in four languages, and discovered that magic isn't tied to one place. It's tucked into the tiniest corners of the world, if you're willing to look.

Grandma Ida would've adored this trip. She would've danced in every plaza, sketched in every journal she picked up in each country, and collected every train ticket like a relic. And maybe we didn't get to go on this trip together, but I think—no, I know—she'd be happy that I'm here. That I'm letting myself live it with someone who makes me feel completely breathtakingly alive and deeply grounded and safe at the same time.

With Eli, every new city is its own kind of magic. Even his obsessively organized travel itineraries have started to grow on me. I still throw in one completely unplanned adventure every weekend, just to keep things interesting. He pretends to sigh about it, but he always smiles when I do.

We've had a few unfortunate adventures too. He held my hair back when I got food poisoning in Marrakesh, then ran through the streets armed with a language guide, and somehow returned from the pharmacy with just what I needed. I've wandered through at least a thousand used book-stores by now, and I've watched him linger reverently over ever brittle page. I've fallen in love with him in train stations and temples, over terrible instant coffee and candlelit dinners, and with every quiet look and shared laugh.

And when we stood on a sun-drenched bridge in Paris and left locks behind to honor Mark and Grandma Ida we held each other as the tears came. The love bloomed there too, tender and fierce, in the safety of someone seeing me fully and loving every inch of me. The fun parts. The hard parts. The parts I used to hide.

Somehow, every step of the way, he's kept his promise.

And I'm keeping mine, too.

After all, I promised to find him the love of his life.

And I have.

I reach into my bag and pull out a weathered volume I'd spotted earlier. Eli's breath catches as he recognizes the binding.

I smile, the soft hum of my magic still tingling at my fingertips. I'd known the moment I brushed past it on the shelf—the way my energy snagged and settled—that it was meant for him. Some books just know where they belong. Some hearts do too.

"Is that...?"

"A first edition Cyrus Whitlock? With annotations?" I dangle it in front of him. "Maybe."

He takes it reverently, his fingers trembling slightly as he opens it. "Rhianna, how did you—"

"Let's just say I have excellent matchmaking skills. Even when it comes to connecting book collectors with their white whales."

My phone rings, interrupting my thoughts. Alex's name

flashes across the screen. I wiggle it in front of Eli then click to answer and shove the phone against my ear. "Hello?"

"Hey, Rhianna!" Her voice is high pitched and rushed. Strange for her.

"What's up?" I ask, watching Eli as he carefully examines each page of the Whitlock book, completely lost to the world. There aren't words in any book that could ever come close to how much I love this man.

"Well..." Alex draws out the word. "Remember how you said you'd kill me if I got engaged while you were gone?"

"You're kidding me!" I screech loudly enough that several customers turn to stare. Eli finally looks up from his book, eyebrows raised. "He didn't!"

"He did! Last night. There were cinnamon rolls involved."

"Of course there were." I'm bouncing on my toes now, unable to contain my excitement. "Was there magic? Please tell me there was magic."

"Officially I'm not allowed to say. Dean Markham didn't approve it. Unofficially... a few stars might have fallen from the sky."

After a few more minutes of squealing and details, I hang up and turn to Eli, who's watching me with a soft smile that makes me want to kiss the expression away.

"We're going to have to make some travel plan changes this winter," I say, trying to keep my voice casual.

"Why?"

The smile that slides up my face almost hurts. "Because Ethan proposed! Alex and Ethan are getting married!"

"What? That's wonderful... that's great, I mean, but I'm surprised he beat me to it."

Wait. What?

Eli's eyes go wide as he realizes what he's just said. A blush creeps up his neck, and he runs a hand through his hair. "I mean... I didn't... That wasn't how I planned..."

I step closer and slide my hands up his chest until they rest on his shoulders. "Planned what, exactly?"

He takes a deep breath, then reaches into his pocket and pulls out a small jewelry box. "I was going to do this properly," he whispers. "After the Rhiannon tour today. I thought that would be the perfect place." He huffs out a laugh, a little self-conscious. "I had this whole speech planned. About how you taught me that the best stories aren't the ones you plan—they're the ones that surprise you." His gaze softens. "I've been carrying this ring around, holding out for the perfect moment. But maybe it's not about perfect. Maybe it's about this. Us. And that's even better."

I jump on my toes and kiss him, pouring everything I feel into it—all the love and joy and certainty. When we break apart, we're both a little breathless.

"Is that a yes?" he asks.

"That's a yes so big I can't even find the right words." I throw my arms around his neck. "Also, over-analyzing the situation? For weeks? That's so typical of you, it's adorable."

He laughs as he slides the ring onto my finger. It's vintage, with a small moonstone instead of a diamond. Perfect.

"So," he says, pressing his forehead to mine. "Ready for our next adventure?"

I think about how I almost missed this—missed him—by chasing emotional safety. By trying to protect my heart at all costs. By clinging so tightly to the idea that if I just didn't risk my heart again, I could avoid the pain.

But maybe that's not what makes a life beautiful.

Maybe it's not about avoiding pain at all. Maybe it's about building something so full of joy and laughter and love that, yes, losing it will hurt—but it will also mean it was real. It was good. It was *worth it.*

And here, with Eli looking at me like I'm his favorite story, I realize... that's what I want. A life rich enough to grieve someday. A life wild and bright and messy enough to leave a mark.

A life that feels like magic—because it is.

"You know what?" I say, reaching up to adjust his glasses just because I can. "I think I'm ready for all of them."

We buy the Whitlock book (of course we do), and step out into the Edinburgh afternoon. The sky is a shade of blue that reminds me of the night we watched meteors together. Eli's hand is warm in mine, and my new ring catches the light.

I think about the letter in my bag—the one offering to extend my fellowship for another year. Just yesterday, I was uncertain about what to do. Now I know exactly what I want: to go home to Magnolia Cove with Eli. To build a life there, knowing we can travel whenever we want. To have movie nights with Alex and Ethan, planning their wedding while we plan ours. To create the kind of love story that would make even Stevie Nicks proud.

I reach for his hand, and he laces our fingers together like it's something he was always meant to do.

Maybe the bravest thing isn't chasing something new.

Maybe it's letting yourself be seen—fully, wildly, messily—and facing the fear of heartbreak to take all the beauty of life with it.

And maybe, just maybe... that's where the magic really begins.

Next Book

Loved *Love by the Book*? The magic's just getting started.

If you're craving more swoony banter, small-town magic, and cozy vibes that feel like warm drinks and falling leaves, you'll adore *Strings Attached*—a forbidden romance full of wit, warmth, and just the right amount of magical chaos.

This time, the spotlight's on Missy Sinclair—Alex's younger sister, a human cellist with a tired heart and a half-packed suitcase—and Dean Markham, the town's broodiest head warlock who's sworn never to fall in love... especially not with someone magicless. But Magnolia Cove has its own ideas —and when rules are broken and sparks start to fly, resisting the pull might be impossible.

Forbidden romance? Check.

Grumpy/sunshine (with magic and music)? Definitely.

Cozy fall setting, unexpected kisses, and a guaranteed happily-ever-after? Always.

So grab your favorite fall drink, wrap yourself in something soft, and return to Magnolia Cove for a story that will warm your heart and maybe break a few magical rules along the way.

Pick up *Strings Attached* today and fall under the spell.

Rhianna's Front Porch Pralines

The first time Rhianna made pralines, she stood on a stool next to her dad at the old gas stove, wooden spoon in hand, eyes wide as sugar bubbled and thickened like magic. He kept one steady hand on the pot and quoted Wendell Berry or Langston Hughes, whoever had struck a chord that day, while she stirred and stirred and stirred.

"Patience, chicken. You don't rush something that's meant to melt slow."

Now, when Eli's family visits, he's the one making the recipe Rhianna taught him, passing warm pralines around the porch as they sip tea and watch the sun dip low. Sweet and simple, just like summer afternoons on the porch.

Ingredients:
- 1 cup (200g) light brown sugar
- 1 cup (200g) granulated sugar
- ½ cup (120ml) whole milk or heavy cream
- 4 tablespoons (57g) unsalted butter
- 1 teaspoon vanilla extract
- 1 ½ cups (180g) pecan halves

• Pinch of salt

Instructions:

1. Line a baking sheet with parchment paper and set it nearby—you'll need it ready.
2. In a medium saucepan, combine both sugars, milk, and butter. Cook over medium heat, stirring constantly, until the mixture reaches a rolling boil.
3. Keep stirring. (Seriously—don't stop.)
4. Once it boils, continue stirring for about 3–5 minutes, until the mixture thickens and starts to pull away slightly from the sides. If you have a candy thermometer, look for 235°F (soft-ball stage).
5. Remove from heat. Stir in vanilla, salt, and pecans. Keep stirring until the mixture loses its gloss and begins to thicken—about 2–3 minutes more.
6. Working quickly, spoon onto prepared parchment in heaping tablespoons. Let cool and set at room temp.

Tips from Rhianna's Dad:

• "Use real vanilla. Don't cheat your soul with imitation."
• "Soft and creamy is the goal—like brown sugar butter fudge with crunch."
• "Share them while they're still warm, if you really want to make someone fall in love. Hey, it worked on Alma."

Acknowledgments

Writing a book is never a solo act, and *Love by the Book* owes its magic to some truly incredible people.

Milly—this book wouldn't be what it is without your guidance. Thank you for teaching me so much about writing romance and for being my first and biggest cheerleader. Your insight, belief, and steady hand helped shape this story into something I'm so proud of.

To my dad: I'm sorry the playlist includes remakes of classic rock songs. Forgive me. (lol!) Thank you for always being there—for teaching me how to appreciate good music, change my oil, repair my deck, and find my way (on backroads and in life). Love you.

To my husband, the person so many of my friends believe inspires the men in my stories... thank you for being the safest place, standing by me in the hardest of times, laughing with me in the lightest, and altogether making this life the greatest story of all.

My mom always blamed certain family quirks on the "dirty Whitlock blood." She usually did so with a laugh and a knowing smile. Crankiness? Emotional constipation? Nervous energy? Classic Whitlock behavior. Cyrus Whitlock was a nod to that family lore, my love for mythology, and a reflection of my heritage. (And honestly, Cyrus Whitlock signing only a handful of books and then making sure his signature got covered up? That is *exactly* the kind of behavior my mom would chalk up to our bloodline. Ha!)

To Cal and Jamie, my brilliant beta readers—thank you

for lighting the path and helping me shape this book into its strongest, most magical self. Your insights meant the world.

To Megan, master of margins and punctuation—thank you for making this book shine, one caught typo and cheerful message at a time.

To Karl and Brooke—the first (and only!) real-life friends I've ever written into a book—thank you for letting me borrow your names and your warmth for Magnolia Cove. The love you share is exactly the kind that belongs in this world—genuine, steady, and full of heart. Thank you for your friendship and support.

To my friends and family—thank you for cheering me on, for loving me through the writing chaos, and for never once making me feel like I had to do this alone.

And to you, my lovely readers: thank you for coming back to Magnolia Cove. Thank you for believing in second chances, in slow-burning love, and in the quiet magic tucked between the pages of everyday life. I'm so grateful to share this world with you.

With love and gratitude,

-Noel

www.ingramcontent.com/pod-product-compliance
Lightning Source LLC
Chambersburg PA
CBHW020821260626
47169CB00003B/773